# ABOUT SHOW TIME

## A JUNIPER RIDGE ROMANTIC COMEDY

***Don't mix business with pleasure...especially when it's all on camera.***

Building a small town from the ground up is hard.

Doing it on a reality television show only makes it more complicated.

But that won't stop my family from trying.

I'm determined to succeed...and I *always* maintain control.

Until my new CFO arrives.

Smart and sexy, Vanessa Vincent is the complete package.

And she's doing something to mine.

Somewhere between a sexy waterslide ride and adopting a dog, we share a helluva lot more than spreadsheets.

The only thing riskier than mixing business with pleasure is the threat to our project.

Someone wants to see us fail.

With sabotage on the table, it's more than just the show on the line.

So are our hearts.

***One-click this hilarious forbidden workplace rom-com about a***

*billionaire trying to create a utopia on reality T.V. and the woman who makes him question everything along the way.*

A Juniper Ridge Romantic Comedy

# Show TIME

USA TODAY BESTSELLING AUTHOR

TAWNA FENSKE

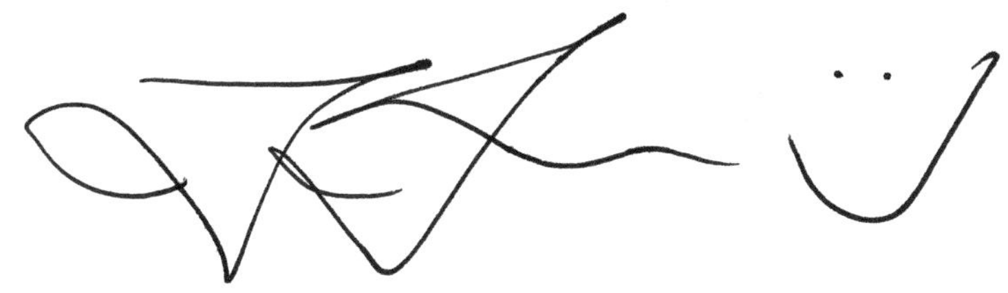

# SHOW TIME

A JUNIPER RIDGE ROMANTIC COMEDY

TAWNA FENSKE

This is a work of fiction. Names, characters, organizations, places, events, and incidents are either products of the author's imagination or are used fictitiously.



www.tawnafenske.com

Cover design by Craig Zagurski

❀ Created with Vellum

## ALSO IN THE JUNIPER RIDGE ROMANTIC COMEDY SERIES

- Show Time (Dean & Vanessa)
- Let It Show (Mari & Griffin)
- Show Down (Lauren & Nick)
- Show of Honor (Joe & Jessie)
- Just for Show (Cooper & Amy)
- Show Off (Lana & Dal)

You might also dig my Ponderosa Resort rom-com series. That's where you'll get your first glimpse of characters from Juniper Ridge, including Val and Vanessa in *Mancandy Crush* and Dean and Gabe in *Snowbound Squeeze*. Check them out here:

- Studmuffin Santa (Jade & Brandon)
- Chef Sugarlips (Amber & Sean)
- Sergeant Sexypants (Bree & Austin)
- Hottie Lumberjack (Chelsea & Mark)
- Stiff Suit (Lily & James)
- Mancandy Crush novella (Valerie & Josh)
- Captain Dreamboat (Blanka & Jon)

- Snowbound Squeeze novella (Gretchen & Gable)
- Dr. Hot Stuff (Isabella & Bradley)

# CHAPTER 1

**CONFESSIONAL 32.5**

JUDSON, DEAN (CEO: JUNIPER RIDGE)

*WHAT? NO, OF COURSE I'M NOT FUCKING CAMERA SHY. JESUS, LAUREN. I GREW UP WITH THE DAMN THINGS SHOVED IN MY FACE JUST LIKE YOU. PRODUCTION VALUE?* [UNINTELLIGIBLE MUTTERING] *CAN'T I JUST RUN THE BUSINESS SIDE OF—YEAH, I KNOW. ALL IN THIS TOGETHER, BLAH BLAH. I STILL DON'T SEE WHY I HAVE TO SIT HERE LIKE A TRAINED PARROT AND—*[HEAVY SIGH] *FINE. BUT ONLY FOR THE BUSINESS. IT'S NOT BECAUSE YOU'RE DOING THE SAD LITTLE SISTER FACE. OR BECAUSE I LOVE YOU.*

*OH, BITE ME.*

* * *

I glance at the clock in my office, trying to decide if I have enough time to grab coffee. In my old life, I had an assistant who'd set a hot mug in front of me before I even *thought* the word coffee.

But my old life was full of dirty money and blinding lights

and the constant stench of desperation, so getting my own coffee is a small price to pay.

Six minutes. That's how long I have until the candidate for chief financial officer makes her appearance. How long does it take to make coffee, anyway?

"Here are the notes for the police officers' screen tests." My sister, Mari, strides in with a folder in her hands and a pencil speared through her lopsided bun. "Lauren emailed you the video files. I think the psych eval on—"

"Doesn't this seem weird to you?" I fold my hands on my desk as Mari stops moving for once and looks at me. "I mean, we're hiring professionals based on how well they'll perform on camera."

Mari sighs and whacks the folder down in front of me a lot harder than necessary. "We're making a reality show, not staffing the Oval Office. And we're hiring them for specific skills they bring to the community." She gives me the look over the rim of her glasses. "Are we going to keep having this conversation? Because if we are, I'll ask Lauren to tape my response and you can hit play by yourself."

"That sounds about right." Our brother, Gabe, ambles through the door grinning. "I only caught the end of that, but if we're suggesting Dean spends his days in here buffing the banana, we should rethink letting him have the big office."

"Get out." I glance over my brother's shoulder at the clock. "I've got five minutes until my next interview gets here."

"She's already here." Gabe drops into one of my guest chairs, in no hurry to get gone. "That's what I wanted to tell you. She's been out in the waiting room for ten minutes."

Punctual. That's a good sign. I make a mental note as Gabe kicks his legs out and folds his hands behind his head. "She's actually sort of related."

A ripple of unease churns my gut. I'm not a fan of nepotism. I saw way too much of that in Hollywood. "Related to whom?"

"To us," he says. "Well, me. My *wife*." He draws out the word like a guy who has not yet exhausted the novelty of it. To be fair, it's been three weeks since the wedding, and also his wife is awesome. "Gretchen's brother, Jon—his dad has this sister—"

"Jon's *late* father," Mari puts in, always big on establishing the human connection. "Who is no relation to Gretchen because she and Jon had different fathers."

I'm already lost in the branches of my brother's new family tree. "So, we're not talking immediate family here?"

Gabe glares. "Will you let me finish, chief tight-ass?"

I sigh and wave him on, glancing at the clock again. I suppose I'll live without the coffee.

"Anyway, Gretchen's brother's father's sister has these twin daughters, and one of them—"

"Vanessa Vincent," I interrupt. I like how the name sounds rolling off my tongue, strong and no-nonsense. "Harvard MBA, two years with PricewaterhouseCoopers, expertise in forensic accounting, compliance, and internal audit management."

Gabe blinks. "You know all of this?"

"I know everything." Not always, but ever since my personal life took a big nosedive, I've made it my business to foresee all possible landmines. Fool me once and all that.

"Anyway," my brother continues, "she completed our Community Compatibility Questionnaire." He pauses here and smiles at Mari. "Nice job on that, by the way."

My sister nods. "Glad to know the psych doctorate is useful to you," she says dryly.

I give them the universal *hurry up* hand signal, my duty as the eldest brother. "You were saying?"

Gabe swings his focus back to me. "Vanessa's answers in the personal information section were really interesting. Under 'level of interest in finding a spouse or mate,' she chose negative three."

I frown at Mari. "I thought it was a scale of one to ten?"

"It was," she says. "Ms. Vincent somehow found a way to alter the online questionnaire to insert a new answer."

Noteworthy. Noteworthy and...interesting.

"The rest of her responses were the same," Gabe continues. "Under 'I see myself getting married in the next five years,' she went with negative six."

Mari clears her throat. "There's also a write-in answer with that one. It reads, and I quote, 'roughly the same as the odds I will wake tomorrow with an overwhelming urge to drive a flaming fork through my eyeball.'"

"I see." I already liked Ms. Vincent's resumé, but this is giving me a new dimension.

A dimension I relate to on a primal level. The CFO will be my closest working colleague at Juniper Ridge. While a part of this social experiment hinges on participants pairing up, the opposite is vital for me.

"Thank you for the information," I tell them. "I'll take it into consideration."

Gabe glances at his watch and stands up. "Gotta go. Lauren and I are filming B-roll over in the residences."

Mari follows, her bun flopping slightly to one side. "Good luck with the interview," she tells me. "Call us when you're done. I want to go over my proposal for the psych profiles of culinary community members."

"No crazy chefs," I tell her. "Or bakers. Or—"

"Yeah, thanks." Mari rolls her eyes. "Without your input, I'd definitely put psychotic criminals in charge of our food supply."

She's out the door before I can retort, which is just as well. I didn't have anything clever to say anyway. I glance at my watch and see there's no time left for coffee.

Heaving myself out of my chair, I make my way down the hall and into the lobby. For a former cult compound, this place is pretty nice. Case in point, this lodge with its high ceilings and springy cork floors and enough offices for all six Judson offspring. There's also an on-site film studio, which I'll be keeping my distance from as much as possible.

Trudging into the waiting area, I'm struck by its lone occupant. Dark hair with just enough wave to leave it rippling around her shoulders as she taps away on a laptop. Slender curves, which I absolutely shouldn't be noticing. I can't see her eyes until she looks up and hits me square in the chest with the full force of liquid brown irises the color of warm cognac.

She shuts the laptop and shoves it in her bag on the chair beside her, then stands with a bright smile. "Hello."

"Ms. Vincent, I presume?" My voice cracks only a little as I extend a hand and do my best to cover the fact that she's knocked me off balance. "I'm Dean Judson, CEO. Thank you for waiting. Would you like coffee?"

"Absolutely." She shakes my hand with a firm grip. "It's great to finally meet you. My cousin told me so much about you."

"That would be—Jonathan." I met him when I first came to Oregon to rescue my brother from himself. Since Gabe wound up marrying into Jon's family, I can't claim much credit for how great my brother's doing.

"I'm glad you brought that up, actually," I tell Vanessa. "The fact that you're here—it has nothing to do with any family connection. Your credentials were simply impeccable."

"Impeccable, huh?" She grins and slings a gigantic purse over her shoulder in a cross-body style. I keep my eyes locked on her face, unaffected by the sight of the strap pressing a soft path between her breasts.

"Impeccable," I repeat. "Former accounting manager for America's second-largest television network. Treasurer and CFO for a Silicon Valley startup." I take a step back, intent on keeping a professional distance between us. "In your last role, you raised more than $50 million in venture capital for a company devoted to establishing sustainable farming practices in third-world countries."

Vanessa gives a low whistle. "You did your homework. Some of that wasn't even on my resumé."

"I believe in being thorough." There's an understatement. "Come on. Coffeemaker's this way."

I lead her into the breakroom, hoping like hell one of my siblings was kind enough to brew some.

No dice. Lana didn't even wash her mug that says, *"I'm actually not funny. I'm just mean and people think I'm joking."*

I rinse it and set it in the drying rack before rummaging in the back of a lower cupboard for my favorite mug. I've had it twelve years and keep it tucked away so it doesn't end up lost or broken or nabbed by one of my five siblings. Turning to face the coffeemaker, I assess the task at hand. Christ, this thing has more buttons than my HP 12C Platinum accounting calculator.

But if I can mastermind a decade of Hollywood's biggest real estate deals and filmmaker financing, I can make a simple cup of coffee. I punch a few levers and yank at something that spurts a sharp hiss of steam. Finally locating the part that holds coffee grounds, I dump the soggy ones in the trash and hunt for a new filter.

"Did you have any trouble finding the place?" I ask.

"Not at all." Vanessa leans back against the counter to watch me work. "The directions you sent were spot on. This is definitely in the middle of nowhere."

"That's by design, I suppose."

"No joke," she says. "The BONK founders wanted their privacy."

One of the few things to admire about the former members of the Benevolent Order of the New Kingdom, the former cult that built this place.

I stare into the vessel where the coffee grounds go. How much do I put in here? I could check the filter I just tossed, but it seems in poor taste to paw through the trash with a prospective job candidate watching. And she *is* watching; I can feel her eyes on me.

"Need help?" she asks cheerfully. "I've got some pour-over coffee packs in my purse. Sugar and creamer, too."

"Nope, I've got it." Noteworthy about the coffee, though. Well-prepared accountants are a plus.

Dragging a flowered tin from the back of the cupboard, I pry off the lid. Coffee grounds. I settle for eyeballing it, dumping in a hefty pile into the fresh filter before slamming the trap door shut. Now where does the water go?

Glancing at Vanessa, I decide to get the interview started. "I assume you've been briefed on the concept of *Fresh Start at Juniper Ridge*."

I cross my fingers she hasn't caught on that I don't know what the hell I'm doing. Not with the coffee, anyway. I've got a handle on the rest.

"Of course," she says. "Reality television show centered around a thoughtfully planned, self-contained community." She's reciting straight from our website, and I admire that. I admire it a lot. "You're bringing in a diverse group of individuals representing a variety of professions, backgrounds, and lifestyles, and setting the stage for them to create a completely sustainable microcosm of society."

"Correct." Seriously, where does the water go? I yank at a lever and end up unplugging the machine. "It's part social experiment, part entertainment, part a chance to resurrect a piece of property with some questionable history."

"BONK was certainly one of the more—*colorful* cults."

I appreciate that she's being tactful, but it's not necessary. "You mean the part where they believed their leader was the progeny of an extraterrestrial prophet and Charlie Sheen, or the part where they touted mass orgies as a means of growing the roster?"

She laughs. "All of it. I take it you won't be shying away from that history?"

"Might as well let viewers learn from others' missteps so they're not doomed to repeat them."

From the corner of my eye, I see her stiffen. When I look up, she's dropped her shoulders again. Or maybe I imagined the whole thing.

Turning back to the coffeemaker, I pry off a piece that turns out to be the water chamber. Now we're getting somewhere.

"The BONK founders created one hell of an impressive town, so we're just giving it new legs." Belatedly, I realize I've just cursed at a job candidate. But if cursing offends her, she's unlikely to fit the Juniper Ridge family. Maybe it's a job test.

Or maybe she's the one testing me, waiting to see how badly I'll screw up the coffee thing before I ask for help. I can't tell from her face if she's judging. Her expression's impassive, patient, even serene.

Damn, she's beautiful.

If I weren't dead inside, I might notice things like that.

"It's a clever concept," Vanessa says, jarring me back to the fact that we're in job interview mode, even though we haven't made it to my office. "And financially speaking, there's high potential for revenue. The files you sent on advertisers who've committed—I took the liberty of setting up some spreadsheets, which I'd be happy to show you."

"That—that would be great." I glance at her, braced for the coquettish smile I've gotten from dozens of social climbing show biz types. The *'show me your private office,'* or *'Let me prove how much I want this job.'*

But Vanessa's slipping a pair of glasses out of her purse and setting up her laptop on the breakroom table. As the coffee starts to perk, she opens up Excel and dives right into the numbers.

"In this table here, I've factored in the living costs for each member of the cast." She glances up and lifts a brow. "Are you calling them cast members or residents or what?"

"Community members." A little dumbfounded, I drop into the seat beside her. "You already started running numbers?"

"I emailed the hiring manger to request some data—Marilyn?"

"Mari." Who, of course, failed to mention this. "Go on."

"Anyway, this takes into account the economic contributions of each community member—for instance, farmers, chefs, grocers—everyone who represents the food supply is shown in this column, while those who contribute to safety—police and fire, for example—are represented here on the grid."

I listen to her rattle off numbers, staggered by how much she's put into this. We had two other candidates make it to this round, and neither took it this far. I listen with rapt attention, impressed she's thought of aspects of this that my five siblings and I hadn't considered in months of planning.

"I'd be happy to email this to you if you'd like a closer look." She smiles and glances at the coffeemaker. "Smells like that's ready. Want me to get it?"

"Definitely not." I jump up like my chair's on fire and hurry to grab mugs. "If we were to offer you the CFO position, I'd want to be clear you're not my assistant. You and I would be partners on the business side of this operation."

She nods and tucks a shock of hair behind one ear. "And your siblings—they're mostly on the production side?" She accepts the mug I hand her, wrapping her fingers around the warm ceramic instead of grabbing the handle. "I find the whole dynamic fascinating."

"Yeah, Gabe's directing, working with our sister, Lauren. She's the producer." I blow on my coffee, conscious of an odd sting in my nostrils. "There's also Mari—Marilyn—she's a psychologist. The social component was her brainchild."

"And Lana." Vanessa twists the mug in her hands but doesn't take a sip. "Public relations, right?"

"Yep, and then Cooper. An actor, though he'll be taking a different role with this endeavor."

I wait for her to ask about Coop. Most people pry for gossip about the Judson family hellraiser, but Vanessa doesn't go there.

"You have a lot of talent in one family." She lifts her mug in a mock toast, then raises it to her lips.

The instant she sips, her brown eyes bulge. "Holy shit!" She sputters into the mug, spraying coffee as she jumps from her chair. "Did you brew napalm?"

I take a sip from my own mug and choke. "My God. It's like battery acid."

She's wiping her tongue with a paper towel, gagging as she does it. "I thought you went heavy on the grounds, but this is like drinking tar."

Handing me the roll of paper towels, she bends to rinse her mouth in the sink. Swishing and spitting, she coughs as she edges sideways to make room for me.

"Sorry," I mutter, scraping my tongue with my teeth. "It's—uh—my first time making coffee."

"I kinda guessed by watching you," she says. "But this is beyond awful."

I finish gulping water from the tap and stand to face her. Water dribbles down my chin, and this is so far from the interview I imagined that there's no point in saving it. "You knew I was screwing it up, but you didn't say so?"

She folds her arms over her chest and stares me down. "It's not my style to micromanage. I was giving you the benefit of the doubt that you had a different way of doing things."

"And that I wasn't trying to kill you?" I shake my head, feeling like an asshole. "I really am sorry."

"Don't mention it. What kind of coffee is that, anyway?"

I open the cupboard and pull out the flowery tin. "Jovan's Special Blend," I read off the label.

"Jovan?" She frowns. "The cult leader? Weren't they raided like two years ago?"

I sniff the contents of the canister. "What does tear gas smell like?"

Vanessa grimaces and dumps the contents of her mug down the sink. "I think I'll skip the coffee, thanks."

"Good thinking." I start to chuck the whole canister, then stop. "Maybe I should have this tested."

She sniffs the contents and shrugs. "It smells like coffee. Really bad, really old coffee, but still coffee."

I smell it myself, and she's right. So maybe it's a case of user error.

"Come on." I put the lid back on and set the canister on the counter. "There's a coffee shop on the other side of the compound. It's not fully operational yet, but at least the coffee is drinkable."

Vanessa cocks her head. "Does this mean we're continuing the interview?"

She's already hired as far as I'm concerned, but yeah. I should do my due diligence. Failing to do that has burned me before, and no way am I repeating that.

A chill snakes down my arms, and I wonder if she feels it. The way she's looking at me is so intense, so intimate, that it stalls the breath in my lungs.

Vanessa takes a step back. "I should tell you up front that I'm here for a fresh start," she says. "I've had bad luck in the past mixing business and—and—*not* business, so this role would be purely professional for me."

I stare at her as my subconscious jumps up and down yelling.

*You're hired. You're so fucking hired.*

But I've learned not to listen to that asshole.

Clearing my throat, I turn toward the door. "Let's get that coffee."

# CHAPTER 2

**CONFESSIONAL 46**

Vincent, Vanessa (CFO candidate: Juniper Ridge)

*Like this? I'm not used to all these lights. It's been a while since—I'm sorry, what was the question? Oh, right. Yes, absolutely it's a change. A good change, though. I like the idea of starting fresh. Running? I wouldn't say running, exactly. Not away from something, anyway. More like toward it. Toward something...different.*

* * *

I wrap my hands around a third—and likely ill-advised—cup of coffee and stare straight into Dean Judson's eyes like I practiced.

"Absolutely, I'm still interested in the job." I offer a small but professional smile. "In spite of the fact that you tried to kill me with toxic coffee."

An even smaller smile tugs the edges of his mouth, and I resist the urge to wilt with relief. This guy is a tough nut to crack. Over the years, the tabloids have pegged him as sort of a hard-ass. The big brother of the legendary Judson clan, he's known for his cool efficiency in business deals and boardrooms.

But I wasn't prepared for his eyes. Hazel instead of brown like his brother's, which I normally wouldn't notice. But there's something almost eerie about Dean's eyes. A greenish silver on the inside, with a faint rim of cinnamon around the edges. I've seen them in magazines, but up close they're quite disarming.

"…would be working closely with me, but also with the individuals we hire to handle banking and legal issues," he's saying, and I order myself to pay attention. "Obviously the level of on-camera time for you would be different from regular community members, but you'd still be participating."

"Of course, I already signed the waiver." I give him my cheeriest smile. "I'm not camera shy, if that's a concern."

He gives me an odd look. "Because of your stint on *Baby Spies*."

Whoa. I mean, it's no secret my twin sister and I starred in a TV show that lasted a single season when we were six years old, but that was more than two decades ago. It's sure as hell not on my resumé.

Surprise must register on my face, because Dean's expression softens. "I hope you don't mind, but I believe in being thorough. I needed to know everything I could learn about you."

"Of course." Here's where I should definitely not admit to internet stalking him. "Is it true you singlehandedly exposed director Dave Wienerman for sexually harassing all those actresses and then fought to upend the Hollywood status quo so it doesn't happen again?"

Shit. I didn't mean to ask that.

Dean presses his lips together and stares at me. "No."

"I see."

"Not singlehandedly."

Oh.

He spreads his hands on the table and looks at me. "I see we've both done our homework, Ms. Vincent."

"Vanessa. Please, call me Vanessa."

"Vanessa." He says my name like he's tasting it. Like he's rolling it around on his tongue like a juicy raspberry.

I uncross my legs and re-cross them, pretty sure I should quit with the coffee. It's definitely hot in here.

"Well, Vanessa" he says. "It's apparent we've both done our research. Due diligence is important, so I'm glad we're on the same page."

I'm struck suddenly by the urge to know more about him. Some detail that's not on his IMDb page or in the gossip columns online. Those sites froth with facts about his family's Hollywood pedigree or his ugly breakup with one of Hollywood's hottest actresses, but I want more. If we'll be working as closely as he says, I want to understand what makes Dean Judson tick.

"Tell me something about yourself." I grip my mug a little tighter and focus on holding eye contact. "It doesn't have to be a big secret or anything, but something that's not on every website."

Dean studies me a moment while I try not to look at his hands. They're splayed on the table like he might take a pen and trace around them, making one of those turkey drawings kids do in kindergarten.

It would be a huge fucking turkey.

"What's so funny?" he asks.

I drag my eyes off his hands to see him eyeing me with curiosity. He doesn't look mad, but I force myself to stop smiling. "Nothing. Just thinking of absurd things to share when first meeting someone. Details that give more information than your usual interview questions."

Dean quirks an eyebrow. "Such as?"

His expression tugs my attention to the edge of his left eyebrow, which sports a crescent-shaped scar the size of a nickel.

"Your scar." I point to his forehead unnecessarily. "How did you get it?"

He hesitates, watching my face like he's looking for clues that I'm worthy of hearing the story. "Bike accident."

Something in his expression tells me there's more to the story, but I don't want to push. "Bike accidents can be brutal," I say. "I had a bad one on a cycling trip through the San Juan Islands."

I was riding with an old boyfriend who insisted he knew where we were going and led us down a treacherous gravel-spiked hill. I wound up with sixteen stitches in my left calf and a growing awareness of my unfortunate taste for controlling yet clueless assholes.

Dean's eyes sweep mine. "How old were you?"

"It was right after college, so twenty-two or twenty-three," I tell him. "How old were you when you had your bike accident?"

"It wasn't me in the bike accident." Again with the hesitation. "My sister, Lana—she's the baby of the family. Our nanny fell asleep, and we went outside to play."

I digest this information, the details he's shared without meaning to. He was raised with a nanny. He grew up playing with his siblings, even though he's at least twelve years older than the youngest.

"Anyway," he continues, "Lana was always trying to copy everything Lauren did, so when Lauren went off a jump on her bike, Lana tried it on her tricycle."

"Ouch." I don't know details, but jumping a trike sounds plenty dangerous. "What happened?"

Dean eases back in his chair a bit, relaxing into the story. "Lana's lying there screaming and bleeding, while Lauren and Mari try to calm her down."

"Were your brothers there?"

"Yeah." He smiles a little at that. "Gabe and Coop were standing guard in case our parents came home or the nanny woke up. They had this whole cover story concocted so we wouldn't get in trouble."

He's given me a snapshot of his whole family in two simple lines, and I'm not sure he realizes it. I'm utterly charmed and irksomely turned on, the latter of which I have no business being in a job interview.

"Was your sister okay?" I ask.

"Yeah." Again, he smiles. "She's got a head like a battering ram. But then our mom showed up."

I've read about Shirleen Judson. Not much, just headlines, but enough to get the full picture. Sex siren of '70s cinema, she graced the cover of hundreds of fashion magazines and won two Oscars before pausing her acting career to get married and make babies.

"Was she angry?" I realize I'm on the edge of my seat and scoot back to avoid looking too eager.

If Dean notices, he says nothing. "Not at us, but she was pissed at the nanny. And she was freaking out about Lana maybe having permanent scars. 'What if you want to model someday?' she kept asking. 'Or star in films?'"

"Jesus." And I thought my mom cornered the market on shallowness.

"She's not that bad," Dean says, reading my mind. "Just wanted us to have all the options. Anyway, Lana starts crying harder saying, 'No scar! No scar!' even though she's four and has no idea what a scar is. So I pick up this bottlecap lying on the ground beside her bike. And real quick, I jam it into my forehead. The same spot where Lana had a cut above her eyebrow."

"Holy—" I stop myself from saying 'shit,' but just barely. "That's some serious sibling sympathy right there."

"I was fifteen," he says, a little shamefaced. "I didn't really think it through. But it made Lana stop crying."

I don't even know what to ask. "Does she have the same scar?"

"Nah, hers wasn't even that deep," he says. "Head wounds just bleed a lot. Mine probably would have been fine, too, but it got infected." He grins and there goes my stomach rolling like a kid doing a somersault down a grassy hill. "Apparently, bottlecaps aren't hygienic surgical instruments."

"You don't say." I'm seriously reeling right now with this tidbit from Dean Judson. Maybe he's told this in magazine interviews, but I don't think so. For some reason, I'm almost positive this is a story few people know.

I peer at the scar, seeing it with fresh eyes. "That's quite the scar. And quite the story."

"Thanks." He picks up his coffee cup and nods at me. "Now you."

Damn. I don't know where to begin. "I can't compete with that."

"It's not a competition."

"Right." I clear my throat, determined to offer Dean the same sort of insight he just gave me. "I've run three ultra-marathons. I've climbed Kilimanjaro and K2. I got scuba certified and went cage diving with sharks in Fiji."

"So you're a daredevil." He looks impressed, though not as much as you might think. "Or an adrenaline junkie."

I shake my head, glancing down at my hands. "I'm actually a huge chicken."

Just ask my mother. I don't say that bit out loud, but Dean's regarding me with intense curiosity.

"How do you figure you're a chicken?"

"I've done all that stuff because I'm scared as hell, and I want to prove to myself I can get over it." Not just prove it to myself, if I'm being honest. "Also, I have severe globophobia."

His brow furrows as he puzzles out the word. "Fear of world travel?"

"Nope." I bite the edge of my lip. "Fear of balloons."

I stare him in the eye, waiting for the laughter that always follows.

Dean sits silent. "You're afraid of balloons."

"Yep. Terrified. If I walk into a little kid's birthday party and see them, I have to walk back out or I'll have a full-on panic attack."

"You're kidding me." It's not a question, so he knows I'm not kidding. "Is it a fear of the balloons or the balloons being popped?"

"Both," I admit. "I've seen several shrinks about it and even got hypnotized once. But nothing seems to cure it."

Dean quirks an eyebrow. "Not even wading through a sea of balloons."

I suppress a shudder, shaking my head. "Not that I've tried that specifically, but no. It's not like rock climbing or sky diving where doing the thing helps me get past my fear. It's been the opposite, really."

"Huh." His expression is thoughtful with a touch of confusion.

It's possible this was not the best story to share in a job interview. I'm about to explain. To tell him it shouldn't be an issue as long as he's not planning some sort of fucked up office party with clowns twisting oblong latex forms into zoo animals.

But then his face breaks into a smile. Folding his hands together on the table, he gives me a nod. "I'd like to offer you the job."

I blink. "Because of, or in spite of my weird phobia?"

He laughs and leans back in his chair. "Neither. I was planning to do it anyway, but you kinda sealed the deal with that story."

I'm honestly not sure what he means, but I don't ask him to elaborate. I got the job, and that's what matters. "Is there a contract I can look over or—"

"Yeah, hang on." He whips out his phone, and I watch as his thumbs fly over the screen. For a guy with such oversized digits, he sure is dexterous. I'm the world's clumsiest typist on my phone, but this guy's fingers move like he's stroking clitoris-covered piano keys.

*Stop staring at his hands.*

"Done," he says, putting the phone down. "Mari will be here in a couple minutes with a contract for you to review. You can take your time looking it over, but we'd love to have a response by the end of the week."

It's all I can do not to fall off my chair. "Wow. That was—uh —quick."

He shrugs. "When you know, you know."

I feel my smile start to falter, though I rally to keep the edges of my lips tipped up. How many times have I been sure—absolutely freakin' positive—that some guy is THE ONE. The guy I'm meant to spend the rest of my life with?

Five times?

Ten?

I'm ashamed to admit it's probably more.

My intuition is busted, at least when it comes to men.

As Marilyn Judson hustles in with a stack of paperwork, I'm eternally glad *that* is not the tidbit I chose to share in a job interview. I'm fine with them knowing I've sworn off dating. I'd prefer they not know the precise ways I've made enough poor choices to give up men altogether.

"Here we go." Dean's sister sits down in the chair beside me and sticks out her hand. "Marilyn Judson. You can call me Mari."

"Vanessa," I say, trying not to stare at the assortment of writing implements sticking out of her floppy bun. Two pens and a pencil by my count.

But Mari's a psychologist. A famous one if her "Shrink to the Stars" label is an indication. She misses nothing. "It's an easy place to store them," she says, plucking a pen from her hair and handing it to me. "Moving out of Hollywood means we're no longer required to conform to those standards of style and beauty."

"Amen to that." I take the pen from her before realizing I have no idea what I'm about to sign. I glance down, expecting a contract, but see it's just a confidentiality form. "I think I already signed one of these."

"This one's different from the preliminary form." Mari pushes her glasses up her nose. "This form is only for prospective community members who receive offers. We ask that you maintain confidentiality about financial information and details of our compensation package."

Dean nods, watching me closely. "We don't want competing networks knowing too much about what we do."

"Ah." I don't have many Hollywood connections, but even I've heard rumblings that the Voltan Network doesn't love the surging competition from the Judsons. I skim the form before inking my name at the bottom. "If it's okay, I'd like a little more time to review the contracts themselves."

"Of course." Mari smiles, revealing an adorable dimple and a hint of freckles on the bridge of her nose. "Have your lawyer look over them if necessary. We want you to feel comfortable about everything that's in here."

Dean's phone—which is still sitting on the table between us—gives a jarring buzz. He frowns down at the screen, and though I try not to stare, I can't help noticing the name that pops up.

*Investigator Brixton.*

He hits the button to force it to voicemail, then makes eye contact with his sister. Something passes between them before Mari gives a quick nod.

Dean clears his throat. "In the interest of full disclosure, there's something you should know."

"Oh?" I try to keep my voice curious instead of fearful. "What's that?"

Mari squares her shoulders. "We're working with authorities to ensure members of the Juniper Ridge community remain safe and protected at all times."

I stare at her, absorbing the words. "And is there a reason to think they wouldn't be?"

"No." Dean clears his throat. "Local police are in the loop, and the private investigator we've hired is verifying whether the threats are credible. So far, he's seen no reason to be alarmed."

"Threats?" I'm not sure how we got from tricycles and balloons to job offers and menacing figures. "What kind of threats?"

Again with the exchange of sibling looks, something I can't quite read. But I have a twin, so I know what it means to communicate without words.

Dean takes a deep breath. "Someone does not want *Fresh Start at Juniper Ridge* to happen."

# CHAPTER 3

**CONFESSIONAL 87**

Judson, Dean (CEO: Juniper Ridge)

*Yeah, I guess I've always been a little too direct. That's one reason I knew I belonged behind the scenes in showbiz instead of in front of the camera. Or behind it. You can't just blurt shit out when you're directing some snot-nosed actor who's convinced his shit doesn't stink. Huh? Who says I can't say shit on camera? Twice. Three times.*

*Goddammit.*

* * *

It dawns on me too late that the moment my top candidate for CFO is ready to sign on the dotted line is not the time to mention her safety may be in jeopardy.

Then again, when is the right time? Before the interview or after she scrawls her signature on this big-ass pile of paperwork?

Vanessa's gripping Mari's favorite myrtlewood pen and looking at me with those big, brown eyes. I owe her an explanation.

With a sigh, I dive right in. "It started with some threatening emails," I tell her. "Stupid sh—stuff."

"Like what?" She doesn't sound alarmed, but she's obviously curious. She sets down the pen and folds her hands on the table.

"It seemed like your run-of-the-mill hate mail at first." I stop myself there, conscious of the fact that non-Hollywood types probably don't get hate mail on a daily basis. "Things like, 'with a show concept that stupid, I hope you fail before the first episode airs.' Or there were a few that made reference to our location—something about asshole Californians swooping in and buying up all the land in Oregon."

At that, Mari rolls her eyes. "Because an abandoned cult compound is such a hot piece of real estate."

"Right." I clear my throat. "Anyway, we didn't think much about the emails. But then Lana got this flower delivery."

"Lana's the youngest." Vanessa's eyes hold mine, and it's clear she's thinking about the story I told. The one about stabbing myself in the forehead to make my baby sister feel better.

"Yeah. Lana's in public relations. The kind where it's her job to make celebrities look less like assholes, so she's had a lot of admirers."

"And the opposite of admirers," Mari adds, deftly avoiding the word *enemies*. "So it wasn't completely out of left field that the flowers turned out to be sunflowers."

"Which she's allergic to," I add for Vanessa's benefit. "It's one of those quirky personal details they mention sometimes in articles, so anyone could have known that."

"Or not known it." Mari rests the tips of her fingers on the table and regards Vanessa with her HR look. "It's difficult to determine motivation or intent from the card that came with the flowers."

Vanessa glances from my sister to me. "What did the card say?"

I clear my throat again. "'Get back to LA soon, Love.'"

"I see." Vanessa's wheels are turning as she digests the information. "And was that the end of the threats?"

I take a deep breath. "We're not sure."

She glances from me to Mari and back again. "What do you mean you're not sure?"

My sister is telepathically urging me to play it cool. I can see the frustration in her eyes, in the way she just picked up the pen Vanessa dropped and speared it back through her bun with impressive force. "Last night, there was an attempt to hack the company email."

"More than an attempt," I say as gently as possible. "Someone managed to fire off about a dozen messages that appeared—for all intents and purposes—to come from members of the Juniper Ridge team."

Vanessa cocks her head to one side, curiosity piqued again. "Do you know what the messages said?"

Mari grits her teeth. "One of them originated from my email address and appeared to inform our top candidate for medical director that in order to be considered for the position, he'd need to email me ten photos of his bare feet."

"Yikes." Vanessa cringes, then lifts an eyebrow. "Wait. Did you find out before or after he sent the images?"

A flush races up my sister's throat. "Before, fortunately. He replied seeking clarification about whether they needed to be prints or digital images. Thank God I was able to clear it up."

"Huh." Vanessa looks at me. "What else?"

Naturally, she's guessed that's only the beginning. I sigh and wish I hadn't opened this can of worms. "There's the one sent from Lauren's email to a local cable station, offering exclusive footage from her private collection of personal sex videos."

"A collection that does not exist," Mari adds quickly. "Neither does the offer from Cooper to star in a miniseries about competitive mooing."

"Competitive mooing?" Vanessa blinks. "That's a thing?"

Mari presses her lips together. "Apparently it's quite popular. They hold an annual Moo-la-Palooza in Wisconsin."

Vanessa looks at me. "I guess the guy gets points for creativity."

And for knowing way too much about my family, though that's not a theory I'm ready to share just yet. "Most of the emails were pretty harmless," I tell her. "But the one from me to our top investor inviting him to a nude tomato fight could have been a disaster if the investor wasn't a good friend."

A friend who knows I can't stand tomatoes, both eating them or being hit in the junk with one.

"Well." Vanessa presses her palms to the table. "That's—inconvenient."

Before I can reply, the café door swings open, and Colleen Carver marches through, a laptop gripped in her hands. Spotting us at our corner table, she moves toward us with a purpose.

"You guys have to see this." Setting the computer on the table, she flips it open and glances at Mari. "Sorry, are you in the middle of something?"

"A job offer." I nod at Vanessa. "We've already brought Ms. Vincent up to speed on the situation."

Mari gestures from Colleen to Vanessa, making the introduction I'm too much of a dumbass to remember. "Ms. Vincent is our choice to be the company's Chief Financial Officer," she explains.

"Vanessa, please." She sticks out her hand and gives Colleen's a pleasant shake. "Pleasure to meet you."

"Same. I'm Colleen, by the way."

"Colleen and her wife, Patti, are wildlife biologists," Mari explains. "They were stationed here when Gabe and Dean first visited."

Colleen laughs, and it's a warm, booming sound I've come to love in the short time I've lived here. "We've been running the coffee shop, and in my spare time, I play around with computers."

"She's one of the top hackers in the country," I clarify, seeing no point in beating around the bush. "And we're very grateful she and Patti agreed to stay on as part of the team."

"Very," Mari agrees.

In the months we've known Colleen and Patti, their homemade muffins and gentle advice have filled a parental need Mari and I have never totally acknowledged. But given our upbringing, it's not surprising we'd cling to their gentle brand of mothering.

"Right back atcha." Colleen boots up her laptop and toggles to something on the screen. "Take a look at this."

She angles the computer so we can see the string of gobbledygook numbers and symbols on the screen. It's all Greek to me.

Vanessa gives me a questioning look. "I'm sorry, do you want me to go?"

I shake my head and glance at Mari. "You may as well be part of this. Not like any of us can understand what the hell that is."

"Right, well, I actually do." Vanessa glances at Mari. "Sorry about messing up your online questionnaire."

That's right, she altered the forms. I'm suddenly reminded of her answers to the questions about marriage.

And as she moves closer to make room for Colleen, I'm reminded of other things. That women smell nice and have hair that tickles pleasantly against the back of my hand. Not that I'm noticing that stuff. Or that her skin is soft where her forearm brushes mine.

"Sorry," she murmurs. "Tight squeeze."

"No problem." My voice sounds strained, and Mari gives me a look.

Meanwhile, Colleen points to her laptop. "You see this string of code right here? Take a closer look at this part."

I know I should be looking at the screen, but I catch myself watching Vanessa's face instead. She slips on her glasses, and the graceful intelligence in her face makes my heart squeeze.

"Wow," she says. "Someone went to a lot of trouble to hide his location. Looks like it's set up to appear as though it's coming from a web portal in Kansas."

"I figure that's the location of the portal's data center, but check this out." Colleen points to another spot. "He slipped up. From what I can tell, this appears to be coming from an IP address right here in Oregon."

Vanessa peers closer and nods. "Great catch. And right below that—what's this about?"

"I noticed that, too." Colleen glances at me and gives a quick nod. "Nice eye."

The two of them banter some more about encryption and firewalls and a bunch of other stuff I don't understand. Colleen keeps glancing at me, and I'm starting to suspect she can read my mind. That despite my best intent to keep my thoughts about Vanessa professional, Colleen's picked up on my attraction to her.

I clear my throat. "We should probably let you get back on the road." I touch the contract in front of Vanessa, aware that my hand is inches from her arm. "It's going to take you a while to get through that."

Mari gives me an odd look before turning her attention to Vanessa. "You're more than welcome to stay in one of the vacant cabins," she says. "It's a long drive back to Bend, and spending a night on site would give you a better feel for the place."

"Right, yes." I swallow hard, the thought of Vanessa sleeping close by filling my head with all kinds of thoughts I shouldn't have. "It might help you to make your decision."

"Thanks, but I should get back to Bend." She grabs the stack of paperwork and stands up, tapping it once on the table. "My cousin's hosting some fancy dinner at the resort. I promised I'd be there."

"Of course." Relief and disappointment wash through me in equal parts. "Let me walk you to your car."

Dumb. What a dumb offer. It's a job interview, not a date.

But Vanessa just smiles. "Thanks." She extends a hand to Colleen first. "Very nice to meet you."

Colleen gives her hand a firm shake. "I hope we'll be seeing a lot more of you."

"Same." Vanessa turns to Mari. "It was a pleasure meeting you as well."

"Likewise." Mari stands and slips a business card out of the pocket on her briefcase. "If you have any questions about the benefits package or the details of the offer, please call me anytime."

"I will, thanks." Vanessa slips the card into her purse and turns to me. "I'm parked out in front of the lodge."

"I'm walking back there anyway." I let her go first, then worry she'll think I'm checking out her ass. Goddammit, I should have paid more attention in that HR workshop Mari gave.

But soon we're walking side by side across the parking lot, the early summer sun bathing us in warm, syrupy light. On the western horizon, the red-gold dirt of the Cascade foothills seems to glow. There's a grassy field to the west where an irrigation system gives a steady *tsk-tsk-tsk*, scolding me for thinking impure thoughts about Vanessa.

"Is all of this part of the Juniper Ridge property?" she asks.

"Yeah, we've got a little over 50,000 acres. Members of BONK planned to expand and eventually build a sports stadium over there by the waterpark."

"That's right, I read about the waterpark." She grins and flutters the papers of the contract. "Definitely a job perk I'll take into consideration."

"There's a world-class climbing area just north of here." I point toward the ridge where the basalt cliffs cling to shreds of late sunlight. "In case that's a selling point."

"Noted," she says. "I do love rock climbing. And I read somewhere that there's a lake for paddling?"

"You haven't seen it yet?"

She shakes her head. "I meant to ask for a tour, but we got busy."

"Damn, I should have offered you one." This is why I shouldn't be in charge of hiring.

"It's okay. I really do need to get back, but maybe I could come out again soon for the tour?"

"We'll make it happen." The eagerness in my voice makes me want to hurl tomatoes at my own junk. Luckily, we've reached the edge of the parking lot, where an older-looking Lexus SUV sits next to Gabe's vintage Mustang.

Vanessa hits the key fob to unlock her car and smiles. "I recognized Gabe's car, so I figured this was an okay spot to park."

"You'll have your own designated parking spot." That's assuming she accepts the job. I shouldn't get ahead of myself. "One of the perks of an administrative position."

Opening the rear door, she sets her bag on the floor of the backseat. "What about lodging? I know the ad said that's provided, but would I have to sleep with someone else?"

Her word choice seems to register in her brain at the same time it does mine, and her cheeks flush crimson. "I didn't mean—"

"No, that's okay. You'd have your own private cabin."

"Great. Perfect." She bites her lip. "This might be an awkward question, but—"

"It's okay, I'm used to it." Fuck, that was dumb. I have no idea what she's going to ask, but experience tells me it's something personal like my breakup with Andrea Knight or the Dave Wienerman scandal. "I mean, you can ask anything."

She gives me an odd look. "Okay, um—I was wondering about pets."

I blink. "Pets?"

"Dogs, specifically." Her cheeks flush just a little. "I've always wanted one, and this seemed like a good chance to adopt a dog."

"Oh. Yes, of course." I'm such an idiot. "You can definitely have pets in your cabin. As many as you like, dogs or cats or zebras or pterodactyls."

She laughs and tucks a strand of hair behind her ear. "Just a dog will do. Thanks."

God, she's beautiful with that color in her cheeks and the sun glinting in her hair.

Which is why I take a step back. "It's been a pleasure, Ms.…Vanessa."

"Likewise Mr.…Dean." She smiles and holds out her hand to shake.

I've just started to reach for it when her eyes blaze wide.

"Ohmygodohmygodohmygod!"

With a shriek, she leaps onto the car's running board, shoes scrambling for purchase. Her heel slips on the metal edge as her arm tangles in the seatbelt, and she flails back with a blood-curdling scream.

"Snakesnakesnakesnake!"

I throw my arms out to catch her without fully registering her words. She lands against my chest with a helluva lot more force than I'm expecting.

"Ooof." I reel to the side, fighting to keep us both upright, but she's struggling and shrieking and still panting "snakesnakesnakesnake!" as I struggle to keep my balance.

I'm realizing she must have spotted one of our resident diamondback rattlers, which I'm not fond of either. My shaky balance makes the snap decision easier, and I topple us both into the backseat.

I fall hard on my back, arms wrapped snug around Vanessa. She keeps flailing, but gravity's no match for her panic. She lands on top of me, collapsing in a sprawl across my chest.

"Ooof." I grunt as her full weight hits me, and I slide my hands to her hips to catch some of her weight.

She blinks down at me, mouth open in a wide O.

*Oh, shit.*

# CHAPTER 4

**CONFESSIONAL 102**

Vincent, Vanessa (CFO candidate: Juniper Ridge)

*Most embarrassing moment? Ugh. I really have to say this on camera? No, it's not that. It's just—where to start? The time I texted my sister asking which brand of tampons she needed me to grab, but I messaged my boss instead. Or the time I mispronounced "organic" as "orgasmic" in a presentation on sustainable farming. Or how about when I offered my seat to a pregnant woman on the subway, only it turned out she wasn't really pregnant. Or the time I—what? Yeah, I could do this all day.*

* * *

There's this moment as I lie spread-eagled on Dean Judson where I consider hurling myself onto the ground to let the rattlesnake have me. It'll be a slow death, but no more humiliating than concluding my job interview by straddling the boss in my backseat.

Somehow, I manage to stop screaming. That might have something to do with Dean's hands gripping my ass.

"Vanessa, stop. Ouch—shit, you're crushing my nuts."

Oh, God. I thought this couldn't be worse.

Scrunching my eyes closed, I fight to get my breathing under control. I keep my eyelids shut tight as I address the man I've inadvertently mounted. "I saw a snake."

"Yeah. I got that."

"I'm, uh—petrified of snakes."

"No kidding." He shifts my weight on top of him, moving my hip off his junk. "In addition to the globophobia."

I open my eyes expecting to see him glaring at me. Instead, there's a look of utter bemusement in his eyes. And something else. Something like…heat?

But that can't be right. I practically maimed the man just now. I'll be lucky if he doesn't have security escort me off the premises.

I look into those silvery eyes and want to kick myself. "I'm so sorry."

I should definitely dismount. Just straighten up and peel myself off his chest, exiting the vehicle with my few remaining shreds of dignity. But something in his eyes leaves me frozen in place.

Also, there's a snake out there. "It was really big."

He shifts beneath me, gritting his teeth. "You don't say."

"Huge." I'm not sure he believes me. "I've never seen one that big."

"Vanessa." He lets go of my ass, jaw still clenching. "I'm gonna need you to stop moving like that."

"What?"

Shit, right, I'm crushing his—wait. *Oh.*

Yeah, that's definitely not a snake I'm feeling. A very intimate part of my anatomy is pressed against a very intimate part of his, and the result is…um. *Intimate.*

"It's a biological reaction," I sputter, pushing off his chest. "I know it doesn't mean anything."

Kill me now. I'm lecturing him about his penis like he hasn't spent three decades with it attached to his body.

Also, I'm still straddling him.

I try to untangle my legs from his but end up pressing my crotch more firmly against the impressive bulge in his pants. This is the most humiliating moment of my life, and I'm praying for someone to fill my whole car with snakes and light it on fire. That couldn't be worse than this.

"Hold still." Dean struggles to sit up, his hand settling in the small of my back. "Your ankle's all wrapped up in the seatbelt. If you'll just stop moving for a second—"

"I'm so sorry." I let my body go slack as I close my eyes again, unable to look at him. "I totally understand if you don't want to hire me after this."

Dean doesn't say anything, so I open my eyes again as he finishes untangling me. His jaw is clenched almost as tight as his arm around my waist.

"There are many things I want to do right now." His voice has gone gravelly, and my ribs buzz with the vibration of it. "But since hiring you is chief among them, it's the only one that's gonna happen."

It takes me a second to catch his drift. That's probably because my heart's hammering like a Clydesdale clomping across a kettle drum.

"Oh." I open my eyes and lick my lips. "Um, yes."

His smile is small and strained. "That wasn't a proposition. Just stating a biological fact, as you so eloquently put it."

"Right." My ankles are free now, so I manage to hoist myself off him. I back out of the car, using the edge of the door for balance.

The instant my shoe touches the ground, I remember what

got us into this mess in the first place. "Rattlesnakes." I start to jerk my foot back, but Dean sits up and nudges me back.

"They're more afraid of you than you are of them."

"I doubt that."

"I'm sure it's long gone."

I have to admit he's right, so I take a step back and offer him a hand up. "Really, I'm so sorry."

"Vanessa, if you apologize again, I'm rescinding the job offer." He ignores my outstretched hand, and I step back to let him escape my car.

"Really?"

"No. But accidents happen." He dusts himself off, deliberately putting distance between us. "I know you didn't intentionally tackle me in the backseat of your car."

"Of course not." But did I intentionally stay just a few beats longer than I should have?

The jury's out on that one.

As Dean straightens his shirt, I scan the ground for any sign of the snake. It's long gone, just like he said.

But the effects of having Dean Judson's warm, solid, masculine body pinned between my thighs?

That's not going anywhere. Not anytime soon.

***

"OVER HERE WE have the Go Kart track." Lana Judson sweeps an arm out over the twisty patch of asphalt as she regards me with a raised brow. "Your guess is as good as mine why a doomsday cult needed one."

I step to the edge of the lined asphalt, surveying the dozen or so vehicles lined up in a covered bay. "If you're expecting end times, you might as well go out with a bang."

"Which can also be accomplished in the bumper car arena." Lana laughs. "We thought about taking them out, but it seemed like something community members could use to blow off steam."

"Plus, you'll get some great footage out of it."

She grins, pleased I'm getting it. "Exactly." She tucks a chunk of honey blond hair behind one ear. "You ready to see the residences?"

"Absolutely."

I follow Lana across the campus, watching carefully for more snakes. And for Dean, who is conspicuously absent for my first tour of the grounds.

When I called this morning to arrange it, Mari volunteered the youngest Judson sib for duty. "Gabe and Lauren are off filming, and Cooper's with me all day doing sensitivity training."

I didn't ask if the training was required for everyone or just the elusive Cooper. I also didn't ask about Dean. It doesn't take a rocket scientist to figure he's avoiding me.

"And here we have cabins one through thirty-five." She gestures toward tidy rows of log structures so adorable, it takes me a moment to remember this isn't summer camp. "You'll be in this block. We haven't assigned you one yet, but they're all pretty similar. Want to see inside?"

"Of course."

She whips out a ring of keys and leads me through the door of the first cabin on the right. It's a single-story darling with a red door and little flower boxes lining the front windows. The space is small, but homey, with a bedroom, a small office, and a surprisingly roomy kitchen. The walls are honeyed pine, and the floors a mix of warm, coppery slate and hardwood.

"We've got catalogues so you can pick your own furniture," she says. "That's included, of course."

"It's gorgeous." I turn in a circle, wondering why the space looks eerily familiar. "I'm having the oddest déjà-vus right now."

Lana laughs and jingles the keys. "They're Armbrust cedar cabins." I must look confused, so she continues. "Nick Armbrust. He's kind of a famous builder. If you've visited any of the Armbrust Resorts around the country, you might have stayed in one."

That's it. Shit. My last boyfriend, Bradley Inkster. We stayed at an Armbrust Resort for a romantic weekend getaway. We ate cheese and crackers in front of the roaring fireplace and made love on a scratchy wool rug.

The next morning, he got a text from his wife.

For the record, I didn't know there was a wife. I dumped him immediately, and we were only together a few weeks anyway, but I still feel lousy about it. He was a controlling, manipulative son-of-a-bitch, but I liked him.

It just goes to show I suck at picking men.

"Are you okay?"

Lana's looking at me with concern in her pretty blue eyes, and I force myself to smile. "Absolutely. It's fabulous. Really. I'll be very happy here." I survey the kitchen, running my hand over the simple quartz counter. "How many cabins are there, anyway?"

"Sixty right now, but we're building more. The idea is that community members will start to pair off, and we'll want more residences suitable for family life."

"Wow, that's thinking ahead."

She smiles. "That's Dean for you."

I'm not surprised it all goes back to Dean. I fight to keep my expression neutral, to give nothing away as far as Lana's big brother is concerned.

"Let's head this way." She leads me out onto the quaint back deck and into the warm sunshine. "This first block is still mostly vacant. Lauren and I are over there, and Mari's place is close to the coffee shop. Gabe and his wife have a bigger one over there by the pond."

I notice she didn't mention Dean, and no way am I asking. But Lana gives me a sheepish look as we trudge back into the cabin. "In case you're worried about it being weird living too close to the boss man, he specifically asked that you be placed in this section."

"What? Oh, you mean Dean." Of course she does; who else would she mean?

Lana just smiles, not fazed by my weirdness. "Also, he's not *your* boss, for the record. But he's way over there in that section near the trees."

"Oh. Great." I have no reason to feel disappointed. God knows I don't want to live next door to my hottie boss. Colleague. Whatever.

But is it wrong to feel just a little hurt he's so eager to put distance between us?

Lana leads me out the front door and locks it. I step around to the side, scanning the spacious back deck and the jagged, snow-capped peaks of the Cascade Mountains. I bet the sunsets are killer here. "Is this cabin spoken for already?"

"No, you like it?"

"It's perfect."

She smiles. "It's one of my favorites, too. It's all yours if you want it. I can show you some others, but—"

"No, this is it."

Lana nods. "Decisive. I like it."

She's smiling, but I can't help hearing my mother's voice in my head. The way she used to chide me for making snap decisions.

*"Honestly, Vanessa. You're so flighty. You'll need to find a man to take care of you. God knows you're not cut out to be on your own."*

I have to swallow a few times to shove down the sour memories surging inside me. I smile at Lana, doing my best impression of a perfectly normal woman.

"Dean told me you might get a dog." She says it like I'm

acquiring a Ferrari and a diamond tennis bracelet, and I instantly love her for it.

"I'd like one," I admit. "It'd have to be the right dog."

"Absolutely. Well, let me know if you need any help. I'm kind of an animal nut."

"Will do." I can see myself becoming good friends with Lana, and the thought makes me smile.

As she leads me along the red dirt path, she chatters about the community. "They're looking to get essential skills hired first. Doctors, nurses, cops, grocers, stuff like that. I know Dean plans to have you help with that, since these are key financial decisions."

"Sounds great."

She gives me a measured look. "Dean's got some pretty clear ideas how he wants things done. Just—don't be afraid to push back, okay?"

I nod, appreciating her candor. "I'll do my best."

"I figured you would."

She turns and keeps walking, and I feel that bitter surge again. I like to picture myself as a strong, confident woman who'd speak up when the boss made questionable choices. I've tried hard to be that woman, both at work and in my personal life.

But deep down, I wonder sometimes if my mother had a point.

*"You should be more like Valerie,"* she said once when my twin was in the other room packing for her internship with a famous clothing designer. *"Choose a ladylike career where you won't need to go toe-to-toe with powerful men. That's not for you, Vanessa."*

Goddammit. I hate that I recall every word of these conversations. I hate that it still bugs me.

Lana keeps walking, and I hustle to keep pace with her. We're almost to the lodge, and she turns to face me on the cinder-lined pathway. "By the way, Dean hired an expert herpetologist to snake-proof the residence areas. They'll be cutting back grass, moving all the dead wood away from structures, that sort of thing. You should be totally safe."

My cheeks flame, and I wonder how much he told his family about what happened. How thoroughly I humiliated myself in the parking lot. "Um, yeah. About that—"

"Hey, Lana." Dean ambles out the side door of the lodge and does a double-take when he sees me. "Vanessa. I didn't realize you'd be here today."

"Yep. Yeah, I copied you on the email."

"Huh. Sorry, but I'm glad Mari got you taken care of."

Lana gives him an exasperated shove. "Hello? I have a role here too, you know."

"Of course you do." He throws an arm around her, yanking her close so he can ruffle her hair. "You're the only Judson universally liked by everyone. The rest of us are assholes."

"Get away from me, asshole." She's laughing as she shoves at him.

Dean lets go and nods at me. "Are you getting all your questions answered?"

"Absolutely." Except the one about whether I'll ever live down what happened in my backseat. "The grounds are amazing. I don't know what it looked like before, but you guys must have done a lot of work."

"Not as much as you'd think," Lana says. "It's amazing how much of the infrastructure was already in place."

"Even the grocery store," Dean adds. "We had to replace a bunch of the coolers and upgrade the flooring, but the basics were already there."

"Lana gave me the tour," I say. "It'll be great once it's up and running."

"Same with the rest of the shops." He drags his fingers through his hair, drawing my attention to those damn hands again. "Speaking of which, are you free to go over some figures?"

"Right now?"'

"Yeah, sorry. I know you're still deciding if you'll even take the job—"

"Actually, I decided." I rifle through my bag and find the folder containing the contract. "Here. All signed and everything."

Dean takes it from me and whistles low under his breath. "Wow, you're fast." His hazel eyes scan the first page, landing on my signature at the bottom. "I'm surprised you didn't have any questions. There's some weird stuff in here."

Lana rolls her eyes. "'Weird' meaning you're pretty much a normal CFO, except you live with us and agree to let us tape your whole life?"

I shrug and offer an easy smile. "Nothing weird about that at all." I turn back to Dean. "My cousin's an attorney. Well, he's also the CEO at Ponderosa resort, but he was a lawyer before that. He looked it over for me."

"You had James Bracelyn look at this?"

"Yeah, is that okay?" Crap, I hope I didn't screw this up already. I mean besides dry-humping my boss in my backseat.

"No, it's great," Dean says. "I met James a few times. Great guy. Gave me some tips for getting this place up and running."

"That sounds like James. He seems like a hard-ass control-freak, but he's a marshmallow inside."

Lana gives a knowing smirk and pats her brother's chest. "Now why does that sound familiar?" She jumps out of the way before he can grab her again, laughing as she dances back down the red cinder path. "I'll see you at dinner, yeah?"

"Yeah," Dean mutters. "Are we at Gabe's place tonight?"

"No, Cooper's. Don't you read the schedule?"

"I have a lot on my plate right now."

"You won't tonight," she says. "Coop's making some vegetarian dish."

"Ugh. Remind me to grab a Big Mac beforehand."

As Lana saunters off, Dean watches her go. The second she's

out of earshot, he turns back to me. “Everything go okay with the tour?”

“Yeah, perfect.” I shove my hands in my pockets. “You told her about me pouncing on you yesterday?”

He cocks his head. “Of course not. Why? What did she say?”

“She said you ordered snake-proofing for all the yards.”

“It’s a safety issue.” The smile he gives me shoots straight to my lady bits. “I don’t just mean my safety. Pretty sure you cracked one of my ribs.”

“God, I’m so s—”

“Nope.” He throws out a hand up to stop me, an easy smile gracing his handsome face. “I’m kidding. My ribs are fine. And I promise I didn’t tell Lana about being in your backseat. Your secret’s safe with me.”

“Thank you.” I take a few deep breaths to wash away any lingering humiliation. “You said you had some numbers to go over?”

“Right, that was just to get Lana out of here.” His smile dims just a little. “We heard from our troublemaker again.”

“Troublemaker?” I frown. “Oh, you mean the hacker? The guy who’s been sending flowers and weird notes and stuff.”

“That’s the one. Only there’s something different this time.”

“What?”

Dean’s jaw clenches. “This one’s about you.”

# CHAPTER 5

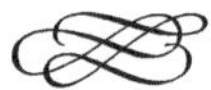

**CONFESSIONAL 141**

JUDSON, DEAN (CEO: JUNIPER RIDGE)

*LET'S SEE, BIGGEST CHALLENGES SO FAR...WELL, WE'RE JUST GETTING THINGS OFF THE GROUND, SO OBVIOUSLY THERE'S FINANCING AND NEGOTIATING WITH INVESTORS. INSURANCE AND LEGAL DETAILS, PLUS THE LOGISTICS OF BUILDING A WHOLE DAMN TOWN PRACTICALLY FROM SCRATCH. WATER, SEWER, ELECTRICITY—WHAT? PERSONNEL? I MEAN... YEAH. FINDING THE RIGHT PEOPLE IS PRETTY FUCKING IMPORTANT. THAT'S ONE THING YOU DON'T WANT TO SCREW UP. NOTHING BLOWS IT ALL TO HELL LIKE ENDING UP WITH THE WRONG PERSON.*

* * *

I'm alone in my office with Vanessa Vincent, reminding myself that it's no big deal. We're going to be in this position thousands of times over the course of our working relationship.

That doesn't stop me from thinking about other positions. The one in her backseat is top of mind.

"This came in today's mail." I hold out a postcard with the

written side facing her. It's typed, which is odd for a postcard, but that's not the weirdest thing.

I watch her eyes as she scans the words.

*"She's trouble. This is not the person to hire if you know what's good for you."*

She looks up at me, brown eyes curious. "You think it's about me?"

I flip the card over, and she gasps. It's a headshot of Vanessa as a teen. She's wearing a fuzzy pink sweater and a fierce scowl that's not even a little hidden by the dark curls falling over her face. I've never seen this picture before, but I'd know those brown eyes anywhere.

Seeing it has clearly knocked her off her stride. "Where did this—how did someone—"

"No idea. You're familiar with the photo?"

She nods, looking slapped. "It's from a bunch of headshots our mom made us do when we were sixteen. She wanted us to get back into showbiz, but I wasn't interested."

"That explains the pissed-off look." Even pissed off, she's stunning. I don't say this out loud. I've gone through Mari's damn sensitivity training.

"I look like a raging bitch," Vanessa agrees. "Weirdly enough, it made some people want to work with me."

"I thought you didn't act again after *Baby Spies*."

"If you can call that acting." She snorts. "I refused to read for any of the roles. It's one of the only times I stood up to my mom."

I turn the photo back around for another look at it. The girl in the picture is young, but there are signs of the fire I've seen in this woman sitting in my office now. "I never came across this picture online."

"Hardly anyone had access to it. Like I said, my re-entry into showbiz never got off the ground."

"So how the hell did it end up here?"

She shakes her head, shock giving way to frustration. "I don't have a clue. I can call my mom and ask if she's given it out to anyone." She starts to reach for it, then stops. "Wait. Do you need to have it dusted for fingerprints or anything?"

"This is a copy. I handed the real one off to our private investigator."

Plucking the copy off the desk, she flips it and studies the words again. "Does he think he'll be able to learn anything?"

"Not likely. Even if he could lift prints off a postcard, this was in our PO box. Probably dozens of postal workers touched it."

Her brow furrows, and I watch her reach the same conclusion I already did. "I don't understand." She looks up at me, brown eyes bright and clear. "I interviewed days ago. You didn't offer me the job until then. How would someone have time to mail a card like this?"

"Good question." I steeple my hands on the desk, trying to decide how much to tell her. "We've been tight-lipped about who we're interviewing for these positions. But if someone had the ability to hack into our email, they'd have learned you were our top candidate."

"I see." Her frown deepens, and I can't help noticing how sexy she is when irritated. It's no wonder directors wanted to cast her. "Are you thinking this whole vendetta thing is about me?"

I hesitate. "I don't think so."

She quirks an eyebrow. "That doesn't sound very certain."

"The initial threat came when we'd only just started advertising your job."

"I applied the first day."

I did consider that. "I still don't think it's about you."

She doesn't look convinced. As she flips over the card, I wonder if it's so she doesn't have to see her teenage scowl anymore. "Why would they pick that photo of all things? Where did they even get it?"

"Whoever this guy is, he's showing off. Letting us know he can get to us from a lot of different angles."

She looks me in the eye, unflinching. "Do you have any theories who'd do this?"

I shrug. "The Judsons have plenty of enemies. It could be any one of them."

I watch her face as she processes this. "Or someone tied to the Benevolent Order of the New Kingdom." She sets the card back on the desk and grips the armrest of my desk chair. "Weren't they still trying to get the land back?"

That had crossed my mind. "There are a few outspoken kooks. The ones who didn't end up in prison, I mean."

I can see the wheels turning in her head. "I assume your PI is working on this?"

"Yeah. We also brought the local police into the loop last week. One of their Lieutenants is our top contender to be the police chief at Juniper Ridge, so she's been looking things over."

I should give her a copy of this card. Lieutenant Amy Lovelin is on my list to call today, along with a thousand other people. I could ask one of my siblings to help, but I don't want to scare anyone unnecessarily. It's best if I handle this myself.

Vanessa glances around the office. I follow her gaze with mine, trying to see the space through her eyes. The expensive leather sofa that looks like no one's ever sat on it. Just yesterday, Lana tried to add a bunch of bright orange throw pillows, but I shooed her out. Above that is a framed family photo on a polished black shelf. Vanessa's gaze lingers there a moment, then shifts to the corner of my desk.

I watch her survey my mug, my special edition red Swingline stapler, the remote control for my office television. They're lined up in a perfect row, and my ex-fiancée's voice whispers in the back of my head.

*"You're such a control-freak, Dean. Loosen up. You work too much."*

"This must be a special mug?" Vanessa picks it up, and I fight the urge to grab for it.

"Yeah. I mean, it's not sentimental or anything." I watch her set it back down a good five inches from where it rested before, and it's all I can do not to move it back to where it was. "I've had it a really long time. It holds the exact right amount of coffee."

"Huh." Her gaze shifts to the remote control and her brows lift. "Your TV remote is attached to your desk?"

I was hoping she wouldn't notice. "I hate when it wanders off."

I hate even more when other people mess with my TV stations or the volume, but no way I'm admitting that. She already thinks I'm a creep after what happened in her backseat. I still can't believe I got a hard-on. That I grabbed her ass and—

"Has the PI swept for bugs?"

I blink. "What?"

"Bugs. Listening devices. I was just wondering if someone might be listening in somehow."

Well, shit. "It hasn't come up." Probably should have. "Maybe I should fire the PI and hire you to do all the investigating."

She laughs and slips out of her chair, dropping onto the floor like she does this sort of thing all the time. "Don't they usually stick them under tables and stuff?" Her voice echoes under my desk as she crawls beneath. "Or is that just in movies?"

Her hand brushes my foot, and I jump like someone hit me with a cattle prod. This should definitely not turn me on. "Do you even know what a bug looks like?" My voice croaks weirdly.

"No, but I keep a mini recorder in my purse. Maybe something like that?"

"Smaller." I suck in a breath as her body heat seeps through my pantleg and radiates up, headed for parts growing less small by the moment. "They're actually pretty tiny."

"Well, I know what nails and screws and wood look like," she calls. "If I see something other than that, I'll consider it suspicious."

And I'll consider it a miracle if I don't pass out before she's back in her chair. "Vanessa, I think you should—"

"Whoa, I can come back later." Cooper skids to a halt in my doorway, eyes boggling at Vanessa's backside sticking out from under my desk.

*Oh, God.* "No, that's not—It's not what you—"

"Hey, I'm Vanessa." She pops out from under the desk, spitting her hair out of her mouth. "You must be Cooper?"

Of course he's Cooper. His face has graced the cover of every magazine on the planet, but I appreciate Vanessa pretending this is normal.

"Pleased to meet you." My younger brother shakes her hand and does a lousy job wiping the smirk off his face. "You're the new money geek?"

"That's what it'll say on my business cards." She grins and turns to me. "Look what I found."

She holds up something that looks a bit like a watch battery, only with weird wires poking out of it. "It was stuck to the underside of your desk. I'm assuming it's not yours?"

I shake my head as she sets it down in front of me. Picking it up between my thumb and forefinger, I hold it up to the light. "Ever seen a bug before, Coop?"

"What, like a listening device?" The stupid grin vanishes as he steps into my office. "I did that spy film a few years back. I'm guessing the technology's changed, but yeah—that does look like a bug."

"Huh." I should probably stop touching the damn thing. Setting it down on my desk, I pull out my phone and snap a few quick pics. "I'll send these to the PI."

Cooper's brow furrows. "What, you think someone's eavesdropping now?"

"No idea. But I won't feel good about this until we have the whole place swept for bugs."

"Good call." He turns his attention back to Vanessa. "So you'll be keeping this bastard in line, huh?"

She quirks an eyebrow at me. "I don't recall seeing that in the job description, but I'm up to the task."

Grinning, Cooper starts to back out of my office. "He's an overbearing son-of-a-bitch but he's good at his job. Also, we love him."

Vanessa glances at me, assessing. "I was raised by an overbearing bitch. Does that trump the son of one?"

"Maybe so." Cooper laughs. "I didn't mean to insult Mom."

I'm only half listening as I fire off a text to the PI. I attach the photos, then set down my phone and address Vanessa across the desk. "I don't know about you, but I'm not feeling great about analyzing sensitive data in here."

"Agreed." She settles back in her chair and crosses her legs. "How about one of the studios or something?"

"Two are occupied, and one's being painted right now." Cooper snaps his fingers. "Shit, that's what I came here to ask you—Gabe and I want to bring out that beer guy for an interview. You have any issues with us showing him the brewing facility?"

I struggle not to flinch. Not to fret about my kid brother being tempted to drink again. "That's fine. I want to be part of it. Can you add it to my calendar?"

"Aye-aye, Captain." He gives me a mock salute as he retreats for real. Before he slips out of sight, he puts a hand over his heart and makes a swooning gesture toward Vanessa.

I'm not sure if Coop's half in love with her or suggesting I might be, but either way, I want to throw something at him. Vanessa's looking at me, so she misses my brother's stupid gesture, but she doesn't miss the glare I shoot him.

Her expression melts into something softer. "You're making me miss my sister."

For some reason, this charms the hell out of me. "You're twins, right?"

"Yep. She's traveling with her husband, doing this TV show

where she makes wedding dresses all over the world. We talk every day, but I miss seeing her."

I love that she's close with her sister. It's one of those things we'd never put in a job description, but that grasp of human connection is what Mari says is crucial to making this show work. "All right. The studios are off-limits, and I don't trust the conference room until my PI gets in here with a bug sweeper. How do you feel about one of the picnic tables out in the meadow?"

Vanessa frowns. "Normally, I love the outdoors. But didn't Lana say they're doing snake-proofing today?"

Crap, she's right. I open my mouth to suggest my cabin, then shut it again. That's exactly what we *don't* need. "I don't suppose the bumper cars are a good spot to have a budget meeting?"

She laughs. "I like how you think, but maybe not ideal for spreadsheets. What about the waterpark?"

It's my turn to shoot her a baffled look. "You've got a waterproof laptop or something?"

Rolling her eyes, she gets to her feet. "We don't need to be in the water. But Lana showed it to me on the tour, and there's that indoor area next to the big slide. I saw a bunch of tables there."

"Right, yeah. That'll work." I get to my feet, appreciating Vanessa's ability to think on hers. "Sounds like a plan."

She falls into step beside me as I head down the hall and toward the lodge's side exit. The high desert sun blazes warm and bright as we make our way along the crushed cinder pathway toward the building that houses the waterpark. Sunlight glints in her dark hair, and something warm sloshes in my belly. I'm not sure if I'm smelling desert wildflowers or Vanessa, but I'm enjoying it either way.

"I can't get over the idea that I have a waterpark just a few hundred yards from my house." She laughs and shakes her head. "Bumper cars, too."

"There's a lot of weird stuff the BONK members built out

here," I admit. "Even a bomb shelter under one of those big wheat fields to the north. It can hold several hundred people in a pinch."

"Wow." A thick wave of chlorine smacks into us as she pulls open the door, and I'm transported back to childhood summers at my family's estate. "I had no idea most of this stuff was out here. I watched the news when BONK was getting shut down, but I'd written them off as just a crazy cult. I didn't realize they were so...."

"Organized?"

"Resourceful." She beelines it toward the tables at the far edge of the space. I follow her past the indoor wave pool and a smaller, shallower pool filled with play equipment for kids.

Vanessa picks her way around spouting fountains toward the five-story enclosed waterslide that empties into a deep pool of turquoise. There's a table close to the edge, and she sets down her bag and pulls out her laptop. "Thanks for sending over those advertiser profiles last night. It's helpful to know what we've got to work with."

I take a seat across from her and set down my own laptop. "Some of the advertisers have very specific requirements for the sort of content they'd like tied to their brands."

"I can imagine." She cocks her head. "Isn't it tough to control that in reality television?"

"There are always ways to control things."

Something flashes in her eyes, and I wish I could take back my words.

"Good to know," she says simply, and goes back to powering up her laptop.

I clear my throat and toggle to my desktop files. "I'm AirDropping you some of the storyboard stuff that Gabe and Lauren put together. There aren't any guarantees with unscripted reality TV, but this should give you an idea what sort of content we're aiming for."

"Got it." She slips a pair of glasses out of her purse, then reaches in again and pulls out a full-sized bag of tortilla chips. "Want some?"

"Uh—thanks." I glance at the purse, wondering what else she's got in there. "I forgot lunch."

"I've got salsa, too." She extracts a sealed jar and pops the top, then reaches back into her bag. "Apple or pear?"

"Are you traveling with an entire grocery store?"

She laughs and sets both pieces of fruit on the table. "I like being prepared."

I can't imagine how heavy her purse must be, but I'm grateful for the snacks. I bite into the apple, savoring the crisp tartness as Vanessa gets to work opening the document. "Just give me a couple minutes to skim through this."

"Take your time." I should probably fire off another message to the PI or the police, but I catch myself watching Vanessa instead. I love how she's hit the ground running. How she's taking charge and fitting right in.

*Stop staring at her, you fucking creep.*

I drag my gaze off her and take another bite of apple as I survey the space. There's a faux rock grotto in the corner, complete with waterfall. It reminds me of the resort in Jamaica where Andrea and I vacationed together. This was a month or two before the split, and the sight of those mossy rocks fills me with—

"Longing and lust."

Vanessa's voice yanks me back to reality with a thud, and I respond without thinking. "Definitely not."

She blinks. "What?"

I'm such a dumbass. "Sorry. What were you saying?"

Her expression is bemused as she nods at her laptop. "That's a common theme for a lot of these story setups. Try to find community members who seem compatible, then arrange for them to be together in close proximity."

"Oh. Yeah. That's part of the social experiment, I guess.

Watching people fall for each other. Filming the fallout when they split up."

Vanessa's brow lifts as she dips a chip into the salsa jar. "That's a very cynical view."

"We spell it out pretty clearly in the contract," I point out. "Not that we're going full-on matchmaker with this, but the romance drama will be a cornerstone of our programming."

"I meant the assumption that they'll split up."

I shrug, dragging a thumb over my laptop's trackpad. "You disagree?"

"Not at all. But what about the rest of your family? I've gotta think at least a couple of them are hoping for happily ever afters."

I consider that. "The social experiment component was all Mari's idea, so yeah—I guess scientifically speaking, it's expected maybe some of the couples will make it."

But most won't. I'm smart enough to know that.

"Probably a good thing you and I aren't in charge of programming, huh?" She picks up the pear but doesn't bite into it. "It'd just be episode after episode of 'tune in this week to see who's breaking up.'"

I laugh, grateful she's found the humor in it. My sisters just call me an unsentimental ass. "As long as you and I keep the lights on and the production crews paid, it'll all work out."

Vanessa seems to hesitate. There's something she wants to ask me, I can tell. "What is it?"

She doesn't beat around the bush. "We both spent time cyberstalking each other," she says. "So I couldn't help reading about you and Andrea Knight."

Hearing that name turns the apple into lava in my stomach. I fight to keep my expression neutral. "That was a long time ago."

Not that long. Eight months since we split, though more than a year since I heard rumors she'd been screwing around. I tried to ignore it, burying my head in the sand and the rest of me in huge heaps of work. Andrea denied it, I believed her, and we went along like that for months before I found out the truth.

I won't make that mistake again.

Vanessa glances down at her laptop. "It sounded like a messy split, so I don't blame you for being cynical about love and romance and all that."

"Yeah." This is my opening. My chance to ask about her responses on that questionnaire, the reasons she's so adamant about avoiding relationships. "I take it you've had some ugly breakups?"

She shrugs and keeps her gaze on the laptop screen. "There's this guy I dated—Raleigh—and I was so sure he was going to propose. Instead, he traveled all the way to Oregon with me for my cousin's wedding, then dumped me after getting a free vacation."

"Ouch."

Her smile doesn't quite reach her eyes. "That's barely the tip of the iceberg. My last boyfriend forgot to mention he had a wife. The guy before that was a co-worker who took credit for my ideas and got promoted over me."

Holy shit. "I'm sorry. They sound like assholes."

"Sure, that's true." She waves a hand like that's inconsequential. "But I'm the one picking them, so what does that make me?"

*Kindhearted. Trusting. Optimistic.*

I know those aren't the answers she wants, so I don't bother saying any of that. For some reason, I find myself wanting to share my own stupid story. "You're right, my breakup was ugly. With Andrea?"

"I'm sorry." She swirls another chip in the salsa. "I only know what I saw in the headlines, but it sounded rough."

"Yeah." I don't know why I'm telling her this as sordid details spill from my mouth. "I worked too much. That's the main thing. I kinda can't blame her for what happened."

*What happened.*

I make it sound like she tripped and fell on some guy's dick. In reality, there was probably more than one guy. More than one instance of cheating. I'll probably never know, and it doesn't matter anyway.

Vanessa folds her hands on the table. I can tell she wants to ask, so I spare her the trouble.

"Yeah, it's true."

She blinks. "What's true?"

"I ended the relationship over text." It was a dick move; I know that now. "It was a long time coming, and I didn't expect her to go on all the talk shows and discuss it, but yeah. I handled things poorly."

Vanessa's eyes fill with sympathy, and I brace for her to defend my ex. Andrea Knight is Hollywood royalty, and everyone loves her films. "It must have been painful for everyone," she says. "I'm sorry you went through that."

I watch her face for signs of sarcasm, but there isn't any. Just openness and kindness and an eagerness to move forward.

With work.

That's what we're here for. I shake myself out of my sharing-time funk and reach for the chip bag. "Let's take a look at the figures in column two on the third page of the spreadsheet."

Vanessa looks at me a moment, then nods. "Absolutely. Let's stay focused on the job."

It's the reminder I need. Maybe we both need it. We're here for one reason, and that's to get Juniper Ridge off the ground.

I scoop a mountain of salsa onto a chip and shove it in my mouth, savoring the sting. I feel it burn all the way down my throat, along with the reminder of what I risk by getting distracted.

If I forget for one moment that the whole family is counting on me to keep my eye on the ball.

# CHAPTER 6

**CONFESSIONAL 189.5**

VINCENT, VANESSA (CFO: JUNIPER RIDGE)

*NO, THAT'S NOT WHAT I'M SAYING. I DO BELIEVE IN LOVE. FOR OTHER PEOPLE, I MEAN. TAKE MY SISTER. SHE'S COMPLETELY BONKERS FOR HER HUSBAND, AND HE'S NUTS ABOUT HER. IT'S AWESOME, TOTALLY AMAZING. I'M THRILLED FOR THEM. AND I'M GLAD I'VE REACHED THIS POINT WHERE I DON'T NEED A RELATIONSHIP TO BE HAPPY. I'M ONE HUNDRED PERCENT SATISFIED WITHOUT—WHAT? OH. SORRY. I DIDN'T REALIZE I WAS YANKING IT. NO, GO AHEAD. I'LL LEAVE THE CORD ALONE. LET'S JUST PLUG IT BACK IN AND START OVER. YES, TOTALLY FINE. I'M GREAT!*

* * *

I know I shouldn't interrogate my new colleague about his love life, but curiosity got the best of me. Besides, I wanted some reassurance we've got zero risk of falling for each other. I've sworn off men, he's sworn off women, and we're both committed to making *Fresh Start at Juniper Ridge* a kickass show. Easy, right?

So why do I keep catching myself ogling him?

"...If ad revenue comes in the way we're hoping in Q2, that'll give us some major purchasing power for media buys in Q3, you think?"

"Absolutely." I nod to underscore the fact that I'm paying attention, even though my brain got stuck wondering what Dean Judson looks like with his shirt off. I blame the smell of chlorine, which is giving me crazy urges to strip off my clothes. For *swimming,* not for anything else.

I clear my throat and order myself to focus on the spreadsheet in front of me. "What do you think about the estimates I've plugged into column six?" I ask. "Too high or too low?"

"They seem spot-on to me. If we need to shuffle things around, there's some extra padding in the line item for social media marketing."

"Ah, yes. I see that. I'll make a note of it."

See? We can do this. We're totally doing this. Look at me being professional and no-nonsense and not at all ogling Dean's massive hands on the laptop keyboard.

*Dammit to hell.*

I'm about to suggest we break for the day when the door swings open. Gabe, who just married my cousin's half-sister, strides in with one of the biggest cameras I've ever seen. Beside him, lugging an armload of studio lights, is a fierce-looking brunette with sun-streaked hair and a no-nonsense scowl.

"We can at least get some shots in," she's saying. "Even without bodies, we'll get a sense of what pops."

Gabe's grumbling something as he heads toward the towering waterslide in the corner. "Is there a reason you make everything sound like the setup for a horror film?"

"Maybe because I'm thinking about murdering my brother?" the brunette fires back.

"We should definitely ask Mari to head-shrink you."

"Or to be my accomplice. She's got a mean streak, and besides—shrinks know the best ways to get rid of bodies."

Across from me, Dean sticks two fingers in his mouth and gives a sharp whistle. His two siblings jump, then scowl at him.

"You're such an asshole, Dean." The brunette heads for our table, then spots me and seems to soften. "Sorry. I don't usually swear in front of strangers."

"Vanessa Vincent." I stick out my hand, which she shakes with a firm grip. "We're not strangers now, so swear all you want."

She laughs and drops into the seat beside Dean. "You're the new CFO. I'm Lauren."

I try to recall the birth order, pretty sure she's the oldest girl. "Glad to meet you."

Gabe slides into the seat next to me. "For the record, she swears at everyone." He looks from me to Dean, scrubbing a hand over his chin. "Is there a reason you're working in the pool house instead of your absurdly huge office?"

Lauren snorts. "Probably because they want to be left alone." She gives me a pointed look. "Judsons aren't great at respecting personal boundaries."

"Not all Judsons suck at it." Dean leans back in his chair, fixing them with a frown I can tell is just an act. "We're trying to work here."

Interesting that he dodged the question about why we're in the waterpark instead of his office. His posture is relaxed and easy, but I'm picking up an odd, coiled energy about him.

"We're working, too." Lauren jerks her thumb toward the waterslide. "We need some shots for the opening sequence."

Gabe's got the camera on his lap, fiddling with buttons and switches. "I'm telling you it's pointless. It'll be a lame shot without people."

Lauren fires off a look of intense exasperation. "We'll get people in it eventually. We just need to get the lighting figured out."

"Hey!" Gabe looks up and points a finger at Dean. "How about you do it?"

Dean frowns. "How about I do *what?*"

"Ride the waterslide." Gabe laughs so hard he nearly knocks the camera off his lap. "Come on, we won't use the footage. We just need a sense of composition and setup."

Lauren cracks the first smile I've seen from her. "Excellent idea. Make yourself useful, big brother."

Dean gives her a withering look. "I'm in the middle of making myself very useful. Maybe you're familiar with the need for funds to get this show up and running?"

Lauren turns her steely-eyed gaze on me. "It's after five. Doesn't seem very nice to keep the new CFO working late."

I open my mouth to insist I don't mind, but she keeps going. "How about it, Vanessa? Come on, you've gotta be dying to try the waterslide, right?"

She does have a point. My inner kid has been squealing and bouncing from the moment Lana showed it to me.

I flick my gaze to Dean, expecting him to answer for me. I can't read his expression at all, but my brain grabs hold of a memory I'd forgotten. I was eight years old, and my sister and I were at a waterpark outside LA with our mom. Val and I desperately wanted to ride the waterslides, so I stepped up to make the plea.

*"Absolutely not,"* our mother said, tossing her perfect hair. *"These places are breeding grounds for germs, and besides, you might get hurt."*

*"But—why are we here then?"* I tried not to let my lower lip quiver, but I couldn't help it. *"You brought us to a waterpark and we can't play in the water?"*

"It's a place to be seen." She stretched out on a lounge chair, adjusting her wide-brimmed hat as I tried to figure out what on earth she meant by that. Be seen?

*"Go play."* She waved me away before I could ask. *"Just stay*

*away from the water. Go work on your tan or something."*

I blink myself back to the present, looking from Lauren to Gabe to Dean. "I'd love to try the waterslide."

Lauren blinks. "Really?"

"Absolutely." I glance up at the swirling spiral, my insides churning with excitement. "It looks like fun, and I brought a bathing suit."

It's Dean's turn to look surprised. "You have a bathing suit?"

"Yep. Right here." I pat my bag, grinning.

He shakes his head slowly. "I'm seriously impressed by that purse. Should I worry what else is in there?"

I ignore the question, but yeah, there's a lot of crap in my bag. I'm big on being prepared. "I was hoping I'd have a chance to swim laps at the end of the workday."

"Which it totally is." Lauren makes an exaggerated show of pointing to the clock on the wall. It's definitely after five. "Let's get to it, girlfriend."

Gabe's full-on smirking, staring down his older brother. "You're not going to make her do this alone, are you?"

Dean glares at him. "Let me just pull that Speedo out of my back pocket."

"Ha!" Gabe smacks the table. "I've got trunks in my car right outside. Next excuse?"

Dean looks over, and I can see him trying to read me. "You don't have to do this if you don't want to. Lauren can be kind of a bully sometimes—"

"Hey," she protests.

"But she does know how to take no for an answer," Dean adds firmly. "So if you don't want to do this, it's definitely not a job requirement."

"No, I want to." I hop to my feet and rummage through my bag. "It looks like fun, and we were wrapping up anyway."

I can't tell from Dean's expression if he's horrified or amused. This is the downside of working with someone from a big acting family. They're impossible to read. He's watching me with those eerie hazel eyes, his big hands spread on either side of his laptop.

I hate how much I notice his hands.

Lauren's on her feet again, lugging the lights toward an open patch of concrete near the waterslide's exit. "This is going to be great. Gabe, how about we try for the low angle shot first?"

As the two of them get lost in a chatter of lights and camera settings, Dean shoots me an apologetic look. "I'm guessing this isn't how you envisioned your first day of work."

I shrug and drag my simple red tank suit out of my bag. "Nothing about this job is really normal, is it? Come on, boss man—get changed."

I can't believe I'm being this bold with the CEO. I can't believe he's going along with it, lumbering to his feet with another glare at his brother. "Is your car unlocked?"

"Yeah, of course. Gym bag's in back."

With a resigned sigh, Dean ambles toward the door. The second he disappears, Lauren calls my name.

I shuffle toward her, red maillot tank suit gripped in my hand. "What's up?"

She's adjusting one of the lights but turns to look at me. "Just wanted to congratulate you. I can't believe you got him to do this."

"Me? Gabe was the one badgering him."

Gabe looks up from adjusting his tripod. "He'd have turned me down in a heartbeat. That was all you, my friend."

Lauren nods her agreement. "He knew he'd look like a big pansy letting you do it by yourself."

I'm strangely pleased by this. Not just that I have the power to influence the stoic, no-nonsense CEO, but that I'm getting to have a little fun.

In all my adult relationships, I've taken my cue from the men. Bosses, boyfriends, all of them have called the shots. Not that I was this withering little damsel in distress, but I always felt content to let someone else drive the ship.

Not anymore. And seeing Dean Judson take cues from me is a powerful thing.

"I just hope you get your shot," I tell Lauren, hoping she can't read my mind.

Her steely eyes hold mine for a few beats. "I always get my shot." She points toward a turquoise door in the corner. "Ladies' dressing room is over there. There's a shelf by the door with robes and towels and stuff. The showers should be all stocked with supplies."

"Thanks." I turn and head for the locker room, fighting against the niggle of self-doubt creeping up on me. Is it weird to strip on my first day of work? It's not in the employee handbook, and this seems like a gray area.

I push the worries out of my head, reminding myself this job is like none I've ever had before. It's new and different and a completely fresh start. Exactly what I wanted.

Peeling off my clothes in the locker room, I thank my lucky stars I had a bikini wax last week. My toes could use a pedicure, and I could stand to lose five or ten pounds, but to hell with all that. I'm here to be respected for my brain, not the way I fill out a swimsuit.

Still, I can't help glancing at myself in the mirror as I adjust the straps of my suit. Not bad. My sister tells me I look good in red, and she might have a point. I pull my hair up into a messy topknot, then grab one of the fluffy white robes by the door.

By the time I get back to the base of the waterslide, Lauren and Gabe have everything set up. Lauren smiles as I wander over to join them. "Way to be a team player, Vincent," she says. "First round of post-work cocktails is on me."

"As soon as we have a bar," Gabe points out. "Why wasn't that the first thing we hired for?"

"Because doctors and firefighters are slightly more important than gin and tonics." Dean saunters in looking like sex on a stick, and my jaw falls open.

Literally, my whole mouth unhinges like in cartoons. Somehow, I manage to pull it back together, but I can't stop my gaze from sweeping hungrily over his torso. Everything ripples with lean muscle, from the curve of his perfect biceps to the slope of his pecs dusted with fine, dark hair. Does he seriously have eight-pack abs? I've never seen that in real life and *ohmygod I need to stop staring.*

I whirl back to face Lauren. "Is that—uh—lighting all set up?"

It's clear she's fighting a grin as she presses her lips together and nods. "Yep. All ready to go. Dean, why don't you grab one of those big inner tubes over there?"

Gabe flicks a switch on the camera and glances at me. "When we're open for real, we'll have someone up top handing them out. This is just for practice."

It's taking all my self-control not to watch Dean walk across the wet concrete to grab one of the massive floatation devices the size of a small boat. I've seriously never seen such a perfect ass.

Lauren's still watching me, looking like she knows I'd like to eat her brother for lunch. "You look a little flushed. You're not afraid of heights, are you?"

I swallow hard and struggle to croak a reply. "Nope, not afraid of heights at all."

That's the least of my fears. I'd rather hang naked by my toenails from the top of this five-story staircase than let myself fall for Dean Judson.

Speak of the devil, Dean rejoins us with a massive yellow innertube anchored under one arm. It bumps his leg as he walks, and he catches my eye before gesturing to the giant column of stairs beside the waterslide. "After you."

Squaring my shoulders, I turn and begin my march. My knees are Jell-O, and my tongue keeps sticking to the roof of my mouth. Halfway to the stairs, I realize I'd better ditch the robe. I drop my hands to the knotted belt and unfasten it with clumsy fingers. Shrugging off the terrycloth, I fold it neatly on a nearby table.

There's a long, slow hiss of breath, and I turn to see Dean staring. "Fuck."

"Close your mouth, bro." Gabe slaps him on the shoulder so hard he lurches forward.

"Dean's definitely afraid of heights." Lauren's smirk tells me that's not true at all, though I admire that she's covering for her brother.

Gabe gives Dean another nudge forward. "Give us a sign when you're at the top. All that stupid lattice means we can't see you, so stick your hand out or something."

With a pained look, Dean trudges toward the steps. I'm relieved he seems to have forgotten the whole "after you" thing, since I'd rather not climb several hundred steps in a bathing suit with a hot guy walking behind me.

He starts up the stairs, and I wait a few beats before beginning my own ascent. No need to make this more awkward by placing my face at butt level, even if it is a fantastically fine butt.

I concentrate on putting one foot in front of the other, enjoying the scratch of the sandpapery treads beneath my feet. I'm doing pretty well not staring at Dean's ass when his voice startles me.

"So this is awkward."

A bubble of surprised laughter flutters up my throat. "I don't know what you mean. I always start new jobs by stripping down and climbing five flights of stairs with my new boss."

"Not your boss." He stops abruptly, and I nearly crash into the big inner tube under his arm. "Just so we're clear."

I throw him a mock salute. "Crystal."

"Seriously, this shit matters. I don't want this being any weirder than it needs to be between us."

"Weird?" I fold my arms over my chest, belatedly wondering if he can see right down my suit from four steps above me. "You mean the part where you poisoned me during the interview, the part where I tackled you in my backseat, or the part where we're both half-naked my first day on the job?"

Dean gives me a pained look. "Weren't you supposed to go first up the stairs?"

"Hell, no."

With a shrug, he continues up the steps ahead of me. We both fall silent, so the only sounds are the slosh of water and the thud of our footsteps on the sandpapery treads. Even Lauren and Gabe are quiet below, and I wonder if they can hear us.

"How come you didn't mention the bug we found in your office?" I've lowered my voice so it's practically a whisper. I'm not sure he hears me, and he doesn't turn around. "Or the postcard with my picture. You didn't say anything to them just now."

Dean doesn't respond at first. I'm figuring he's not going to, so when he stops this time, I plow head-on into the tube. I start to bounce back, but Dean catches me by the arm. "Sorry."

"No problem." I swallow hard, conscious of the heat of his hand around my biceps. "Uh, sorry if I startled you."

"You mean the questions?" He glances back to where Gabe and Lauren are working, though we can't actually see them. "Coop will fill them in about the bug. Maybe they already know. But the postcard—" He stops himself, and I watch an odd mix of emotions play across his face. Uncertainty. Determination. Maybe a little worry. "I don't want them jumping to any hasty conclusions," he says at last. "Not until the PI has a chance to give us a report."

"Hasty conclusions," I repeat, not sure I understand. "You mean, like—that I'm the target?"

He nods once. "I want to get the facts before we bring everyone into the loop."

I can't decide if I'm flattered by his protectiveness or exasperated by how controlling he is. Can I be both?

"Do you think it's about me?" My voice is a whisper, barely audible over the rush of water.

Dean hesitates. Drops his hand from my arm. "No."

His silvery eyes search mine, and I watch him swallow again before turning. This time when he starts up the steps, I let him get ten ahead of me before I begin climbing again.

"There are plenty of people who hate the Judsons," he says. "Individual family members or all of us collectively."

"Oh?"

I wait for him to elaborate, not sure he will.

"There's the Dave Wienerman scandal," he says slowly. "The film director accused of assaulting all those women."

"He was shot at your brother's premiere."

"Yep." Dean clears his throat. "Some are pissed Gabe worked with him in the first place. Wienerman's defenders are pissed he got shot. Others are pissed that he's dead and won't stand trial."

"That's a lot of anger aimed in one direction." Or is it multiple directions? It's not like all the fury is aimed at the Judsons, exactly.

Dean keeps climbing. "I've got my own fair share of enemies."

"Yeah?"

His shoulders lift like he's sighing. "When it came to business deals in Hollywood, I was always fair." There's a hesitation, both in his voice and in his step. "But I wasn't always kind."

"I got that from the headlines." If I had a nickel for every one that referred to Dean Judson as "ruthless," I'd be lying on my private island in the Caribbean instead of climbing these slippery stairs. "You don't think it's enough for someone to come after you, do you?"

"I don't know."

He stops short, and I bounce into the tube again.

"For crying out—"

"Sorry." He catches me by the waist this time, dropping the

tube. It goes bouncing down the stairs behind us, smacking against the wall fifteen feet down.

Neither of us moves. I watch Dean's throat as he swallows. "Look, I don't have any idea what's going on here."

"With the threats, you mean?"

He hesitates, and I'm not sure at all that's what he means. "Right. Maybe it's a prank. Wouldn't be the first time."

"What do you mean?"

"People love to fuck with celebrities." He shakes his head like he can't believe he used that word to describe himself. "Gabe's a big name, and Lauren. Cooper, too. But all of us have been in the spotlight since we could crawl, and people get off on messing with that."

"Example?"

His arm is still looped around my waist, and I can't believe how good it feels.

"Let's see." He frowns. "Right after Gabe got that Mustang, he came out to find this three-foot scratch all the way down the driver's side."

"That's awful." And maybe not surprising. I've seen firsthand the resentment toward people with flashy cars and money.

"Yeah, it wasn't real, though. You know how you can pull those long, sticky threads off strips of duct tape?"

I nod, not sure I get where he's going. "I think so."

"That's all it was. But someone took the trouble to make one that long and to stick it on so it looked like a deep scratch. One helluva prank, really."

"Damn." That's impressive. "Fairly harmless, though."

"Yeah. Not a big deal in the grand scheme of things, only we never found out who did it."

"You're sure it wasn't just a coincidence?"

He shakes his head. "Someone had scrawled 'fuck you' on the windshield with a Sharpie marker."

"Ah, okay." That does sound a bit more targeted. "So that's one example. Any others?"

He hasn't let go of my waist, and I wonder if he realizes he's still got an arm looped around me. I can't bring myself to mention it.

"Another time, someone leaked Lauren's mug shot to the press."

"Lauren has a mug shot?" Everyone knows Cooper as the family bad boy, but I had no clue about Lauren.

"It's one of those things we tried to keep under wraps," he says. "But shit has a way of getting out. We contained it, so everything was fine, but still."

"Yikes." I suppress a shudder, but not very well. "It must suck being famous."

He shrugs. "It has its advantages. Point is, that stuff was mostly harmless. Maybe what's happening here is just more of the same. Meaningless pranks."

I look into his eyes, mesmerized by the intensity there. For the threat to his family or something else? I lick my lips and taste chlorine, even though I haven't set foot in the water. "You think this is meaningless?"

Still holding my waist, Dean shakes his head slowly. "No."

I nod and shift my weight. Just slightly, but it seems to jar him. He glances down and sees his arm around me. "Shit, sorry." He takes a fumbly step back.

Tries to, anyway. He's still on the stairs, so he stumbles with a yelp. I grab his hand, intent on helping.

But Dean outweighs me by a good hundred pounds, so instead I topple toward him. I'm headed right for his chest when I grab the handrail at the last second.

"Dammit." The force yanks me back so hard my boob nearly pops out of my suit. "Shit." I straighten and yank the straps up over my shoulders. I've just cursed twice and nearly flashed my tits at the boss, which is a great start to a new job.

But Dean blinks up at me from the spot where he's landed butt-first on a stair tread. "Is it just me, or is gravity conspiring against us?"

I laugh back the blush creeping into my cheeks. "We're almost to the top, right?"

"Yeah, but who knows how we'll manage to maim each other with two flights to go."

"I'll take my chances." I turn and start back down the steps. "And I'll take the tube the rest of the way up. It's only fair."

He hesitates. This is not a man who likes surrendering anything, even if it's just a float tube. "Fine."

I can't help feeling a sense of jubilation. I also feel his eyes on me as I move down the steps, but instead of making me self-conscious, I feel sexy. Straightening my spine as I reach the landing, I grab the tube and turn to start back up. Dean's on his feet now, and he gestures me to go ahead of him. "Want to take the lead?"

"No, thank you." I grip the tube tighter and tip my chin toward the stairs. "Keep going. Eyes on the stairs."

"Yes, ma'am." He grins and turns back around, giving me the perfect, unobstructed view of his butt for the remaining flight of stairs.

We arrive at the top to an array of signs directing us to line up with our water buddies, no more than four per tube. "The signs are left from BONK days," Dean explains. "We didn't see any reason to change them."

"They're cute. And they get the job done." I lean the float tube up against the wall and adjust my updo. "So how does this work? Do we get in together, or one at a time?"

He shrugs and surveys the fast-moving flow at the mouth of the tube. "Beats me. I was working the day they all came up here to test it."

"You mean you haven't done this yet?" That can't be right. "You own a freakin' waterslide that you've never tried."

"Correct." He grabs the tube and plunks it in the water, anchoring it in place with his foot. "How hard can it be?"

"Don't say that. You'll jinx us."

He laughs and steps into the center of the tube, holding the handrails for support. "What, like you'll be knocked unconscious and sue the company for millions?"

"I was thinking more like your swim trunks falling off or something." Shit, bad example. Now he thinks I'm picturing him naked. "Or one of us will get a splinter in our foot."

He looks down at the AstroTurf-surface separating the two of us. "I think we're good. You ready?"

"Hang on." I stick my hand through an opening in the lattice, waving for Gabe and Lauren's sake.

From miles below, Gabe bellows "Action!"

I turn back to Dean. "Okay, let's do this."

"Hop in on that side. I'll hold it steady."

It's just now dawning on me that this is like one of those corporate trust-building activities. The ones where you take turns falling backwards and counting on your co-workers to catch you. I bite my lip as I look at Dean, admiring the flex of his biceps and the tightness in his core as he anchors the tube in place with his body.

But I suppose he has to trust me, too. Trust that I won't jump in too fast and knock him off, leaving him stranded up here solo. I step carefully to the edge and dip a toe in the water. "Brrr."

"It's not that cold." His eyes flick over my chest then dart away. There's the faintest hint of a blush beneath his stubble, and I realize my headlights are blazing.

I start to fold my arms over my chest, then stop. "It doesn't mean anything," I say, parroting my own words from the back-seat of my car. "Just a basic, biological reaction."

His eyes lock with mine and he nods. "Of course."

But it's not just the cold, and we both know it. It's the proximity of Dean's body as I brush past him and clamber into the tube. There's a handle on the edge of it, so I grab that with one hand and the rail at the mouth of the tube with the other. I'm conscious of my breasts aimed at his face like beacons, conscious of the warmth of his thighs as he slips in beside me.

Our knees knock together and the bottom drops out of my stomach. Dean turns and looks at me. "Ready?" he asks.

I nod because odds are good my voice will come out as a squeak if I answer. "Mmhm."

"Let's do this." He lets go and the tube starts to move. It's slow at first, a gentle glide. Then we start to sway, gliding back and forth up the edges of the slide.

The lights dim, and I give a startled yelp as we hit some kind of dip. I can't help it, I grab Dean's arm. "We do this in the dark?"

"Guess so."

I suck in a breath as we swoop through another turn. Gravity pushes me so I'm almost in his lap. I squirm against him, knowing I should move, but not sure how to.

We hit another bump, and water splashes up like a curtain, slicking my thighs and arms and breasts with a breath-stealing blast of mist. I clutch Dean harder, and I swear I hear him groan.

"The dark must be part of the experience," he says as the next turn pushes him my direction. I bite my lip to keep from moaning as his shoulder sinks into my breast.

"Sorry," he murmurs, and it comes out a little hoarse. "The lack of light, it's probably to make it more exciting."

Like someone envisioned all this accidental groping and the need to hide my flushed face? "Mmhm," I manage again, but it comes out sounding a bit like a moan.

"Probably so the drop-off is a surprise," he adds.

"The drop-off?" I barely get the words out when the floor falls out from under us.

I shriek as we plummet through blackness, Dean's arm flexing under my fingers as he fights to hold us in the tube. I scream again, laughing this time as Dean clutches me against him and gives a shout of his own.

"Holy shit." He's laughing and sputtering and holding me tight as we land with a splash. Our tube swoops up one wall, then veers left and climbs the other side. We're moving so fast I swear we're about to do a full circle. I'm dizzy and laughing and more turned on than I have any right to be in a freakin' waterslide.

"You okay?" he asks.

"Yeah, you?"

"Perfect."

Perfection doesn't begin to describe this body tangled with mine in the dark. I know this is meant to be a family-friendly attraction, but it feels decadent and dirty in the damp, dim heat.

"I think there's another drop-off coming," he says. "I noticed it from below."

"Okay, I've got a good grip." I know I should be holding tighter to the handles than to Dean's arm, but I can't seem to let go.

He shifts his weight, probably trying to stabilize us, but I lean into him like a cat arching against the stroke of a palm. I'm horny and pathetic, but I can't control myself.

"Here it comes."

The floor drops again, and I fall into him shrieking. I'm making sounds somewhere between laughter and terror, conscious of every place where our bodies touch as we sail through another turn. My belly rolls as we hit the next curve. It's like riding a roller coaster, only hot and wet and practically naked and ohmygod my hand just brushed his abs.

"Sorry," I murmur.

"S'okay," he croaks out. "Just don't move any lower."

"Right, no, of course."

There's a faint glow up ahead, and the sound changes just a bit. A rhythmic sputter instead of the gentle swoosh and splash. "Is that the end?"

"I think so."

A wave of disappointment washes through me, and I struggle to put some space between us. To peel my thigh off his and release my death-grip on his arm.

"Here we go," he shouts.

And then we're launched into the light, laughing and coughing as our legs twine together and we go airborne.

Dean gives a shout and then we hit the water, splashing down into a pool of swirling blue. His hand finds mine underwater, and he pulls me to the surface, moving us toward the edge.

"You okay?"

I'm laughing as I come up, shaking the water from my hair. "I'm great. You?"

"That was amazing."

The brightness in his eyes, the slickness of his fingers gripping mine, all of it is overpowering. Our forgotten tube bumps me in the back, knocking me into him. Dean releases my fingers and dips his hand into my low back. His eyes lock with mine, and I can feel our bodies moving closer, our lips drawn like magnets as we—

"Got it!" Lauren's voice is followed by applause, and I jerk my attention to the side of the pool.

She's clapping and flashing a knowing look while Gabe drives the camera.

"That was amazing." Lauren steps to the edge of the pool. "I can't wait to see the footage."

Footage? That's right, they're filming, and holy crap on a cracker, I almost kissed Dean Judson. What the hell was I thinking?

But it wasn't just me thinking it. I can tell by the way he's watching me, by the way he touched his lip like he's convincing himself it didn't really happen.

It didn't. Thank God it didn't.

But holy inner tubes, we came close.

And that thought alone is enough to send me scampering out of the pool. "That was fun, really great, it was awesome."

I'm chattering like a drunk teenager trying to pass herself as sober at a frat party. I'm tugging my swimsuit top and wringing water from my hair and doing anything to keep from turning to look at Dean.

Lauren catches my eye and smiles. "Was it like you expected?"

Not even a little. Not one a tiny bit like what I thought I was signing on for when I agreed to be the new CFO for this crazy community-slash-reality show. I'm trying to play cool, but I feel Dean's eyes burning through the back of my head.

"It was great," I tell Lauren, forcing a smile that I pray doesn't reveal how I'm tingling all over. "Totally amazing."

I turn and dash for the locker room, fingertips brushing my lips to be sure they haven't burst into flame.

# CHAPTER 7

**CONFESSIONAL 231**

Judson, Dean (CEO: Juniper Ridge)

*Yeah, I like to be in control. You say that like it's a character flaw or something. I'm the oldest of six kids, for Christ's sake. Someone had to be in charge. Our parents...I mean, they're great and all, but—[mumbling]. Look, it was just a weird upbringing, that's all. I don't regret anything. Not from my childhood, anyway.*

* * *

"Are we almost done with this business plan, or should I order more coffee?" Lana spins her enameled tin mug on the table, the words "sex kitten" twirling above the photo of a vicious feline with fangs dripping blood.

Mari flips a page in the document and begins polishing her glasses on the hem of her T-shirt. Until six months ago, I'm not sure she'd ever owned a T-shirt.

"Does it look like we're almost done?" She turns a page in

Lana's packet, catching her up to the rest of us. "We're on page 68 out of 171."

Lana rolls her eyes. "Duh," she retorts, leaning on her favorite baby-of-the-family comeback. "I meant are we taking a break or something."

Lauren peers over the top of her packet. "There is no break. Only numbers and pie charts and words like 'market penetration' and 'ROI' and 'monetize' until we shrivel up and die a lonely, miserable death."

Cooper breaks into applause. "Very nice performance. Maybe work up a faint sheen of perspiration on the next take."

Lauren picks up a pencil to throw at him, but Lana beats him to it, flinging her empty tin mug at his head. It's a good shot, but Coop ducks, and the mug clangs off the corkboard behind him.

Mari sighs. "Is there any chance we can make it through one of these meetings without assaulting each other?"

"Nope." Gabe swoops in from the coffee bar across the room, angling himself between Lauren and Mari with a fresh pot in one hand. "Refills for all. Except Lana, who's minus a mug."

Lauren elbows our baby sister. "Open up and he can pour it down your throat."

Mari winces. "Can we please curtail the sexual innuendo?"

"Dude." Gabe shakes his head. "You're the one who went there, Mar. I'm just pouring coffee."

"Tsk-tsk." Lauren gives her sternest finger wag. "Now who's the perv, Mari?"

Hearing my siblings bicker floods me with a bewildering surge of affection. I know I need to step in and bring us back on track, but I'm enjoying this pleasant, nostalgic buzz.

"Dean, where's your mug?" Gabe holds up the pot as Lana scurries across the boardroom to reclaim hers.

Lauren rolls her eyes. "He probably shoved it up his ass to keep us from taking it."

"Ha ha." I pull it out of my briefcase and set it on the table. "Thanks, man."

"No prob."

Across the room, Colleen looks up from her laptop. I'm not sure if she's working on coffee shop business, wildlife research, or hacking the dark web. Maybe all three. She catches my eye and gestures to the state-of-the-art espresso machine behind the bar. "Need more?" she mouths.

I shake my head and turn to the next page in the business plan. "Can we please get back on track? I have a meeting with Tia Nelson at Sun Daisy Organic Ranch."

Cooper perks up. "Is she signing on to be part of the show?"

"Possibly."

I don't want to get his hopes up. He's been nuts about organic farming since he got sober and committed to clean living. I should probably hand the whole thing off to him, but I hate to see him disappointed if Tia keeps declining. Sobriety's a fragile thing, and I'd do anything to safeguard it for my brother.

"Let me know if you want help," Cooper says.

"Thanks. We're making progress." The truth is it's still a firm "hell no" from the testy rancher whose property adjoins ours. I glance at my watch, surprised to see it's almost four. "Vanessa's meeting me in the parking lot so we can drive over together."

Coop takes a swig from his coffee mug. "Good luck."

Gabe flips a few pages ahead in his packet. "Can we talk about this section on competing networks?"

"What about it?" I turn to the page, stifling my frustration at going out of order. "You still worried about the Voltan Network?"

Lauren sits up straighter. "I'm hearing more grapevine gossip. Their programming director isn't thrilled we're planning to go up against their top-rated show."

Cooper kicks back in his chair holding a pen shaped like a hot dog. A vegan one, I presume. "Voltan's ratings have been in a nosedive for months," he says. "If it tanks, it won't be our fault."

"Tell that to the Voltan execs," Gabe mutters, glancing at Lana. "You worked with Bob Voltan on that campaign a few years back, right?"

She makes a face and creases the corner of a page in her packet. "Spiteful asshole. He wanted me to help him figure out how to game the ratings. He didn't give a damn about making good television."

"But we do." Lauren folds her arms over her chest. "And that's why we'll kick his ass."

A niggle of worry moves through me. I've only met Bob Voltan a handful of times, but his network is unquestionably our biggest competitor. Lana's right, he's an asshole. Is he the kind of asshole who'd sabotage a competitor's show?

Something dings across the room, and I glance up to see Colleen pushing her laptop aside and striding into the small kitchen off the coffee bar. Moments later, she emerges holding a plate piled high with muffins.

"Oh my God, you're an angel." Lana stands to take the stack of paper plates from her hand, divvying them up between us. "Are these the marionberry ones you made the other day?"

"Nah, this is huckleberry lemon," she says. "Patti and I were out this morning checking the wildlife cams. We found a whole mess of 'em right below the ridgeline."

"Mmmph, this is amazing." Mari bites right into one, while Lauren carefully cuts hers into perfect quarters. "So good."

Cooper nods his approval around a mouthful of muffin. "You're the most badass baker slash biologist slash internet hacker I've ever known."

Colleen laughs and dusts crumbs off her hands. "Yeah, speaking of that, I've been battening down the hatches on your website. Whoever managed to hack their way in, they'll have to work a lot harder next time."

I try not to hang up on the idea that there might be a "next time," or the fear that our prankster might have more on the agenda than making us look incompetent.

"Please make sure you bill us for your hours," I remind Colleen as I grab the muffin Cooper's handing me. "I know this is a big drain on your time while we're waiting to hire a tech guru."

"Nah, it's just fun." Colleen shrugs. "Of course, it'd be more fun to catch the son of a bitch. Whoever's messing with you is damn good at covering his tracks."

Lauren finishes chewing a mouthful of muffin. "Is there a reason we keep assuming it's a guy? Women can be nasty, too."

"True dat." Cooper shoves half a muffin in his mouth and points at me. "Anything new on that bug in your office?"

I wait for Mari to ask him not to chew with his mouth full, but she's focused on choosing another muffin. I shrug at Coop.

"Turns out it's been there a while," I tell him. "That's what the PI says. The battery's long dead, and it's a model they haven't made for years, so—"

"So the cult people were bugging each other?" Lana asks.

"Or the Feds were bugging them," Lauren suggests.

"You're all kinda bugging me." Cooper helps himself to another muffin.

Mari ignores him and sips her tea. "Or the cult leader's scorned mistress was gathering intel for his wife. There are about a million possibilities for how people might mistrust each other, and most of them are probably justified."

We all take a moment to process that. All except Gabe, the lone Judson who's happily married. He's smiling and tapping something on his phone. Probably sexting his wife.

"How's Vanessa settling in?"

Mari's question jolts me from my X-rated thoughts and onto...okay, more like R-rated thoughts. Is it wrong that I haven't stopped thinking about her slick, soft body pressed against mine? It's been a few days since the waterslide, and we've been nothing but professional since then. Still, my brain won't stop flickering with images of her in that red swimsuit.

"She picked the cabin right down from me," Lana supplies, since I'm too lost in thought to answer. "The one with the red door and the nice back deck and those cute little flower boxes."

"Oh, that's a nice one." Lauren nibbles the edge of her muffin. "I like her, too. She's got spunk."

Mari folds her hands on the table. "Unless it's connected to someone's job, we should refrain from personal descriptions of employees in a public setting."

Gabe surveys the room. "Is this public? I mean, we own the place."

"I only said she had spunk," Lauren points out. "Personal would be if I said I'd kill to have an ass like hers."

"Right?" Lana picks up her mug. "She must do a zillion lunges a day."

Lauren looks thoughtful. "I wonder who does her hair. We should see about having them open a salon here."

Cooper shakes his head and turns back to me. "Anything to report on the postcard?"

That gets Mari's attention. "What postcard?"

Shit. I meant to tell the others, but...okay, maybe I didn't. "It showed up a few days ago. One side had this weird glamour shot of Vanessa as a teenager, and the other warned us against hiring her."

Lauren's brow furrows. "You think maybe it's a former boss or something? Someone pissed that we hired her away?"

The thought had crossed my mind, but I shake my head. "I don't know what to think. I've asked Lieutenant Lovelin to come in and brief us sometime this week. It might help to have someone laying out all the pieces and going over them with us."

Cooper grins. "I approve of this plan."

Lauren rolls her eyes. "Because Lieutenant Lovelin is smart and badass and freakin' gorgeous."

Mari looks pained. "Can we please not discuss prospective employees like pieces of meat?"

"Okay, but real quick." Lauren holds up her hand. "Anyone else have a massive girl crush on Vanessa?"

"Yo." Across the room, Colleen holds up her hand and grins. "Don't tell my wife."

Lana laughs and flicks a muffin crumb off the table. "Your wife adores her, too. We ran into Patti when I was giving Vanessa the tour."

Lauren ignores them to give me a look I can only describe as "calculating." She drums her fingers on the edge of her plate and stares me down. "Our girl crushes will remain unrequited, since she's clearly straight." She holds her hand up to Mari. "I know, I know—we're not discussing employees' sexual orientation. I'm just pointing out that you could power a generator on the electricity zapping around between Dean and Vanessa."

"Really?" Lana bounces a little in her chair. "Think she's got the magic touch to yank the stick out of his butt?"

"Hello, I'm right here." I glare at them all before turning to Mari. "Anyway, isn't it against company policy for co-workers to fraternize or something?"

Mari stares at me like I've got earthworms coming out my ears. "Of course not. That's the whole point of this, isn't it? For people to pair up in mutually-satisfying yet highly-entertaining demonstrations of personal connection."

"Mmm, that'll sound good in teaser reels." Lauren pops a bite of muffin in her mouth.

Mari gives her a withering look. "How are those interviews coming along for building contractors?"

A little fire flickers out of Lauren's eyes. "Fine. I'm working on it."

No one says anything, since we all know Lauren's history. She used to be in a hot and heavy relationship with Nick Armbrust, one of the top building contractors in the country. There's no way she wants to hire him to build our new cabins, and no way we're *not* hiring him, since he's the best. It's driving her nuts, and the urge to jump in and save my sister is overwhelming.

But I've got bigger issues on my plate. "Look, maybe we should call it a day." I push back in my chair and glance at my watch. "We can come back to this tomorrow, okay?"

"Tell Vanessa hi for me," Lana says, flipping blond hair out of her eyes. "Give her a great big ol' kiss."

Lauren smirks. "Oh, he almost did. We got it on video and everything."

I make a beeline for the door with Lana's delighted shriek echoing in my ears. Even Cooper holds up his hand for a high-five as I pass by on my way to the door. I ignore him because (a) I am definitely not hooking up with Vanessa Vincent, and (b) even if I were—which I'm not—it would hardly be something to celebrate. For crying out loud, could things get more complicated?

She did feel amazing in my arms, though. The way her body molded against mine on the waterslide or in the backseat of her car or—

"Hey!" Vanessa steps out from behind a pillar next to the lodge and slips on her sunglasses. "Beautiful day, huh?"

"Yeah, not bad." I pull out my own sunglasses, aware that things might go better if we're not making eye contact. Maybe that's our problem. "Sorry I'm late."

"You're not late." She glances at her watch. "Okay, you're two minutes late." She folds her arms over her chest and glares. "Goddammit, Dean."

I laugh and fall into step beside her as we head for the parking lot. "How about I drive? That way you can flip through the prospectus for Sun Daisy Organics on our way over."

"She sent us a prospectus? That's a good sign."

"Maybe." I pull the printed packet out of my briefcase and hand it to her. "She's still not budging on being part of the show."

"Did she share her objections?"

I shrug. "Reality TV is the devil. Wealthy developers are worse than the devil. We're raping the land and not using it for its intended purposes. Take your pick."

"She sounds like a peach."

"She's actually really cool." It's the main reason we'd love to have her on *Fresh Start at Juniper Ridge*. That, and her farm generates gobs of amazing meats and produce.

Vanessa walks around to the other side of my truck and gets in. She's flipping through pages before I start the engine. "Everything's organic, huh? Even the meats she raises."

"Yep. For a farm that size, they've got amazing yield."

She turns a page, looking thoughtful. "Maybe there's more to her animosity than you think."

"What do you mean?"

She shrugs and keeps scanning the page. "Maybe she wanted to buy the BONK compound before you swooped in."

"The thought crossed my mind." I'm not sure who we bid against when the property came up for sale, but it's possible Tia wanted to expand her farm. "Sorry, I'll shut up and let you read."

Vanessa gives a mock salute and keeps flipping. I try to keep my eyes on the road, on the craggy hills of red basalt in the distance or the snow-capped mountains with carpets of grassy meadow laid out like carpets at their doorstep.

But I keep catching myself glancing at Vanessa, admiring the side of her face. Her dark hair is pulled back in a ponytail, and she's wearing a red chambray shirt knotted at the waist and a black tank top beneath. She looks damn good in red. All fire and passion and—

"So, Tia's looking to expand distribution." She looks up and catches me staring. "Even if she won't join the show, it's possible she'll sell her products directly to us."

"That's not ideal." At the risk of sounding like a control-freak, I continue. "We're trying to stay self-contained, so having an on-site farm dedicated to our needs would be the best option."

"Where does she distribute now?"

"Mostly farmers' markets and organic grocery stores. I just need to convince her she stands to make a lot more money with us."

"Money's not everything." She says it mildly, but there's an undercurrent of tension in her voice.

"True. But it really would be a win-win for everyone. She keeps her land but becomes our exclusive supplier for fresh meats and produce."

"Makes sense." From the corner of my eye, I see her rest the pages across her knees. "Well, hopefully we can persuade her."

We're approaching the turnoff to Tia's ranch, so I fix my eyes on the road. Vanessa looks up from her packet as we bump onto the gravel road. "Oh! What a great barn. It looks like something on a postcard." She bites her lip, and I wonder if she's thinking about the other postcard. The one with her picture on it. "How long has she had this place?"

"The ranch has been in her family for generations," I say. "Tia's been running it alone for a few years."

"Nice." She points out the window at the tidy rows of plants whizzing past. "That must be potatoes. Oh, and cabbage."

"Beats me. But yeah, I know she grows that stuff." We're approaching Tia's house, but I drive on past and head for the barn. "She wanted to meet us out here. Said she's expecting a new intake."

"Intake?"

"She rehabilitates dogs," I explain as I park the truck. "Injured or sick or stray. I guess she's some kind of dog whisperer."

"Dogs." Vanessa's voice goes soft and wistful, and I remember what she said about wanting one.

"You've never had a dog?"

She shakes her head. "My sister and I used to beg for one, but our mom said no."

I kill the engine and pocket the keys. "What about cats? Or hamsters or bunnies or—"

"Nope, nothing." She gives a sad little shrug. "We had this fat orange goldfish once. I won it at a carnival, and Val and I got so excited. We named him Cheeto and built this whole fairyland castle for him in an aquarium."

The furrow between her brows makes me almost afraid to ask. "What happened to Cheeto?"

She frowns and spins the ring on her pinky finger. "Our mom said the water smelled bad. She wanted us to flush him down the toilet, but I convinced her to let me give him to the neighbor."

"Jesus." Her mom sounds like a piece of work. "We didn't have a ton of pets growing up, but we did have two cats. Oh, and Lana had a hamster."

That sparks some light in her eyes. "Names?"

"Puma Thurman and Catrick Swayze for the cats." I grin when she busts out laughing. "Lauren and Lana fought for weeks over those names."

"And the hamster?"

"Neil Patrick Hamster," I tell her. "That was Lana."

"How come Lana and Lauren got to name all the pets?" she asked. "Mari's between them in age, right?"

Leave it to Vanessa to zero in on this family quirk. "For some reason, Lauren and Lana have always been super-close. Mari—Mari's just been—" I fumble for the right word but can't come up with it.

"In the middle?" Vanessa fiddles with the end of her ponytail. "I've heard that's sometimes the case with middle kids. I mean, I know there are six of you, but—"

"Yeah, Mari's a classic middle kid." I'm not sure I really thought about this before now. "Lauren's the oldest girl, and Lana's the youngest kid period. Gabe and Coop and I were always just kinda *there*, but it was Lauren and Lana who had this special bond."

I've never considered if that bugged the shit out of Mari. My brothers and I, we pissed each other off in equal measure, but I never felt like any two of us were tighter than the other two.

"You're definitely a classic oldest child." Vanessa's voice brings me back to the conversation. "I'd have guessed it even if I didn't know."

"How do you mean?"

"Control-freak." She grins. "I have a big brother."

"No kidding?" I don't remember learning that in her background check.

"He's quite a bit older. Almost ten years, so we weren't supertight growing up."

"And let me guess," I say. "You're older than your twin?"

"Correct." She grins and pops open her door. "Five minutes and twenty-three seconds, thank you very much. If Val had been just two minutes later, she'd have been born after midnight and we'd have had different birthdays."

I come around the truck to join her, and we walk together along the dust-blanketed path to the barn. "Cooper and I have birthdays only three days apart, but there's six years separating us."

That used to feel weird when we were kids, but our mom always made sure we got separate cakes and parties with all our friends. That we were made to feel special.

A few months after Andrea and I got engaged, she threw a huge surprise birthday party for Coop and me. Cooper had a blast and landed in the tabloids for public drunkenness. I worked late and spoiled the whole thing, promising I'd be home in an hour, then two hours, then three.

Eventually, Andrea gave up on me. Not just the party, but all of it.

I can't say I blame her.

We've reached the door of the barn now, so I shake myself out of that dark place and knock on the door with Vanessa behind me. I can hear rustling inside and the bleating of sheep or goats or whatever the hell makes that noise.

Then Tia Nelson swings into the doorway wiping her hands on her jeans. Her dark hair is braided off to the side, and she smiles warmly when she sees us. "Good timing, I was just finishing up feeding."

Vanessa steps forward, eyes saucer-wide. "What are you feeding?"

Tia laughs and sticks her hand out, and Vanessa shakes it automatically. "Chickens, cows, goats, you name it. I'm Tia. Tia Nelson."

"Vanessa Vincent. I'd love to see your animals."

That earns an even bigger smile from Tia, who is damn serious about every living thing on this ranch. "Come on." She turns, dark braid swinging. "Most everyone's outside right now, but I'll give you a barn tour first."

"Sounds wonderful."

Vanessa and I follow, hustling to keep up with the quick stride of Tia's dirt-caked boots. "I just finished feeding most of the livestock," she calls over her shoulder. "Maybe you want to help with the dogs?"

"Yes, please." Vanessa flashes me a celebratory fist pump, and I laugh in spite of myself. "I know we're here to talk crop yield and livestock units, but this is all part of it, right?"

"Absolutely." Tia nudges a door with her hip, leading us past a pen filled with the tiniest goats I've ever seen. "Those are Nigerian Dwarf goats," she says. "Very friendly."

Vanessa gasps. "They're so cute."

"They produce a huge volume of milk for their size." Tia stoops to scratch a tan and white goat behind the ears. "We're making cheese next week if you'd like to come watch."

"I'd love that." Vanessa's bright cheer makes it obvious she really means it.

"Great." Tia beams. "I love showing off the farm to folks who really have an interest."

"Oh, I do." Vanessa leans in and rubs a little black and white goat between its nub antlers. "You have Saanen, LaMancha, and Toggenburgs as well, right?"

Tia doesn't mask her surprise. "You've done your homework."

"Always," Vanessa says, and it's all I can do not to high-five her. "Sounds like there's been a high demand lately for the Saanens."

"It's the high milk yield with low butterfat content." Tia turns and keeps walking, pausing to stroke the neck of a shaggy donkey. "The health food junkies can't get enough of it."

She leads us down another row of stalls. This section of the barn is quieter and smells different. Straw crunches underfoot, and a cow moos somewhere in the distance. "Roughneck is down here. We've been slowly introducing him to people so he's ready for adoption. You can help feed him."

"Roughneck?" Vanessa stops walking as Tia halts in front of a pen.

"He came in as a stray a few months ago," Tia says. "He'd been on his own a couple years with this ratty old mesh collar embedded in his neck."

Vanessa gasps. "What? How?"

There's a flash of fury in Tia's eyes. "Someone put the collar on him as a pup and then abandoned him."

"That's awful." Vanessa's blinking hard, and my urge to comfort her is overwhelming. "People can be so cruel."

"It was pretty infected by the time we got him." Tia reaches into a cupboard and pulls out a dish that's already filled with kibble. "I called in a favor with a vet who operated and got him fixed up."

"Thank God." Vanessa peers over the edge of the stall, and I step up beside her to look. A brown and black mutt—some kind of herding mix, I think—peers back at us with liquid brown eyes. The fur around his neck is missing in an odd, two-inch wide band, a bald patch that looks like a collar. He lifts one edge of his lip to show a tidy row of sharp teeth. He's not growling, and while I don't know much about dogs, it looks more like a smile than a snarl.

"He's not a biter, right?" I ask.

"Not unless you bite him first." Tia unlatches the stall door. "He was pretty skittish the first couple weeks. Air-snapped anytime we got close enough to feed him or check his wounds, but he never made contact. He's practically a teddy bear now."

The teddy bear gives a tentative tail thump and eyes us warily. He looks from Tia to me and pauses, tail tucking slightly. Then his gaze shifts to Vanessa.

"Oh, now there's a tail wag." Tia laughs and surveys Vanessa. "He likes you."

It's true; the dog is on his feet, tail wagging fiercely as he approaches Vanessa. He comes forward and puts his paws up on the edge of the stall, sniffing the air around her.

Vanessa steps closer, holding out a hand. "Maybe I look like someone he used to know?"

"Could be. Here." Tia hands her the food bowl. "He's not a runner. Just ease in gently. No quick movements. Low and slow, that's the key."

For someone who's never had a dog, Vanessa seems to know just what to do. She slips through the stall door, moving like her boots are dragging through honey. She's murmuring words I can't understand, but there's something soothing about them.

"Hey, buddy." She holds out her hand, and Roughneck sniffs it, then gives a gentle lick.

Vanessa laughs, and the dog jumps, then skitters back to lick her again. "It's okay," she soothes. "I won't hurt you, I promise."

The dog cocks his head, and I swear to God he understands her. Tail wagging again, he sets to work giving her arm a thorough tongue bath. Vanessa laughs and scratches behind his ear with her other hand.

"How did you rehab him?" Vanessa asks. "He's so tame for a dog who ran wild for years."

"Reading was a big part of it," Tia says.

"Reading?" I stare at Tia, pretty sure I've heard wrong. "What, like books?"

"Yep." Tia smiles. "I sat in his pen for hours, day after day, reading pages of whatever books I had on hand. Eventually, he got used to my voice. Then he got used to the idea that people weren't evil and might not hurt him. Also, that we had food."

Vanessa's stroking the dog's head, laughing when he licks her face. "So you're a literary buff, eh boy?"

The smile on Tia's face isn't one I've seen before. Usually she's glaring and crossing her arms over her chest, insisting there's no way in hell she'll partner with us. "You're a natural," Tia says to Vanessa. "You must be a dog person."

"I always wanted to be." Vanessa sets the bowl in the straw, then smooths her palm down the dog's smooth back. "This guy is a sweetheart."

Tia leans on the edge of the stall door. "He's never been like this with anyone else."

"I'm not surprised," I tell her. There's a gentle energy to Vanessa, a presence that leaves me feeling like I've known her forever. Roughneck's no dummy. He must sense it, too.

"There you go," Vanessa coos as the dog starts to eat. "That's a good boy. Yummy stuff, huh?"

Roughneck wags his stump of a tail but doesn't lift his snout from the bowl. I'm not even sure he's chewing. He's just inhaling the kibble, hoovering it up until the stainless-steel surface is bare. Licking the last few crumbs, he pops his head up and grins. I swear to God, that's what it looks like.

"Good boy." Vanessa sits down in the straw and uses both hands to scratch behind his ears.

The dog gives a groan of pleasure and heaves himself into her lap. He must weigh eighty pounds, and Vanessa topples laughing onto her back as Roughneck licks her face.

Tia turns and looks at me. "Looks like maybe you two are going home with a dog."

"What?" I glance at Vanessa, who's too busy soaking up dog kisses to realize Tia assumes we're a couple. "Oh, we're not—"

"I love this guy!" Vanessa sits up, still laughing as she pulls bits of straw from her hair. "Is this what they mean by love at first sight?"

My breath snags in my throat as I stand there on the outside of the stall, watching Vanessa light up the whole barn. "Yeah," I murmur. "Could be."

# CHAPTER 8

**CONFESSIONAL 263.5**

VINCENT, VANESSA (CFO: JUNIPER RIDGE)

*I really didn't. Want to be in show-biz, I mean. Doing Baby Spies was fun when I was a kid, but mostly because they gave me candy and let me play video games between takes. But having a career in Hollywood?* [makes a face] *No thanks. My mom wanted me to. Both of us, my sister and me, but...I don't know, it seemed like she pushed me harder. We had this screaming match about it. I must have been sixteen, seventeen. She starts yelling about how I didn't have any idea how to run my life. That the best thing I could do was find a man to keep me in line. I know, right? Crazy thing to say to your own daughter. I don't know, I guess I set out to prove her wrong. Sometimes, I'm not sure I've done that.*

* * *

"I adopted a dog."

I blurt the words before my sister manages "hello." That's how excited I am to tell her.

"Oh my God, a dog? What kind? How old? Does it have a name yet? Tell me everything!"

See? This is why I called Val the instant I got Roughneck settled at my cabin.

*My cabin. My dog. My life.*

All of this sounds nuts, but I'm giddy it's my new reality. "The lady who rescued him estimates he's about four," I tell her. "She thinks he's maybe McNab and Bernese mountain dog."

"I've never heard of either of those things. Hang on, let me Google."

I hear her fingers tapping the keys of her laptop, and I picture her curled up on the sofa in her little Parisian sublet. It's six in the morning there, but my sister has always been an early riser. The feeling of missing my twin nearly takes me out at the knees, and I breathe deep to keep from crying. Dean's lucky to get to work with his siblings every day.

Thinking of Dean has the edges of my smile quirking up. On the way back from Sun Daisy Ranch, he let Roughneck ride right up front, perched between us on the bench seat of Dean's truck. He drove us straight into town to grab supplies, shaking his head in disbelief as he followed me through the pet store.

"I can't believe Tia's really considering it," he said as I loaded the cart with dog bowls and kibble. "For months she's said there's no way in hell she'd be part of the show."

"She's still a long way from signing on." Truth be told, I don't hold much hope she'll partner with us. She's got a good thing going and doesn't need us one bit. I envy her in a way.

"Still, you made good progress. Better than I've been able to do."

The surprise in his voice made me look up from the soft-bristled brush I'd been holding. Dean grabbed it, then scooped up the red plaid dog bed I'd put back because it was too expensive. "Let me get this stuff, okay?"

"What? No, you're not buying my dog gear."

"Please." He slipped out his wallet and extracted one of those metallic black credit cards my mother always covets. "It's the least I can do. Besides, we'll definitely want your dog to be part of the show."

I decided not to argue. Now, talking to my sister, I still can't believe this is real. "He's amazing."

My sister laughs. "The dog or Dean?"

"Very funny." Also, not wrong. "He really is the best dog."

Sensing he's the center of conversation, Roughneck perks his ears from his dog bed in the corner. Stub tail thumping, he picks up the purple stuffed tiger we bought him at the pet store. He chewed the tail to a two-inch nub about an hour ago, breaking it in just how he wanted it. Clutching the toy in his mouth, he rolls to his side and heaves a sigh.

"I'll rub your belly in a minute," I assure him.

"Thanks, I could use a good belly rub," my sister quips. "Holy cow, these are big dogs."

"Which ones?"

"The Bernese things. They look like bears."

I glance over at Roughneck, who does look a bit bearlike. "McNabs are herding dogs," I tell her. "Tia said that's what makes him smart."

Ready to demonstrate his intelligence, Roughneck abandons his toy and trots over. He looks up at the couch where I'm sitting, waiting for an invitation. "You can join me." I pat the cushion and my dog hops up. Curling into a half-moon crescent, he rests his head on my thigh. His ears are warm velvet as I stroke my palms over them.

"I'm deciding whether to keep calling him Roughneck." I explain the story to my sister, tearing up as I recount the details of the embedded collar. "Is that a mean thing to call him after he suffered like that?"

"Seems more like a badge of honor to me."

"That's what I was thinking." I scratch behind his left ear, earning a groan of pleasure. "I started reading to him already. I guess that's something Tia did to tame him."

"What are you reading?"

"Irving Stone's *Lust for Life*. It's a fictionalized history of Van Gogh."

"Sounds interesting."

"Roughneck seems to like it." I scratch behind his ears, and he gives a low moan. "How are things in Paris? Did you finish that gown with all the beading?"

"Yes!" As my sister chatters about her latest wedding dress creation, I feel the tiniest twist of envy. Not for her career, which is pretty kickass.

But I've got the kickass career, too. What I don't have is the sexy husband murmuring in the background asking if I want waffles or crepes for breakfast.

"Either one's good, babe," my sister says to Josh. "I'm talking to Nessie."

*Nessie*. She's called me that since we were little, and I always loved the sound of it. "Say hi to that super-stud husband of yours," I tell her.

"Hi, super-stud," she parrots, laughing at something he murmurs in return. "He wants to know if you're running the place yet."

"Not yet. Maybe in a week or two. Did I tell you Dean and I are interviewing chefs?"

"Mmm, I hope you get a taste test." She laughs. "Of the food, not Dean."

It's the second time my sister's probed this particular tender spot. I swear I've told her nothing about my growing attraction to the hottie CEO, but twin intuition is strong.

"Dean's very professional," I manage as blandly as possible. "Smart, too."

"I'm sure he is. Just pointing out that it wasn't too long ago we were all crushing on him."

"What?" I have no idea what she's talking about.

"Come on—Dean Judson? Don't you remember every girl in middle school had his picture tacked up in her locker?"

"I have zero memory of that."

"Come on, Nessie." My sister makes an exasperated noise. "Haley Montfort and Ashleigh Styles and Candace Chrisman—remember how they used to argue about which Judson brother was the hottest?"

Sometimes I think my twin and I had completely different childhoods. "I guess I missed that."

She laughs. "Probably because you were smart enough to chase after real guys," she says. "I mean real guys at our school. The ones you could date instead of the make-believe ones."

I snort at that. "Yeah, that worked out really well for me."

"Ugh. Colton, you mean?"

"Colton Lawrence the Third." This is a good reminder that Raleigh was far from the first poor choice I've made with men. My high school boyfriend was only the start.

"What a toad," Val says. "You dated him the last couple weeks of sophomore year, right?"

"That I told you about," I admit. "It was actually a few months."

"What? Why?"

Why did I date him? Why didn't I tell her? All good questions.

"I didn't want to give Mom the satisfaction of knowing I was dating a guy from the country club set."

"Who turned out to be an asshole." My sister makes a disgusted noise. "What guy thinks it's okay to pick out a girl's prom dress for her?"

"Not a very nice one." I stroke my hand down Roughneck's back. "I'm doing better. I picked a good one this time."

"Oh, you mean D—"

"Dog, yes." I know damn well she was going to say Dean. "My dog is amazing."

"I can't wait to meet him." Val's quiet for a bit. "Did I tell you I ran into Raleigh last week?"

My sister's mention of my ex jerks me back to the conversation. "Ugh, no. Where did you see him?"

"Here in Paris." She makes a disgusted noise. "The network made me go to this big charity event."

"Kind of a random place to run into someone from home." I brace for a wash of emotion—anger, disappointment, nostalgia. I thought I'd marry Raleigh, after all.

But there's nothing but blankness in the center of my chest. Blankness and a bit of regret.

"He was hanging out with this pack of overgrown frat boys," Val continues. "Must have been a business function or something. He was holding court over this ridiculously expensive bottle of wine."

"That sounds like Raleigh." And also like a guy I should have seen right through from the beginning. "I can't believe I thought I was going to marry him."

"He charmed us both," Val points out. "I had a crush on him before you did, remember?"

"Yeah, but I was the one dumb enough to wait around for him to propose."

"Hey." Her voice is serious all of a sudden. "That's my twin you're calling dumb. Don't make me fight you."

I stroke Roughneck's side, surprised how much it soothes me. "Sorry, I'm a little emotional. I'm a dog mom now; I process things differently."

"I hear ya. Send me a picture?"

"Of course." I flip the phone around, framing up a selfie of Roughneck and me together on the couch. I swear to God he looks up and smiles.

"Done," I tell her, firing it off to Val.

"Oh, you both look great." There's some murmuring in the background, and I hear my sister showing the pic to her husband.

"Gotta go, Ness," she says. "Breakfast is almost ready. So, everything's good there?"

"Perfect." Mostly. "Enjoy that tasty mouthful. Have a good breakfast, too."

She laughs. "Thanks. Congratulations on the dog."

I hang up the phone and look at my dog. "Roughneck." He cocks his head to the side. "You're good with that?"

He gives a soft little "uff" and thumps his odd little half-tail.

"Because I don't want to give you a name that's traumatizing." I stroke the bald ring around his neck, careful to be gentle. Tia said it's fully healed, but it feels fragile like new baby skin. "Would you prefer something bold like Duke or King or Champ?"

Wagging again, my pup jumps off the couch and goes to fetch his purple stuffed tiger. He trots back to the sofa and plunks it on my lap. That's when I see he's chewed a faint, furless band around its throat.

"Very nice," I tell him. "Okay, Roughneck it is."

Again with the tail wag. I swear he understands me. "Who's a good boy?" I scratch his throat, earning myself a groan of pleasure. "You're a good boy. *You* are."

A bright chime rings through the cabin, startling us both. Roughneck perks up his ears and gives a soft little "uff."

"I didn't even know we had a doorbell." I stand up and head toward the front of the cabin. "Should we see who it is?"

"Uff." He says it more forcefully this time, bounding to the front door with his head high. He sniffs the door and gives a low whine.

"Hi, Roughneck." It's Dean's voice from the other side, and instantly my belly flips over. "Don't maul me, okay? I've got your dinner."

Dinner? I unlatch the deadbolt, mentally inventorying everything I bought at the pet store.

"Oh, crap," I say as I fling open the door. "I left the kibble in your truck, didn't I?"

He stands there on my front steps in fitted jeans and rumpled hair and looking sexy as sin. His arms flex from the weight of the forty-pound bag of dog chow on his shoulders, and I feel my mouth go dry.

"Not a problem. Where do you want this?"

"Over there's great." I point to the door of the small pantry just off my kitchen. "Thanks for bringing that. He had dinner at Tia's, but I would have been in big trouble at breakfast tomorrow."

"Wouldn't want a rift between you and your new dog." He eases the bag onto the floor, then turns to scratch Roughneck's ears. "Hey, buddy. You settling in okay?"

Roughneck wags his tail, sniffing the bag of food. He's a lot more eager to see Dean than he was earlier today, which seems like a good sign he's loosening up.

Or maybe he's picking up on my excitement. My belly's fizzing with joy, behaving like a glass of cola topped with baking soda. So dumb. I just saw Dean an hour ago, so no way should I be this happy to see him.

But he's even sexier in post-work mode. He's changed clothes, and the fitted black T-shirt reminds me what it felt like being pressed up against all that lean muscle on the waterslide.

"You want something to drink?" I'm suddenly conscious of how dry my mouth is. "I've got beer in the fridge, or there's some red wine open."

"Beer sounds great, thanks." He points to my back window, which faces east over the ridgeline. "Want to sit outside? Looks like it'll be a great sunset."

I steal a glimpse out the window, surveying stripes of mottled pink and orange streaking the skyline. "Oh, wow." I start toward the fridge, trying to act natural instead of like someone trying not to ogle the hot guy in her living room. "You want a glass or the bottle?"

"Bottle's fine, thanks."

"You can head out if you want. There's a cute little set of patio furniture I haven't had a chance to try yet."

"That's all Lana." There's a hint of pride in his voice. "She wanted everything to be homey before people started moving in."

"Mission accomplished." I pull two IPAs from the fridge, hoping Dean's okay with hoppy beer.

He's at the door now with my dog staring up at him with an imploring gaze. "You want Roughneck to join us?"

My dog wags his tail and shoots me a look that can only be described as "please, Mom?"

"For sure." I point to the hook beside the door. "That harness is pretty easy to put on."

"Blue's not really my color, but okay."

I bust out laughing, splashing beer on the counter. "Funny guy. Tia said the harness would be less traumatizing for him than a collar. That one's padded."

"Got it. Let's get this on you, buddy."

Roughneck gives a sharp yip and bolts away. I'm sure we've scared him with the leash, but he scurries over to the couch where the purple tiger lies soggy on its side. Stump tail wagging, Roughneck snatches the plush creature and trots back to drop it at Dean's feet.

"Thanks." Dean bends down to pick it up. "You've done a number on this, huh?"

"He's telling you he wants to take it outside." I've owned this dog a few hours, and I'm translating for him?

"We can do that." Dean clips the harness in place, then hands the tiger back to him. "It's like a self-portrait. Missing tail, bald patch around the neck."

I laugh and dump half a bag of pretzels into a bowl. "He's artistic. I've been reading to him about Vincent Van Gough."

"Very nice." Dean holds the door open, and Roughneck trots out ahead of him. I hear the rumble of Dean's voice as I set the beer and pretzels on a tray, wishing I'd thought to grab more food at the grocery store. I'm not much of a cook, but I could at least offer dinner or something.

*This isn't a social call. Don't get attached.*

A good reminder all around.

I carry the tray to my back door and out into the cooling high desert evening. Roughneck settles in a patch of fading sun at the edge of the deck. The end of his leash is wrapped around the leg of Dean's chair, while Dean watches him with a fondness I feel deep in my gut. Roughneck's holding the tiger between his paws, lovingly grooming the fake purple fur.

Dean looks up as I push the door open. He's sprawled in one of the wrought iron chairs, legs kicked out in front of him. I hate how my heart stutters at the sight of him framed against the backdrop of mountains.

"Here you go." I set the beer in front of him, then walk around to the other side of the table to plant the pretzels in the middle. No sense sitting any closer than I need to. "Wow, what a great view."

"Yeah." Dean sips his beer. "I love that about the high desert. The smell of sage and juniper and all these kickass sunsets."

"I spent the summer over in Bend after high school." I pick up my beer and take a small sip. "This was back when Ponderosa Resort was just a rich guy's ranch, and I was out visiting my cousins."

"The rich guy was...your uncle?"

"Yep." I sip my beer and try to recall if I told him this at some point, or if it's another bit of trivia he picked up while snooping into my background. "Anyway, the sunsets were my favorite.

That contrast of all the bright pinks and crazy oranges against the mountains."

"It's certainly different from LA."

We sip our beers in silence for a moment as crickets start to chirp. It occurs to me I could do this. Just be friends with Dean, ignoring the sexual attraction. That'll go away, I'm almost sure.

But then he looks at me again, and I'm lost in those hazel eyes. "Roughneck sure likes that toy."

I glance over at him and smile. "He's barely let it out of his sight since we got here."

"Mari would probably have an explanation," he says. "Something about attachment issues or fears of abandonment or whatever."

"Did she always want to be a psychologist?"

Dean shrugs and lifts his beer again. "Yeah. Things took a weird turn after she became a celebrity shrink to the stars. Don't mention that, by the way. She's still weird about it."

"Noted." I nibble off one edge of a pretzel and glance at Roughneck again. He really does look happy, sucking on the tiger's purple fur like it's his pacifier. "Did you have stuffed animals as a kid?"

Dean smiles a little sheepishly. "Yeah. Probably a lot longer than I should have."

"What do you mean?"

"When you're one of the young kids in a big family, you do all this stuff to avoid looking like a baby. Give up your binky or try to stay up late like the older kids."

"Ah, I see." I try to recall if that was Val and me. Probably yes, compared with our big brother. "And when you're the oldest?"

Dean grins and grabs a handful of pretzels. "You head off to middle school thinking it's cool to bring a stuffed lion named Lucy Fur."

"Lucifer?" I bust up laughing. "Did you get teased?"

"A little," he admits. "At least I didn't pick the stuffed bunny."

This is too adorable for words. "Did the bunny have a name?"

"Yep." He grins. "Rabbit Downey Junior."

"No!" I laugh and take a sip of my beer. "Val and I had matching teddy bears. She named hers Eddy and wanted me to name mine Freddy."

"Let me guess. You picked something else?"

"Guilty." Not really, though. I always felt kinda proud of my attempt to march to my own beat. "Mine was named Frig."

"Frig?"

"Yeah, I heard my dad say it, and I knew it was a bad word." I grin at Dean's confused look. "He'd say 'frig' instead of 'fuck' when we were kids. I had no idea what it meant, but I felt naughty calling my bear that."

He laughs and takes another sip of beer. "I had a stuffed turtle named Shelly," he says. "And a teddy bear named Weenie for reasons I can't recall."

"Probably because boys will seize any excuse to talk about weenies and boobs and bajingos?" I hold my breath, hoping I didn't cross some line.

Dean just laughs. "Says the girl who tried to name her teddy bear 'fuck'?"

"Fair point." I realize I'm staring at Dean and order myself to admire the sunset again. The sky over the mountains has gone from peachy pink and lemon to a kaleidoscope of magenta and burnt orange. "I had a stuffed seal I named Angst."

"Angst?"

I shrug and pick up another pretzel. "I'd heard the word on TV and thought it sounded pretty."

He looks at me for a long while. "You must have been an odd child."

"Quite possibly." I toss two pretzels in my mouth, enjoying the salty crunch and the smell of Dean's shampoo. I noticed it when I was pressed up against him in the waterslide, the grassy sharpness of it filling my senses.

*Stop thinking about that.*

"Do you still have any of them?" I ask. "Your childhood stuffed animals, I mean."

"My mom does," he says. "She keeps all kinds of stuff in case we want to pass them along to our kids someday." His brow furrows just a little. "Mari had a toy rat named Svetlana that she used to carry around everywhere. Pretty sure Mom saved that. Lana was more into dolls. She had this creepy one she named Shirleen."

"Wait." I frown at him over the lip of my beer bottle. "Isn't that your mom's name?"

"Bingo."

"That seems like something Mari would have a heyday with."

"No doubt." Dean sips his beer. "At first, Mom thought it was cute. Then it just got weird when Lana would be all, 'Shirleen needs her diaper changed' or 'Shirleen was bad and needs a spanking.'"

"Oof. Awkward."

"No kidding." He laughs, and I love how loose and easy this is. How pleasant he is to talk to. "How about you? Does your mom have all your childhood toys?"

A bitter puddle forms in my gut, and I take my time answering. "My mom's not very sentimental."

"You must have had a favorite toy, right? Something she held onto for you?"

I picture it in my mind. An abacus, the old-school kind with beads for counting. My brother bought it for my birthday after I said I liked numbers and wanted to learn math. I played with it until my chubby little fingers grew raw. While Val played with dolls, I played stockbroker under the covers.

"I had this great abacus," I say slowly, not sure why I'm sharing with Dean. "It had painted wood beads—red and yellow and blue. They moved around on these curved steel wires painted green."

"I had one like that," Dean says, tilting his head fondly. "They're for teaching kids to count, right?

"Yeah." I swallow hard, trying to budge the lump in my throat. "I loved that thing so much."

Dean frowns, catching the dark note in my voice. "What happened to it?"

I peel the label off my beer bottle, stalling for time. "I came home from school one day to find my mom cleaned out my room. She'd thrown out the abacus. Said math wasn't a good vocation for girls. Gave me a doll and told me to ask Val to teach me to make clothes for it."

"Damn." Dean takes a sip of his beer. "I'm sorry. That's really shitty."

"Thanks." Talking about this is giving me a sick feeling in the pit of my stomach. I try to recall what we were talking about so I can steer the conversation back there. "Tell me about the rest of your family's stuffed animals. What did Cooper have?"

Dean studies me for a split second, then takes his cue. "A cow. I'm positive Mom kept it."

"Cooper had a plush cow?"

"Yep. Moorio."

I laugh, but something about that snags in my brain. My expression must give something away because Dean gives me a sharp nod. "Yeah. Same thing crossed my mind."

My heart stutters in my chest. How did he know what I was thinking?

"You mean your email hacker saying Cooper was going to do a movie about mooing competitions?"

"Exactly." Dean's brow furrows. "I mean…it could be a coincidence."

But he doesn't think it is. I can read that plain as day on his face. I take another sip of beer and remind myself to tread carefully. "Has anything else happened lately?" I ask. "Anything suspicious, I mean."

He shrugs and lifts his beer again. "Remember that chef I told you about? Becca La Blanc, the one who asked about flying out early for next week's interviews?"

I try to remember all the test footage we reviewed with Lauren. "The one from New Orleans? The gorgeous blonde who sent all the headshots with the box of macarons?"

"Yeah, her. She bowed out."

"What? When?"

He scratches a thumbnail over a fleck of something on the table, not meeting my eyes. "A couple hours ago. Said she got a letter in the mail. Something suggesting she shouldn't get mixed up with the Judson family. She wouldn't tell us much, except that she wanted to withdraw her name."

"But—that's libel." I think. I'm not up on all my legal terminology. "Did you ask for a copy of the letter?"

"Lauren's the one who talked to her," he says. "I guess Becca was pretty tight-lipped about the whole thing. Didn't say too much. She wasn't our top pick anyway, but still."

"I can't believe it." But in a way, I can. It's getting clearer someone doesn't want *Fresh Start at Juniper Ridge* to get off the ground. "What does the PI say? Or the police—have you told them yet?"

"I left a message with Lieutenant Lovelin," he says. "And emailed the PI. There's not much to go on, though."

I can tell Dean's more worried about this than he's letting on. I see it in his furrowed brow, in the set of his shoulders as he gazes out over the horizon. The sun's sinking lower now, a glowing orange gumball gobbled up by jagged mountain teeth.

Dean drains his beer and stands up. "I should get home."

"I'll walk you out." Roughneck lifts his head as I get to my feet, but he doesn't move from his patch of fading sun.

Dean glances out at the open meadow, at the cinder path leading toward the lodge and the other banks of cabins. "I can walk from here. No need to trespass through your personal space."

The laugh that slips out is tinny and self-conscious. "You afraid I'll jump you if I get you in my house?"

He looks at me for a long, long time. "If you must know, yeah."

I blink. "What?"

"Not that you'll jump me." He drags his hand through his hair, and there's that sheepish look again. "But yeah, you and me being alone together in a private cabin after dark…that seems a little risky, doesn't it?"

The question hangs there between us for a few beats. I think I stop breathing. "I can keep my hands off you, Dean." I'm trying for cool and aloof, but even I hear the wobble in my voice.

"Yeah." He takes a deep breath. "I'm more worried about keeping my hands off *you*."

"Oh."

He's studying my face again, eyes searching mine. "I almost kissed you in a public pool in front of my brother and sister. How reckless is that?"

"A little?" Okay, it's out in the open now. We're talking about this instead of pretending it didn't happen. "But we didn't. Kiss, I mean."

"Barely." He glances back into the house. "But we should probably keep it from happening."

Odd how his voice tilted up at the end. Something about that makes me bold. "Was that a question or a statement?"

He looks at me. "What?"

"It almost sounded like a question."

"You mean whether or not we should kiss?" His smile is halfway between amusement and a grimace. "We'd have to be idiots."

"Stupid," I agree, trying to sound like I mean it.

"Next-level morons."

"Yep." I nod, pretty sure I've convinced myself. "I mean, we've both sworn off relationships."

"Right? There's that." He glances at the mountains again as a cloud passes over his face. "So we can just be grownups about this—this—whatever this is between us."

He waves a hand, and I don't know if the word he's looking for is "chemistry" or something else. Something neither of us could describe, but both of us are feeling. I'm not the only one; I can see it in his eyes.

I try to step back, to put a bit more space between us.

But my feet hear the message wrong and move toward him instead. I'm inches away now, close enough to smell the grassy shampoo and something else. Something uniquely Dean Judson that sets my blood bubbling and my breath hitching in my throat.

"We're both adults." I lick my lips, pretty sure this isn't what he meant by being grownups. "If we did kiss—hypothetically, I mean—we'd just be getting it out of our systems."

He stares at me like he's waiting for the laugh track. "What, like one time?"

I nod, even though this is the dumbest idea I've ever had. "Maybe that's all this is. Just sexual tension that'll go away if we let the air out."

"Like a balloon," he says, and I wince. "Okay, no balloons. One of those float rings at the waterpark. Like stabbing a knife in one or something."

"Yeah, this is good." I nod, conscious of how close we are. How I could stretch up and kiss him so easily. "Talking about balloons and stabbing is turning me off already."

But Dean's turning me on. Standing this close to him, breathing in his scent, sharing the same space.

I don't know who steps forward first, him or me. All I know is that we collide like bumper cars, our bodies connecting with an invisible splash of sparks. As his lips touch mine, I hear myself gasp.

Then we're kissing, and this is nothing at all like letting the air out. If anything, I'm filled to bursting, the seams of my skin prickling under pressure. I slide my fingers into his hair, gripping tighter than I mean to. Instead of pulling back, Dean deepens the kiss, his tongue brushing mine as I arch tight against him.

I know we should stop. Somewhere in the back of my brain, there's the frantic ding of a warning bell. But it clangs to the beat of my throbbing pulse, urging me on instead of pushing me away. I kiss him back, hungry to make the most of this.

We can't do this again, we both know that. Maybe that's why we're so frantic, so starving for each other's touch. Dean's got his hand on my ass, and I'm conscious of how big it is, how the rest of him matches. His arms, his chest, the hardness in his jeans that I know I shouldn't keep rubbing against, but I can't seem to help it.

Dean groans but doesn't break the kiss. His fingers are tangled up in my hair, his kisses more urgent with each heartbeat. I'm conscious of my fingers clutching the front of his shirt, conscious of how little it would take to rip the thin cotton off his body and run my tongue between those perfect pecs I've already touched. Would this be so different?

"Vanessa." He breaks the kiss, breathless, like he's tearing off a limb. "We should—" He breaks off and glances at the door.

I lick my lips. "We should what?"

Stop? Go inside and have wild monkey sex on the table?

How can both things sound so wrong and so right?

Dean's still holding me, and I move against him. A small movement, so tiny. But my hip grazes the bulge in his jeans, and he groans and closes his eyes.

"You're killing me." It's like the words are being dragged from his throat.

I swallow hard, trying to get a grip. "You seem pretty alive to me."

He laughs, but it's a choked sound. When he opens his eyes,

the intensity in those silvery depths nearly steals my breath away. "We either need to go inside or stop this right now."

I'm honestly not sure which choice is the right one. "Okay."

There I go again, letting the guy call the shots. But I truly don't know the right move here.

As smooth and in-command as Dean has always seemed, I'm not sure he knows, either.

"So...yeah." I swallow hard, willing myself to step back. To stop myself from doing something I'll regret.

But my body's edging toward the door, hungry to keep going. To see where this leads.

A sharp bark stops me in my tracks. I whip around to see Roughneck on his feet, growling into the distance. I follow his gaze to a trio of coyotes trotting across the meadow. They're too far away to pose a threat, but Roughneck growls anyway, protecting his turf.

Something about it breaks the spell between Dean and me. He steps back, dragging a hand down his face. "We shouldn't."

It's the exact opposite of what he said only a minute ago, but it's just as true.

*We should. We shouldn't.*

Both are facts, and neither is particularly convenient.

I edge toward the back door, reminding myself to breathe. To remember the cycle I've been through again and again with men I have no business dating.

"You're right," I say, even though I'm not sure at all what he meant to say. "Um, this was fun, but—"

"Right, totally. We shouldn't do it again."

"Agreed."

"Glad that's out of our system."

I nod, even though I'm nowhere near having anything out of my system. If anything, I'm burning hotter and fiercer for Dean than I was ten minutes ago.

But I can't say that out loud. Can he read it in my eyes as I take another step back and shove my hands in the back pockets of my jeans to keep from reaching for him?

"Right, so I'll go now." Dean moves toward the steps, already out of reach.

At the edge of the deck, Roughneck whines and pulls at his leash.

*I know the feeling, boy.*

That's the thought racing through my mind as I watch Dean walk off into the last, fading embers of sunset.

# CHAPTER 9

**CONFESSIONAL 301**

Judson, Dean (CEO: Juniper Ridge)

*Look, I'm not saying I always know the best way to do everything. Just that I've been making decisions for thirty-two years and mostly I've gotten them right.* [clenches jaw] *Mostly right. Yeah, I've had some fuckups in my personal life. Who hasn't?*

*Next subject, please.*

* * *

I shuffle the pages in front of me, skimming the words at the top of Bill Brandywine's resume. "Tell me what you liked best about your last position. You were the Assistant Manager for Horington National Bank?"

The bespectacled man across the table sits straighter in his chair, glancing between Vanessa and me. "It was a very rewarding job," he says. "Very rewarding. I led a team of thirty-five employees to become one of the top-performing branches in the United States."

At the other end of the table—so far away we may as well be on other continents—Vanessa marks something on a notepad. "And you were there for nearly fifteen years," she says. "That's impressive dedication."

"Yes, well, I love my work."

Vanessa glances at me, and I try to read her mind. About the interview, not anything else. Not whether she's spent the last few days like I have, replaying that kiss over and over until it's like a movie I've watched enough to recite each word.

A faint flush darkens her cheeks as her gaze skitters away. "Tell us about why you want to be part of the show," she says to Bill. "What interests you about *Fresh Start at Juniper Ridge*?"

Bill's smile dims just a little. He folds his hands on the table and directs his response to the empty space between Vanessa and me. "I've had a really tough time since my divorce. Really tough." He clears his throat. "When I read about the idea for starting over again, I thought—" He falters a bit here, fishing for words.

Vanessa gives him an encouraging smile. "Take your time. There's no rush."

There is actually a rush, since our next candidate arrives in less than an hour. But her soothing words put Bill at ease, and he presses on.

"I'm just looking for something different, you know? A chance to start my life again. To make better choices, if that makes sense."

"It does." Vanessa nods and marks something on her notepad.

I take a sip from my water glass, aware that the movement puts my hand that much closer to Vanessa. At some point I need to stop being aware of every molecule of her body and its proximity to every atom of mine.

That kiss was supposed to deflate the tension between us. If anything, it's grown bigger, floating between us like a bright, hot balloon.

I direct my attention back to Bill. "You mentioned choices," I say. "Tell me about a particularly good choice you've made in your career. Something that produced a positive outcome."

He beams, relieved at being back on neutral ground. "My decision to intern with Horington National was a big turning point," he says. "I learned about integrated sales and securities transactions and really the whole banking industry. Also, that's where I met Lydia."

"Lydia?" Vanessa glances down at her notes, like the information might be there somewhere. "Was she your mentor?"

"My wife," he replies, and I can tell from the response that he's not over her. Not even close. "We were so young and so in love. We used to stand by the water cooler for hours, just talking about what we did over the weekend or what TV shows we'd been watching. It took me months to get up the guts to ask her out."

I glance at Vanessa, thinking it's probably not a great sign the guy admitted to hours-long breaks in his workday. But maybe I'm being judgmental. Vanessa's not meeting my eyes. Hasn't met them for a while, actually.

She smiles again at Bill. "Let's stick with that theme about choices, shall we? Can you tell us about a bad choice you might have made, and what you were able to learn from it?"

I notice she didn't specify it had to be a career choice. Deliberate, or an oversight? Either way, I sense what's coming.

"That would be marrying Lydia." Bill leans back in his chair, tugging at his tie. "Not at first. We were so in love. This one time we went to Hawaii, and we made love on the beach beside the—"

"Right," she says, cutting him off as she scribbles something else in her notepad. I squint to see if the words are "embarrassing oversharer," but I can't make them out.

In reality TV performers, oversharing can be a selling point. With bankers, however—

"Let's stick with workplace details for now," I tell him. "We can keep the focus on your career trajectory."

"Oh, yeah, sure." Bill smiles and plants his palms on the table. "Sorry, I think it's the table throwing me off."

"The table?" I glance down at the smooth lacquered surface, not sure I'm following. "What about it?"

"It's funny, actually." Bill's brittle laugh ensures what's coming next won't be at all funny. "We picked it out together, Lydia and me. The bank put us in charge of redesigning the conference room, so we got to choose everything. Chairs, table, even the pictures on the wall."

Vanessa offers an encouraging smile. "That's great. They must have really trusted your taste."

"Yeah, I suppose." Bill's staring down at the table now, his eyebrows knitting together. "It was juniper, just like this one. Sturdy, too. This one time after hours, Lydia and I were working late. We were the only two people in the office, so I laid her back on the table and she pulled up her skirt and we—"

"Okay." I rap my palms on the table, the drumbeat cutting off the story. "I think we have all the info we need. Vanessa?"

She nods, jaw twitching as she fights back a smile. "Absolutely. Bill, did you have any questions for us?"

Ugh. I know she has to ask, but—

"Am I understanding right that part of the show's premise involves putting a bunch of single people together and seeing if they pair off?" Bill is achingly earnest as he looks from Vanessa to me.

I relax a little, grateful the question is an easy one. "More or less," I say. "We won't be doing any matchmaking, per se, but if things just happen between two people…" I trail off there, hoping he can put two and two together.

But it's Vanessa who jumps in to fill in the blank. "Or not," she says. "If someone's not looking for a relationship or not interested in being paired up, that's absolutely not a requirement. Right, Dean?"

"Right." My answer comes out quick and sharp, making Bill

jump in his chair. "If someone's got past relationship trauma they need to work through, we have a psychologist on the team who'll be helping with that."

Bill's looking from Vanessa to me, and I can tell there's something he wants to know. "May I ask a personal question?"

Vanessa stiffens in her chair. "We're not sleeping together."

Bill blinks. "What?"

"Sorry." She looks like she wants the floor to swallow her up. "Your question?"

"Oh. Um." Bill tugs his tie with an uncomfortable little laugh. "Have you cast anyone yet who—well—this is embarrassing. Um, anyone who might be a good match for me?"

His sincerity almost breaks my heart. So does the fact that there's no way in hell we're hiring Bill the Boardroom Bangin' Banker. "It's pretty impossible to figure out who'd pair up well with anyone else, isn't it?" I offer.

Vanessa looks straight ahead, nodding her agreement. "Right. Totally impossible to predict who might hit it off and who'd be an absolute disaster together."

"Yes, definitely." I clear my throat again. "Some people absolutely should not be in a relationship together."

"Or any relationship," Vanessa adds. "Sometimes, it's nothing personal. Just where people are at in the process."

"Yeah, okay." Bill's eyes ping-pong between the two of us. "That makes sense."

I'm not sure we've answered his question. To be honest, I've forgotten what the question was. "We're still in the early stages of things."

"Of casting people," Vanessa says quickly. "That's what he meant. Again, to reiterate, we're in a strictly professional relationship."

"Okay." Bill grabs a pen off the table and tucks it in his briefcase. I recognize it as one of Lana's custom ordered Montblanc ballpoints with the rose gold accents, but she has plenty. It's time to get Bill out of here.

"Thank you for your time, Bill." I stand up and offer a handshake. "We'll be in touch."

"Right, yes, thank you." He shakes my hand, his grip limp and clammy. "I appreciate the opportunity."

"Let me walk you out." Vanessa stands and gives me such a wide berth you'd think I have leprosy. "It can be tricky to find your way around all these corridors."

Their voices fade down the hall, and I hear Vanessa telling him we have half-a-dozen candidates left to interview. Not entirely true, but maybe it'll soften the sting when he doesn't get the job.

A few minutes pass, and I hear the chime of the door opening and closing. Then footsteps tapping closer as she returns to the conference room. I swear my heart stops as Vanessa floats back into the room, looking like a dream in a slim black skirt and silky purple shirt that brings out the color in her eyes.

"Well, that was....enlightening." She sits down about as far from me as she can get and still be at the same table. "What did you think?"

"I think Bill might need therapy." I press my palms against the table, then catch myself imagining Vanessa spread out on it with her skirt hiked around her hips. I fold my hands in my lap instead. "Seriously though, not the right fit."

"Agreed. We still have three more on the list, right?"

"Right. You think we should call them up and pre-screen to make sure they've never had sex on company property?"

She laughs, though from the way her cheeks just pinkened, I'm not sure she's thinking about Bill. "Would that really be an issue if he were the right candidate?"

I consider that for a moment. "Probably not. I'd guess most people have done something like that at one time or another."

She studies me for a moment, throat moving as she swallows. "I suppose so."

"It's more about having the poor judgment to share that in an interview."

"Exactly. The last thing we need is a banker with bad judgment." She looks down at the table again, and I wonder if she's thinking what I'm thinking. That this table looks very sturdy. What would it be like to tip her back against the glossy surface and—

"Have you?"

I blink at her. "Have I what?"

A full-on flood of color rushes her cheeks. "I'm sorry, it's none of my business. I got caught up in the oversharing."

"Have I what, Vanessa?" I smile to let her know I'm not pissed. "Had sex at work?"

"Sorry, just being nosy." She shakes her head. "It's definitely not my business."

"No, but I'll answer if you want."

I'm baiting her, I know. There's a sick little part of me that wants her to be curious. That wants her to see me as a sexual person and not just the guy in charge of the company.

"You don't have to…" she begins, cheeks still heated.

"Yes." I fold my hands on the table. "That's one of the perks of working for yourself, I suppose."

Her eyes widen just a little. "Having sex at work?"

"Having the option if the mood strikes."

"I see." The way she's looking at me makes me wish we were alone in this building. But Lauren and Gabe are right down the hall, filming test footage of candidates for an assortment of shop owners. Anyone could walk in here at any time.

"Was it—was it someone who worked for you?"

Her question throws me off guard, and it takes me a second to answer. "No."

"No?" Something that looks like relief flickers in her eyes.

"No. My ex-fiancée. Andrea."

She nods, processing the information. It doesn't seem to bug her, but I'm no mind reader. "You two were together a long time."

It's not exactly a question, but I nod anyway. "Yeah." I hesitate, not sure how much to share. "I mean, sort of. The relationship lasted a while, but the cumulative time we spent together wasn't that much."

"What do you mean?"

I shrug, pushing back the faint remaining traces of guilt and anger. "I worked so much we hardly saw each other. Or she'd be off somewhere filming, and I'd be too busy to go visit." No, that's not true. "I wouldn't *make* the time," I amend, knowing that's how Mari would have me frame it. I can take ownership for my fuck-ups. "Of course she'd look to someone else for companionship."

Vanessa's brow furrows. "You can't blame yourself."

"Sure I can."

She shakes her head slowly. "Accountability's one thing. But you're not to blame for her cheating."

I quirk an eyebrow at her. "And are you to blame for the dick-heads you've dated?" Her face registers surprise, and I realize the blow landed harder than I meant it to. I soften my approach. "At the waterpark the other day, you blamed yourself. For dating guys who screwed you over or turned out to be married or whatever."

She looks at me for a long time, then nods. "You're right. It's not entirely on me that I pick guys who manipulate or patronize or talk down to me." She looks down at the table. "It's sort of on me, though."

"Or your mother."

She looks up sharply. "What?"

I kick myself, pretty sure I've overstepped. "The way you've described her, it's like you ran straight from one controlling relationship and into a series of others. Repeating the pattern or something."

A faint smile tugs the corners of her mouth. "Does having a sister who's a shrink give you an honorary degree?"

I laugh and press my palms to the table. I can't help but notice her gaze lingering, and I wonder what that's about. "Maybe a little. So how about you?"

"What about me?"

I pat the table and her eyes flick to my hands again. "Scandalous workplace hookups. Not your thing?"

She smiles and shakes her head. "No, but I made out with my sister's husband while we were dangling a couple hundred feet off the ground on the Morning Glory at Smith Rock," she says. "Does that count as scandalous?"

"What?" I gape at her, too stunned to come up with a better response.

Laughing, she tucks her hair behind her ear. "This was long before my sister met him. I was eighteen, visiting Oregon for the summer. We had this hot fling for a few weeks."

Relief floods my system, along with a little intrigue. "Sounds…exciting." My voice sounds weird, and I'm trying not to picture Vanessa having a hot fling.

She shrugs. "*Hot* may not be the right word. I was young and inexperienced, so we maybe only got to second base."

It takes all my mental control not to picture second base. Not to recall the curve of Vanessa's breasts brushing my arm in the waterslide or pressed against my chest when we kissed. "Is that awkward? Having your sister married to a guy you used to date?"

"Not at all," she says. "He's a great guy. Just not the right one for me."

"I see." I'm not sure I do, though.

I wait for her to share more, but she's pressing her lips together now. "Sorry, I kinda derailed things for a bit." Reaching across the table, she grabs the notepad she used for the interview. "So that's a no on Bill, right?"

"Right." And the end of our conversation, as far as I can tell. I glance at my watch. "Next contender will be here in just a few. Maybe she'll be a better fit."

"Maybe."

I can't help thinking about the scars we both carry. About the ghosts of past relationships hovering above, waiting for the moment to swoop into the space between us.

***

It's after five when I roll into the coffee shop. I know it's late to be chugging gallons of espresso, but I can't resist the siren call of caffeine.

Apparently, I'm not alone.

"Hey, buttface." Lana waves from the table she's sharing with Lauren and Mari. It's rare to see all three sisters together, so I'm beelining it for their table before my brain catches up and reminds me I came here for some alone time.

Mari's got her hands wrapped around a mug of tea. "How'd the interviews go?"

"Bankers, right?" Lauren scrunches up her face. "Please tell me you're not hiring the guy who cried about his ex-wife in the screen test."

"That would be Bill." Poor bastard. "Nah, we had a really good interview with the woman from Minnesota. Angie someone."

"Waller." Mari gives a nod of approval. "I liked her answers on the questionnaire."

Lana cocks her head. "We've got a female CFO, a female banker, and if Amy Lovelin signs on, a female police chief. Are we going to start hiring men at some point?"

"Do we have to?" Lauren makes a face. "Maybe we could find a female building contractor and scrap the idea of hiring Nick Armbrust."

I'm not sure what to say to that, so I settle for letting Mari and Lana give her sympathetic pats. I always liked Nick, though I have no idea what happened between him and Lauren.

"Want me to have him murdered?" I'm only half joking. "Pretty sure Dad has some mob connections."

"Thanks, I'll consider it." Lauren swipes a hunk of muffin off Lana's plate. "How's Vanessa doing?"

"Great." I fight to keep my face from giving anything away, from breaking into a big, doofy grin.

"I got to meet Roughneck." Lana beams like she met Santa or George Clooney. Or George Clooney dressed as Santa, which I'm pretty sure happened at one of our family Christmas parties. "She says I can go over anytime and read to him."

"Read?" Mari cocks her head. "Is that some sort of therapy?"

"I guess so." Lana shrugs. "Anyway, I get to walk him every day at ten. I bought my own leash and everything."

My baby sister, the animal nut. It still kills me to think of the day her hamster went to the big sawdust heap in the sky. Lana cried for days, stopping only when I forced Gabe and Cooper to help build the biggest blanket fort she'd seen in her life. The thing had two stories, and Lana sat inside singing while we tacked up a roof made from our mom's best French linens.

"So really, how *is* Vanessa?" Lauren shoots a smug look at Lana, and they both start giggling.

"What?" I look from Lana to Lauren, then Mari. "What the hell is wrong with them?"

She shrugs. "I've wondered that my whole life."

Lana swats her arm, then leans forward to grin at me. "Lauren and I were making dinner the other night," she says. "The evening of that really pretty sunset?"

I sigh, knowing what's coming. Lana's kitchen looks out over Vanessa's back deck. "We were just getting it out of our systems," I insist. "It wasn't a big deal."

The three of them exchange a look. "Wait, what?" Lauren laughs. "You mean something happened?"

"Yeah, we just saw you bringing dog food through the front door." Lauren grins at Mari. "Apparently, that's not all he delivered."

"God." I put my head in my hands and consider what my life would be like without three sisters. I might like to find out. "I'm going to recant my statement."

"Actually," Mari says, coming to my rescue, "there's some scientific basis for the notion of getting someone out of your system like that."

"Yeah?" Lauren perks up. "How do you mean?"

"There was this study a few years ago through the University of Washington." Mari shoves her glasses up her nose. "They investigated the theory that it could be therapeutic for exes to plan a mutually-agreed-upon sexual encounter with carefully established parameters as a means of establishing closure for the relationship."

Lauren cocks her head to the side. "You mean a bunch of shrinks invited random exes to bang it out for the sake of science?"

Mari shrugs. "In a manner of speaking, yes."

"Damn." Lana steals a bite of Lauren's cookie. "What did they find out?"

Mari folds her hands on the table. "They determined that a structured regimen with established guidelines for physical contact led most couples to feel a stronger sense of closure. Roughly seventy percent of participants responded 'definitely yes" when asked if they felt ready to move on from the relationship. That was more than a fifty-percent increase from their responses at the start of the study."

"No kidding?" I'm trying not to sound too interested, but the look Lana shoots me suggests I've failed. "So there really is something to the idea of getting it out of your system."

Mari's brow furrows. "In terms of data, it's a strong possibility. Of course, there were couples who emerged from the exercise intent on giving the relationship another try."

"And we're talking about exes, right?" Lauren lifts an eyebrow at me. "Not relative strangers who have the hots for each other."

I open my mouth to defend my honor, but Mari interrupts. "Theoretically, it could work either way," she says. "But yes, there's a different set of psychological and emotional factors at play with exes."

Lana laughs and pats my hand. "Good try, big brother."

"What?" I force myself to keep a neutral face, not giving anything away. "I was just curious about the research."

"You were curious about getting into Vanessa's pants," Lauren points out.

Lana nods. "Which all of us would approve of, for the record."

I glance at Mari, my lone sister who doesn't seem to be jumping on the bandwagon of...well, me jumping Vanessa. "I'm not saying I'd go there," I begin. "Because I probably wouldn't, and it's not up to me anyway and—"

"Yes." Mari takes off her glasses and folds them beside her empty mug. "In theory, the act of demystifying your physical chemistry by establishing parameters around a desired connection before engaging in some mutually pleasurable contact could produce satisfactory results."

Lana makes a face. "That's hot."

"Not everything needs to be hot," Mari shoots back.

"Fair point," Lauren agrees. "Maybe it's the act of eliminating the hotness that leads to...well, whatever the opposite of hot would be."

As my sisters launch into a discussion of hotness or lack thereof, I'm saved by the ringing of my phone. Slipping it out of my pocket, I catch sight of Vanessa's name and number. My heart ticks up, and I take a second to collect myself before answering.

"Hey, Vanessa. How's—"

"Oh my God, Dean! I need help right away."

# CHAPTER 10

**CONFESSIONAL 316**

VINCENT, VANESSA: (CFO, JUNIPER RIDGE)

*I HATE BEING VULNERABLE. THERE, I SAID IT.* [HEAVY SIGH] *I HATE IT SO MUCH. MY MOTHER, SHE'S THE ONE WHO USED TO SAY ALL THE TIME, "DON'T LIFT THAT HEAVY THING, VANESSA. ASK A MAN TO HELP, VANESSA." ALWAYS, FROM THE TIME I WAS A LITTLE KID. IT DROVE ME BONKERS. I MEAN, COME ON. I'M SMART AND CAPABLE AND CAN DO EVERYTHING FOR MYSELF. EVEN ORGASMS, THANK YOU VERY MUCH. I KNOW WHAT I NEED, OKAY? WHAT I LIKE.*

*YOU'RE NOT GOING TO USE THAT, RIGHT?*

* * *

By the time Dean shows up at my front door, I've stopped hyperventilating. Roughneck, on the other hand, is losing his shit.

"Roo-roo-roo-roo-rooooooo!" He's at the other end of my cabin, shouting though the back door as he lunges at my worst nightmare lying on the deck.

The doorbell chimes again, and I snag Roughneck's harness to pull him across the living room and over to the front door. Swinging it open, I take a few breaths to slow my heartbeat.

God, Dean looks good. And worried. But also really, really good.

"I'm so sorry," I tell him as I struggle to keep Roughneck from jumping up on him. "I just found the booklet with the number for maintenance. I should have called them first."

"No, you shouldn't." Dean shoulders past me, pausing to pet Roughneck, who promptly settles down. "You did the right thing."

"By calling the CEO for a maintenance issue?"

He ignores that and starts toward my back door. "Show me. The police are on their way, but I want to see it for myself first."

That gives me pause. Is there a reason he'd want to check things out before the cops? Or a reason he's not contacting the PI first?

I don't ask questions as I hustle through the living room and to the back door. The window beside it overlooks the exact spot we stood just days ago, kissing and touching and edging closer to crossing that line we'd never be able to uncross. Still, it was hot. Hot and sexy and—

"There," I say, pointing through the window. "Right on the edge."

Dean stares through the window for a long, long time. I look, too, even though the terrifying image is burned into my brain. At the edge of the deck lies a long, greenish-brown snake. It's huge, maybe five feet long, but that's not the worst part.

Looped around its neck is a rubber band cinched tight at the base of a pink balloon. At the other end, tied to the snake's rattle—yes, *rattle*—is a blue balloon.

Dean glowers. "That's fucked up."

I feel myself shiver, though it's plenty warm in here. *Fucked up* barely touches the surface. Even from here, I can read the words scrawled on the bobbing orbs of horror.

*Go away.*

It's inked on each balloon in black, blocky handwriting. I shiver again, and Roughneck whines and licks my hand.

Dean's still staring at the snake. "That's not alive."

"I sure as hell hope not. Otherwise, someone wrestled a live rattlesnake just to fuck with me."

"No, I mean it's a fake snake." He points to the tail. "See how that looks rubbery instead of hard?"

"I tried not to look that closely." But having Dean so close lends me a healthy dose of bravery, so I peer through the window. "Okay, so even if it's not real, that's creepy as hell."

"Agreed." His brow furrows as he stares through the window. When he looks back at me, his eyes are filled with concern. "You didn't see anyone?"

"Not a soul." I shudder again. "Just David Hisslehoff there."

He snorts. "David Hisselhoff?"

"Seemed like something a Judson kid would name a pet snake. That, or Snake Gyllenhaal. I also considered William Snakespeare or Monty Python."

"You named it?"

"I had to do something to keep my mind off how damn creepy it is."

"Glad you could distract yourself." He looks deep in my eyes, concern etching a trench between his brows. "You're sure you're okay?"

I want to say yes, but I can't bring myself to do it. "Balloons, Dean. Not just the snake, but balloons. How many people know I'm freaked out by balloons?"

He frowns. "I don't know; how many?"

"Not that many." I try to think of a number. Phobias aren't really something I advertise. "A couple dozen people, maybe. Family, of course. Close friends. You."

"I feel honored."

"I feel creeped out." I let go of my dog's harness, and he instantly starts pawing the door. "What do we do?"

"Lieutenant Lovelin should be here any minute. She was actually just down the road."

"Is that normal?"

"What do you mean?"

I bite my lip. "I know she's your top pick for police chief, and I haven't met her yet. But we've been speculating about suspects, and it seems odd a cop would be just standing by. We're out in the middle of nowhere."

"Right, gotcha." He considers that. "I don't think so. She doesn't live far from here."

"I'm sure she's fine." I glance back at the balloon-covered snake and try not to gag.

"We'll look into it," he says. "Promise. This will all be okay."

The crazy thing is, I believe him. Maybe it's the certainty in his voice. Maybe it's his big, soothing presence or the heat radiating off his body. I know I'm standing too close to him, and I hate the weakness it signals.

But I can't bring myself to step back.

He looks into my eyes, probably checking to make sure I'm not about to pass out. As his gaze sweeps over me, I feel my shoulders start to relax. No, *relax* isn't the right word. My heart ticks up, but it's not panic this time. It's something else.

As I pray he can't read my mind, I see his hand move. He's reaching for me, stretching out one huge, capable palm to—what?

The doorbell chimes before I have my answer, and we jump apart like naughty teenagers. Roughneck barks and barrels to the front of the cabin. I jog after him, conscious of Dean right behind me as I reach the door and clip the leash onto my dog's harness.

Roughneck takes this as a cue we're going for a walk and proceeds to lose his shit all over again.

"Sorry, my dog's a little keyed up," I shout through the door before pulling it open. "He's harmless, I promise."

"No problem." The woman on my front porch smiles, tawny hair glinting in the sunshine. She wears a friendly smile and a cop uniform that she fills out like a dream. I do my best to ignore the pinch of envy in my gut as she extends her hand. "I'm Lieutenant Amy Lovelin."

"Vanessa Vincent." I shake her hand before stepping aside to let her in. "Come on in. I'll take you through to the back."

"Thanks." She nods at Dean. "Good to see you again. Sounds like there's been more drama."

Dean doesn't try to hide his grimace. "If you call a balloon-covered snake drama, then yeah."

She smiles and adjusts her grip on the black bag she's carrying. "Hardly the weirdest thing I've seen in the line of duty."

That statement alone is enough to make me love her, and my fandom surges when she glances down at my howling dog and smiles. "And who do we have here?"

"This is Roughneck, and I swear he's really friendly. He just sounds awful."

"Roughneck? From Tia's place?" She bends down to pet him, and my dog goes crazy licking and wagging. "Hey, buddy. Good to see you again."

Roughneck melts down completely, groaning with joy as she rubs his belly. I'm guessing Amy Lovelin has this effect on lots of guys. "I take it you know each other?"

Amy scratches behind his ears, laughing when he tries to lick her nose. "I was part of the crew that helped capture him. Tia let me read to him a couple times once he got settled."

"Anything he especially liked?" And now I'm the weirdo who takes book recommendations for her dog.

Amy isn't fazed. "He did seem to like the Bill Cameron crime novel I read him. "Then he ripped the head off a doll and spread the guts all over his pen. I switched to romance novels after that."

"No wonder he's such a lover." I scratch him behind one ear while Amy gives him a good booty rub.

"You've come a long way, buddy." She gives him one last pet and straightens up. "You want to fill me in on what's happening?"

"Right, of course." Dread curdles my gut. "You probably want to see the…the…"

"It's okay, you don't have to say the s-word." She offers a sympathetic smile. "My mom hates them so much that we're only allowed to call them rattlebears."

Dean quirks an eyebrow. "Rattlebears?"

"I guess bears are less scary-sounding than…well, the other animal." Amy smiles at my dog. "Maybe 'rattlepup' would be more comforting?"

I laugh and wrap his leash around my hand. "It's okay, I'm not freaked out by the word." Just by the animal itself. "Sorry, this whole thing probably seems silly to you."

"Not at all," she says. "I'm already invested in what's happening out here, though this does seem like a strange twist."

Dean shoves his hands in his pockets. "It seemed like an odd thing to call the cops for, but considering what's written on the balloons…."

"Absolutely." She picks up her black bag. "Let's take a look."

We all troop through my cabin, Roughneck trotting along beside us. When we get to the door, Amy peers out the window. "Thank God it's just plastic," she says. "I've never dusted a snake corpse for prints before."

"Small blessings." I grip Roughneck's leash a little tighter.

Amy pushes the door open and steps through. She sets down the black bag and extracts a pair of rubber gloves, which she promptly snaps into place. "You haven't touched anything, correct?"

"Correct." I can't suppress another shudder. "No amount of money is enough to convince me to touch anything going on out there right now."

Dean reaches down and laces his fingers through mine, giving my hand a squeeze. "We haven't set foot outside."

"Excellent, I'll keep an eye out for footprints." She frowns, scanning the desert dirt and my small patch of neatly-mowed grass. "Not likely we'll see anything, but you never know."

"Want us to wait here?" Dean asks.

"For now. I'll let you know when you can come out." Amy strides across the deck, surveying her surroundings as she moves. Even if she were wearing street clothes, there's something about her posture that screams "cop." I can see why Dean wants to hire her. We stay fixed in the open doorway, watching her work. Even Roughneck seems mesmerized.

Amy slips a small camera out of her pocket, firing off a few images before she stoops down for a closer look. I watch her a moment longer before turning to Dean. "Sorry to drag you out here. I feel a little silly knowing it's fake."

"You have every right to be freaked out," he says. "Hell, *I'm* freaked out."

He holds out his arm, and I get distracted by big hands and ropey forearm muscles before realizing he's showing me goosebumps. "Same," I murmur, lifting my own arm. The one not attached to the hand he's still holding.

Dean smiles, and there go the goosebumps again. I tear my attention off him and direct it back outside where Amy is busy inspecting the balloons. I keep my voice low, not entirely sure why. "You think this is tied to the other stuff?"

Dean hesitates. "Yeah. I do."

I don't want to ask the next question, but I have to. "It's directed at me, right? I mean, it has to be."

He doesn't say anything for a long time. "Why don't we wait and see what the police think."

Which is not the same as a denial. I know that. He knows that.

But who the hell would target me like this? I comb my brain for thoughts on who I've pissed off recently. My breakup with Raleigh wasn't pretty, but I can't see him setting out to scare me. Besides, Val said she saw him in Paris. It doesn't add up.

Outside, Amy is shoving the snake into an oversized evidence bag. The balloons are still inflated, and even though I know the snake's not real, it makes my skin crawl.

Seeing us watching her, Amy holds up a finger. "One second. Let me log this into evidence, and I'll be right back."

"Is it okay for us to come out?" Dean asks.

"Sure, it's clear," she says. "Just try not to touch anything."

I glance down to where Dean's still gripping my hand. I don't think he notices, and I also don't think that's what she means by touching, but I still feel guilty. The pleasure of feeling his skin against mine far outweighs the guilt, so I say nothing.

Dean gives my hand another squeeze. "Want to go out? It might help with the closure or something."

"You sound like you've been talking to Mari."

He gives me an odd look. "I have, actually."

Before I can ask, he lets go of my hand and strides out onto the deck ahead of me. I wrap Roughneck's leash around my wrist and follow. I don't know why I'm scanning the deck like there's something Amy might have missed. I'm sure she did a thorough job, but I can't help feeling creeped out. Like someone's watching me.

Or maybe that's Dean. His eyes sweep over me as I follow Roughneck to the edge of the deck. Amy comes back around the house, blessedly snake-free. She's got a notepad in one hand and slips a pen out of her pocket as she climbs the steps to the deck.

"I'm not seeing any trace of prints, but we'll see what the lab says." She clicks her pen a couple times. "Have you noticed anything else unusual around here?"

"More unusual than a fake snake covered in balloons?" I shake my head. "Not really."

"What about those cabins over there." She waves a hand toward the bank of them just south of mine. "Anyone living there yet?"

"A few are occupied," Dean says. "Lana's in that one, and

Mari's on the far end. A couple of our new shopkeepers were going to start moving in this week."

"How about beyond that?" She's still scribbling on her notepad. "Past the trees over there. That's the edge of Tia's place, right?"

"That's right." Dean's voice sounds tight.

"Okay, good." Amy does some more scribbling, then looks up. "I'll want to speak with anyone who could have seen anything."

"Of course." Dean clears his throat. "So you think this is more than a prank?"

Amy's pale eyes study his face. "I think in the context of the other things you've had happening out here, we need to examine all angles."

I bite my lip. "Should I be worried?" I hate how my voice shakes when I ask it. I hate even more that I have to ask.

Amy doesn't say no right away. Or at all. "You should be cautious," she says. "But this guy here can help protect you."

I start to argue that I don't need a man's protection when Amy bends to scratch Roughneck's ears. "You're looking out for your mom, aren't you? That's a good boy."

"He is a good boy," I agree. And the fact that Amy Lovelin recognizes it makes me extra eager to hire her. "I'm sure he barked his head off at whoever did this."

"Nice job, buddy." She gives him one last scratch and straightens. "Here's my card." She hands it to me before nodding at Dean. "Obviously, Dean and I have been in communication, but you're welcome to reach out anytime."

"Thank you." Dean glances at me. "It's hard not to want to take this personally."

Amy turns and trails her gaze over the field, scanning like she might have missed something. "It's noteworthy that this message was so tailored to Vanessa's fears," she says. "Snakes are a common enough phobia, but balloons?"

"Right." I glance at Dean, a little surprised he told her about that. Was it when he called this in, or in one of their other conversations? "It does seem pretty obvious someone's targeting me."

Dean folds his arms over his chest. "Not necessarily. Plenty of other stuff has been directed at the rest of us."

"Is there anything you haven't mentioned yet?" Amy clicks her pen again. "Anything that could be connected?"

Dean hesitates. "Not that I can think of."

"We've been trying to think of anyone who might have an axe to grind with any of us," I tell her. "Neighbors, ex-colleagues, former cult members, that sort of thing."

Amy cocks her head. "Any leads?"

Dean shoves his hands in his pockets "Not really."

"Why don't you go ahead and put it in writing," she says. "Make a list. Everyone, not just the two of you. Your brothers and sisters—have them do it, too. Maybe there are things we haven't considered."

"All right." I grip my dog's leash as he tugs me toward a tree he'd desperately love to water. "Thank you for coming out here so quickly."

"No problem." She glances at Dean. "I signed the contract, by the way. Ms. Judson—Mari, I mean—she should have everything she needs to get the ball rolling."

Surprise flashes on Dean's face. "That's terrific." He grasps her hand in a firm shake. "Glad to have you joining the team."

"Likewise." Amy turns and smiles at me. "Vanessa. I look forward to working with you."

"Same." My brain flashes on an image of girls' nights with Amy and Tia and the Judson sisters, and I feel pathetic and hopeful at the same time. "It'll be great to have you here."

She smiles and shoves her notepad in her pocket. "I'm looking forward to it." With a quick wave, she steps back and down the three stairs leading to the grass. "Stay safe, you two."

And then she's gone, moving around the corner to the front of the house. I listen for the sound of her car starting, not sure if she's heading home or going to go interview people in neighboring cabins.

Either way, Dean and I are alone again. Alone and right back on the deck where we kissed a few days ago. I bite my lip, grateful he can't read my mind.

"What are you thinking?" he asks, and I nearly choke.

"I'm thinking I need to let Roughneck water his favorite tree." Moving past him, I let my dog lead me down the steps.

Dean follows, ambling across the grass toward me. "Seriously, are you doing okay?"

"Yeah, just a little rattled." I wince. "Bad word choice."

"We probably need to get your mind off the rattlesnake thing."

I start to ask what he means by that, then stop. *Nothing. He means nothing. Stop trying to read something into this.*

I move around the tree, letting Roughneck get a good sniff. "You told Lieutenant Lovelin about my balloon phobia?"

"It seemed relevant." His brow creases. "I'm sorry, was it a secret?"

"No. I'm just not used to having other people speak for me." Actually, I'm very used to it, which is probably why it's bugging me. "It wasn't a secret," I reiterate. "I just prefer to represent myself."

He looks at me for a few beats, then nods. "Understood."

And now I feel like an asshole. I touch his arm, softening a little. "Sorry, I'm a little on edge."

"No, I get it. This whole thing is creepy."

Roughneck's made a full circle around the tree, wrapping his leash all the way around the trunk. I follow after him, doing my best to stay focused on tending my dog instead of the heat of Dean's body so close to mine.

I should ask him to go. I should beg him to stay.

I should definitely stop thinking about kissing him.

"Have you had dinner?" I blurt the question without thinking.

"A cup of coffee." He makes a face. "I need to do better about eating real meals, but I've been busy."

"Stay." Where the hell did that come from? "I mean, I'm not much of a cook, but I can grill burgers. I grabbed frozen patties the other day, and some buns."

"Hamburgers?" The excitement he infuses into those three syllables is enough to make me laugh.

"That's the plan." I tug my dog's leash, trying to lead him back around the other side of the tree. "Pretty sure I have some cheddar if you want to make it a cheeseburger. I can't promise I've got your favorite condoms, but there's ketchup and mustard and—"

"What?"

I stop talking, registering the odd look on Dean's face. "What do you mean?"

"My favorite *condoms*?" He leans back against the porch railing, eyes flashing with amusement. "Glad to know I'm not the only one with illicit thoughts on the brain."

My cheeks flush with heat. "I did *not* say that." Only I'm pretty sure I did. "That's not what I meant, anyway."

"Okay," he says, still grinning. "I'd love burgers. With or without the condoms."

Kill me now. "Come on," I tell him. "I'll get the grill fired up, and we can see what I've got for sides."

"I make a mean macaroni salad." He pushes off the railing and follows me into the house. "That's assuming you've got the ingredients."

"You can make macaroni salad, but not coffee?"

"I'm a man of varied talents."

"I believe it." And right now, I can't stop thinking about one in particular. I blame it on being back on the deck where we kissed before, so things should be better in the house. More neutral.

I lead the way into the kitchen, trying to recall everything I grabbed at the store the other day. "I definitely have macaroni," I tell him. "And mayonnaise. What else do you need?"

He moves to my sink and starts washing his hands. "Onion would be good. Celery if you have it, plus whatever spices you have lying around."

I unclip Roughneck's leash and sweep a hand toward the bank of cupboards behind him. "Go ahead and paw through my panties and—" Oh, shit. I did it again. "My *pantry*. That's where my spices are. The pantry right behind you."

Dean busts out laughing. "I love where your mind goes."

"Pantry." I repeat feebly, closing my eyes against a wave of embarrassment. "Goddammit, Dean Judson."

He laughs and catches me by the elbows before I can go hide behind my couch. "I learned something new from Mari," he says. "Want to hear about it?"

"Maybe." I crack one eyelid to peer up at him. "Is it about my deep-seated sexual frustration?"

"Not specifically, but let's put a pin in that."

"God." I hate myself sometimes. "What did Mari tell you?"

"She read this study about exes trying to get over each other by having sex."

Jealousy pinches the edges of my heart as I fight to keep my expression flat. "Did you—are you wanting to—" This is not coming out right. I'm distracted by his palms cupping my arms, by the warmth of his breath ruffling my hair. "You're talking about having sex with Andrea Knight?"

"What? God, no!" He shudders exactly like I did when I spotted the snake. "I'm talking about the science of getting over someone. Kissing to get it out of our system or whatever. Mari says it's a legit thing."

I'm not sure where to start with that. My heart's hammering in my ears, and have I mentioned he's still touching me?

*Get it together, Vanessa.*

I swallow hard and order myself to focus. "You told your sister we kissed?"

"Not exactly." He sighs. "Lauren and Lana saw us the other night."

"On the back deck?"

"Actually, they didn't see us." He grimaces. "I only *thought* they saw us and I confessed the whole thing because I'm a huge dumbass."

I laugh, delight swirling through me to mix with the arousal. He smells so amazing, that grassy-good Dean smell, clean and woodsy. Is this affecting him like it's getting to me?

His pupils are wide, black pools in oceans of glittering hazel. A sign he's turned on, or is it just really dim in here? I can't control my breathing. It's like I'm running a marathon, only instead of a marathon, I'm naked and Dean's naked and we're pressed up against each other in bed.

What were we talking about again?

"So this study," I press, struggling to stay focused. "It seriously found that physical intimacy is a good way to get over someone?"

"I might be paraphrasing," he admits, color seeping under through his stubbled cheeks and jaw. "Reading something into it based on what I wanted to hear."

"Which is what?" I need to hear him say it. I need to know we're on the same page.

Dean smiles into my eyes. "I want you, Vanessa. And maybe I'm being presumptuous, but I think you might want me, too."

My breath stalls in my chest. This is it. My opportunity to insist we keep things professional. That we not cross this line that can't be uncrossed.

But as I look into those flecked hazel eyes, there's a heat there that flips a switch deep inside me. Lights, camera, *action.*

"Yes," I hear myself breathe. "I want you."

"Good." He smiles. "Now what should we do about it?"

# CHAPTER 11

## CONFESSIONAL 329.5

JUDSON, DEAN: (CEO, JUNIPER RIDGE)

*BIGGEST WEAKNESS? JESUS, WHERE DO I START?* [LONG PAUSE] *BELIEVING WHAT I WANT TO BELIEVE, EVEN WHEN I KNOW GODDAMN WELL IT'S NOT TRUE. HOW'S THAT FOR FUCKED UP? I'LL KNOW SOMETHING LOGICALLY IN MY BRAIN, BUT THE REST OF ME GETS CAUGHT UP WANTING SOMETHING DIFFERENT TO HAPPEN, AND IT'S LIKE I'VE GOT BLINDERS ON. I DON'T KNOW, I GUESS I'M WORKING ON IT. TRYING TO, ANYWAY.*

* * *

When I looked deep into Vanessa's eyes and asked how we should handle the fact that I want her and she wants me, this was not on my list of expected options.

"A little more salt, you think?" She holds out a spoon dipped in the homemade Caesar dressing she's been working on for sixteen hours, give or take.

Maybe not that long. It's probably been ten minutes, but time crawls for a guy who thinks he has a shot at having sex with the hottest girl he's ever met.

But I'm determined to give her time or space or whatever else she needs, so I lick that spoon like a champ. Vanessa's eyes flicker a little, filling me with hope I'm not the only one whose mind is in the gutter.

"It's perfect," I tell her. "Want to eat?"

She nods and surveys the spread we've laid out on her counter. "Burgers, buns, macaroni salad, green salad." Glancing back at me, she smiles a bit self-consciously. "And all the *condiments* of course."

"Your attention to detail is impeccable."

Still grinning, she thrusts a paper plate into my hands. "Load up. You're going to need your energy."

Wait, what? I don't ask what she means because I don't dare hope, but yeah...I'm still optimistic about where this is going.

We pile food on our plates, brushing elbows like old friends. Only the sparks crackling between us are not remotely friendly, and I wonder if she feels it, too. By the time we've settled at her dining room table, I'm pretty sure my skin is on fire.

"So." Vanessa clears her throat and spears a leaf of romaine in her salad. "How should we do this?"

I've just shoved Caesar salad in my mouth, and it's all I can do not to choke on a crouton. "Wait," I wheeze. "What are we talking about here?"

"Sex, of course." She picks up her glass and takes a sip, then holds it up. "This is water, by the way. Not wine or beer or anything else that could cloud my judgement."

"Way to plan ahead." I'm still not sure what's happening here. "Clever forethought."

"Or foreplay." She gives me a sheepish look. "Sorry, is this weird?"

A little, but no way am I saying that out loud. "Not at all."

"It's just—I'm trying not to leap without looking, you know?"

"Yeah, of course. It's smart to talk things through beforehand." I'm not sure if she's wanting to talk birth control or hookup spots, but I can roll with it. "Okay, well…how about the bedroom?"

"Clean sheets, check." She grins and picks up her burger. "Also, condoms."

"Good. Well, that's good." Okay, so that's settled. I've never had this sort of pre-hookup communication, and my mind reels with what else to ask. "Any particular kinks I should be aware of?"

"Not for our first time." She smiles a little sheepishly as her cheeks color. "I know it's just a one-night thing, but you can… um…more than once?"

"No pressure." I take a sip of beer, wondering if I should stick with water. "Yeah, I'm pretty sure I can manage."

"Excellent." The grin she gives me shoots straight to my groin. "For the record, I'm generally okay with a little light hair pulling and maybe some dirty talk."

"Who's doing the talking and hair pulling?" We should definitely get this out in the open, and also it's turning me on. "I'm open to either. Just want to make sure I meet your expectations."

Vanessa takes her time chewing a bite of burger before answering. "Let's play it by ear. How about you? Any particular turn-ons I should know about?"

*You. Everything about you. Your face, your scent, your brains, your smile, the way you eat a hamburger, for crying out loud.*

It's on the tip of my tongue to say that. All of it, the whole big mess. To tell her everything from the light in her eyes to the way she holds her fork gets me hot, but I need to maintain some kind of control. "Ear nibbling," I admit. "Also the way you touch my face when we're kissing."

"Oh, yes." Her eyes flash, and I can tell this is getting to her, too. "I can definitely do that."

"Good. Um, right." I clear my throat, trying to get some blood back into my brain. "All right, anything off-limits?"

"Being called someone else's name isn't awesome."

"Of course." Shit, has that happened to her? "What else?"

"Let's see." She taps her fork with her fingernail, and I wonder if it's a nervous habit. Like maybe a tell in poker. "I'm not into strangulation or pony play or dressing up in each other's clothes."

"Okay, we're on the same page there." I start to pick up my burger again, then stop. "But really, I'm pretty open. If there's something you want..."

"You." She grins and stabs into her salad. "That's pretty much it. I want you."

Electricity zings through me, and I fight to hold it together. "Same. And seriously, if there's anything special you like, just tell me. Or show me." Hell, she could ask me to light my hair on fire and say I'm a Roman Candle, and I'd beg for some goddamn matches.

"Okay, so we're compatible." She grins. "How about you? Anything in particular you do or don't like?"

I swallow my macaroni salad before answering. "I can't stand it when people pet my eyebrows backwards."

Vanessa bursts out laughing. "This happens to you often?"

"My sisters used to do it to bug me." I drop my fork and reach out to trace a thumb over her brow line. "See, it feels nice if someone pets your eyebrow in the direction the hair grows."

"Okay, yeah, I get it." She flushes under my touch, and I love seeing her react.

I switch directions, stroking my thumb toward the center of her forehead. "But if they go the wrong way—"

"Stop, no, I get it." She laughs, swatting my hand away. "Okay, I can promise I won't pet your eyebrows. Not forward or backward or upside down or any way at all."

I grin and draw my hand back, already missing the feel of her. "Just covering all our bases."

"Absolutely." She takes a swallow of water. "Okay, on that note, I'm not a fan of being tied up. I like my hands free for—well, for whatever I might want to touch."

Any blood remaining in my brain heads south in a big hurry. "I think I can manage to forego bondage this one time." I swallow back the urge to grab her right fucking now. "Anything else?"

"Uh, well, that thing where guys want women to call them 'daddy' or baby-talk in bed?" She shrugs. "Not my thing."

"Mine, either." I nod and pick up my burger. "I'm okay with being called Goliath, He-Man, or Waldhar the Wonder Penis Warrior."

She bursts into laughter, hair falling over her eyes. "Okay, I'll take She-ra, Your Majesty, or My-God-You're-The-Hottest-Woman-On-Earth."

"I can manage that." Without a touch of irony, I might add. "So, uh…do you want to choreograph positions, or are you open for spontaneity there?"

She's still smiling, but bright sparks flash in her eyes. It's clear I'm not the only one who's aroused by this conversation. "Let's play it by ear." She fiddles with the edge of her napkin. "I know this all seems silly, but I like having things out in the open."

"Not silly at all." I take a sip of water. "More couples should probably do this before they start taking off their clothes."

She bites her lip. "I'm not ruining the mood?"

"Honey, I couldn't be more in the mood if you got naked right now and laid down on my plate." I move my fork aside. "Here, I'll make it easy for you."

She laughs, but there's hesitation in her eyes. Something telling me there's more to this little exercise than titillation or consent. "I've been thinking about what you said. About running straight from my overbearing mother and into the arms of men who were just as controlling. I'm just—I'm trying not to do that, you know?"

I nod and slip my hand over hers. "I get it. I do."

God knows I'm trying my best not to repeat mistakes I made with Andrea. Pushing my plate aside, I turn to fully face her. "Look, I won't pretend whatever happens between us—whatever we decide to do—is going to be all stars and rainbows and angels singing on high."

She laces her fingers through mine. "Voyeur angels sound creepy anyway."

I squeeze her hand, wanting to be sure she hears what I'm saying. "First times can be awkward." I stop, realizing I'm selling myself short. "Look, I can promise I'll get you off. How's that for straightforward?"

Her throat moves as she swallows. "That's…um…promising."

Maybe I'm being too cocky. I can't wait to get my hands on her body, but I can do this all night if she needs reassurance. "Whatever you need, Vanessa. If you want to cuddle or make out or—"

"Let's do it." She pushes her plate aside and grins.

My heart nearly explodes through my chest. "Really?" I let out a slow breath. "You're sure."

"Positive."

I stand up so fast I knock over my chair, startling Roughneck from his nap on the sofa. I gather up our plates and rush them to the kitchen counter. When I return to the table, Vanessa's fiddling with the top button on her blouse. "Are you nervous? Because I'm a little bit nervous, but—"

I pull her close and kiss her slow and soft and deep. When I draw back, I look right into her eyes. "I'm not nervous. But we can take this as slow as you like."

Her eyes flash with hunger. "Not nervous anymore." She licks her bottom lip. "Kiss me again."

So I do, taking it slower this time. As my lips touch hers, I thread my fingers through her hair. It's unbelievably soft, but no match for her mouth. She moans as my tongue grazes hers, pressing her body against mine.

When I draw back this time, we're both breathless. "Dean," she breathes. "Take me to bed right now."

I don't need another invitation. I take her hand in mine, thankful I know the floor plans for all the cabins. I make a beeline for her bedroom, fighting to keep myself from sprinting. We've got all the time to do this right.

Roughneck sighs as we pass him on the couch, resting his head on his paws and regarding us with a look of intense boredom.

There's a lot I'm feeling right now, but boredom's not on the list. Excitement. Desire. A little bit of nerves, if I'm being honest. I haven't been with anyone since Andrea, but I push her out the door of my mind like an unwelcome guest. There's only room for Vanessa here.

"Oh, good." She turns to me at the threshold of her door and smiles. "I remembered to make my bed."

Her bed could be covered in ants right now, and I wouldn't care. "I'm definitely judging whether you have hospital corners."

She laughs and pulls me inside. "The bed just arrived a few days ago. It's really comfortable."

My mind struggles to stick with the conversation about beds instead of what I want to do on one. "I like your throw pillows."

"Thanks." She surveys the rainbow row of them. Square, round, cylindrical, and in every bright color I can imagine.

I expect her to have some ritual for setting them neatly aside, so I'm surprised when she drops back on the bed, grabbing my hand to pull me with her. "Don't make me wait any more."

"Me?" I laugh, grateful for the invitation as I ease back on top of her. I'm careful to brace my weight on my elbows, not wanting to crush her.

But Vanessa wraps her legs around my waist and pulls me in tight. "You," she breathes, kissing the side of my neck. "I've wanted you so much."

"Same." I murmur it against her throat, kissing a warm, gentle path into the space between her breasts. "You have the softest skin."

She laughs and draws her hands to the sides of my face. "Kiss me, Dean."

I move back up, melding my lips with hers. This time, the kiss is urgent and hungry. I try to hold back, but she's urging me on with her tongue against mine and the soft little moans in the back of her throat.

When she draws back, she's wild-eyed and panting. "Dean," she says, thrilling me with the sound of my own name. "God, you're good at that."

I laugh and kiss her again. "That's Goliath," I say between kisses. "Or He-Man."

"Or Waldhar the Wonder Penis Warrior?" She giggles, but it turns to a groan as I cup her breast through her shirt. "Oh, God."

"That works, too."

I can't stop kissing her, laying claim to every inch of her flesh. Collarbones, breasts, that narrow trail down her abdomen as I unbutton her blouse and tug it from her skirt. The sight of her lacy pink bra fills me with a fresh wave of desire.

Dropping a kiss into the hollow of her waist, I move to her belly button. I'm fighting to go slow, to give her a chance to catch up.

"Dean. Don't stop."

Thank God. Her moan fills my ears as I hike up her skirt and slip between her thighs. There's a thin strip of lace barely covering her, and she gasps as I hook a finger and slip the fabric aside.

"Please, Dean," she begs. "I'll do anything."

Slowly, I trace the tip of my tongue along her slippery seam. Vanessa cries out and clutches the back of my head. "Yes."

I smile and lick her again, drawing her clit into my mouth. "I take it this isn't one of your turnoffs?"

"Don't stop," she pants. "Please don't stop."

"Wasn't planning on it." I lick her again, savoring the honey-sweet slickness. I slip a finger inside, groaning as her tight walls clench around me. "You taste so good."

"Dean." There's an urgency in her voice that wasn't there a second ago.

I lick her again, feeling her pulse around me. The instant I draw her clit into my mouth, she breaks apart beneath me.

"Oh, God." She screams, clutching the back of my head. Desire floods my system as I keep licking, keep fucking her with my fingers. She arches way off the bed, and I anchor her in place, wringing every last spasm out of her.

Her screams subside as she comes back down. Roughneck trots in and cocks his head but doesn't move to join us.

"Go lay down, Buddy," I tell him. "Everything's okay."

He considers that, then flops down in the corner and instantly falls asleep. Vanessa angles up on her elbows. "I was reading to him from this book called *Take a Nap, Change Your Life*," she says. "It's written by a neuroscientist and sleep researcher."

"Good to see he's taking it to heart." I turn back to her. "You okay?"

"More than okay." She pushes her hair out of her eyes and grins. "Holy God. That was unreal."

I smile and move up the bed, kissing my way along her body the same way I got down here. She pulls me to her, kissing me deep and soft and hungry. When she breaks the kiss, she's laughing. "You taste like me."

"That's a turn-on," I tell her, kissing her again. "For the record."

"Mmm." She closes her eyes, but her hands have a mind of their own. She's working my zipper, tugging it down as she shoves my pants down over my hips. It's a marvel of science that she manages to remove them while I toe off my socks and shoes. She's already got the condom in her hand, and I don't bother asking where she grabbed it. I'm just grateful she's rolling it on, touching and stroking and—

"Need you inside me," she pants as she pulls me between her thighs. "Please, don't make me wait."

"Wouldn't dream of it." Still, I hesitate. "This is just to get it out of our systems, right?"

She blinks once, then nods. "Absolutely." She reaches between us and guides me to her warm center. Her heels press the backs of my thighs, guiding me in.

I groan as I sink into the softest, slickest heat I've ever felt. "Vanessa. God."

She's so tight, so wet, and for a moment, I forget it might be the only time I'll ever feel this. I want to feel this a hundred times, a thousand, a million. I want to lose count of all the times I make her cry out and clench around me.

I groan as she angles up against me. "Holy hell."

The sound she makes is somewhere between a sigh and a moan. "Jesus, Dean." She opens her eyes and looks deep into mine with a little laugh that turns into a moan. "You're—uh—big."

My ego swells as I push into her again. "You're—uh—hot."

Her laughter becomes a moan as I slide into her and hit what I'm pretty sure is her G-spot. Our bodies move together like they were made to do this. Like we've been careening toward this our whole lives.

My ears start to buzz, and my vision's going fuzzy. I want to last forever, so I try to slow it down. My brain conjures the least sexy things I can think of. Shareholder expense ratios. The cost analysis of yield to maturity distribution rates. Anything to keep my mind off how good it feels to be inside her right now.

"Dean."

She says my name on a gasp, and I'm too far gone to joke about Goliath or He-Man or whatever the fuck I said earlier. Her moans, they're like tiny prayers, and I've never felt so much like a God. I'm going under, slipping past the point of no return.

*Only once. Just this once.*

I close my eyes, reminding myself this can't last. We're just getting it out of our systems, gaining closure.

But this doesn't feel like an ending. It's the brightest beginning I've ever felt, and I don't know how long I can pretend that's not true.

She clenches around me, and I know she's there. "Oh, God!"

Her slick walls spasm with release. I drive in hard as she arches up to meet me. My own orgasm chases hers, barreling along with no brakes. I hear myself shout, though I've never been noisy in bed. Something inside me snaps, and I'm gasping and moaning and murmuring words even I can't grasp.

Slowly, the pleasure recedes. As my vision clears, Vanessa goes slack in my arms. I roll to my side, pulling her against me as I fight to clear my head, my senses, my conscience.

But there's only one thing that's clear as Vanessa curls up against me and burrows into my side.

She's not out of my system. Not even close.

# CHAPTER 12

**CONFESSIONAL 347**

VINCENT, VANESSA: (CFO, JUNIPER RIDGE)

*IT'S FUNNY, PEOPLE MAKE THIS BIG DEAL ABOUT HOW WOMEN CAN'T SEPARATE SEX FROM LOVE. LIKE A COUPLE GOOD ORGASMS RATTLE OUR BRAINS SO HARD WE HEAR WEDDING BELLS, WHILE GUYS ARE JUST THINKING ABOUT...I DON'T KNOW, SANDWICHES, I GUESS. MAYBE THAT WHOLE DYNAMIC IS SUPPOSED TO BE PART OF THIS SHOW? ANYWAY, I DON'T THINK IT'S THIS ACROSS-THE-BOARD KINDA RULE. I'VE NEVER HAD ANY TROUBLE KEEPING MY HEAD AND MY HEART AND MY...WELL, OTHER PARTS FROM GETTING ALL TANGLED UP TOGETHER. I MEAN, WHAT'S THE BIG DEAL? IT'S JUST SEX, RIGHT?*

* * *

That was…

That was…

I don't even know what that was except amazing.

I'm lying snuggled against Dean, feigning sleep because I'm not sure how to deal with the fact that what just happened between us was so incredible, I can't feel my toes. Or my fingertips.

I can feel a lot of other parts, and all of them are humming a singular harmony: *Him. This one. This guy. He's the one.*

Which is nuts, and also why I'm pretending I've drifted into the stupor of a thoroughly satisfied lover.

Eyes closed, I'm conscious of Dean stroking my hair, kissing the edge of my temple. He just lifted one of my curls and held it to his face, brushing it against his lips. I'm drunk with the thought he's loving my scent the same way I do his.

Maybe I can lie here forever. Eyes closed like this, not confronting the fact that I just slept with a guy I absolutely shouldn't sleep with.

"I know you're awake, Vanessa."

His words startle my eyes open, and I look up to see him smiling at me. I blink a few times struggling to think of something to say. Something wise and cool and meaningful.

"This doesn't have to be weird, right?"

That wasn't it.

Dean laughs and tugs a curl at the edge of my temple. "Define weird. There was none of that pony play you mentioned. I don't think you called me 'daddy.'"

"Small blessings." I close my eyes again, not sure what the hell I said in the throes of orgasm. I've never been a screamer, but the ache in my throat tells me I delivered more than polite, ladylike moans.

"Look, I just have to say that was unreal." Dean's voice makes me open my eyes again, and my heart seizes at the intensity in his eyes.

I nod my agreement, not positive my voice still works. "It was pretty great."

*Pretty great?*

Chocolate lava cake is pretty great. A trip to Greece is pretty great. Eating chocolate lava cake on the balcony of a Greek villa with Oprah Winfrey and Meryl Streep would be pretty great, and none of it compares with what just happened between Dean and me.

But the inner turmoil turning my brain to mush doesn't seem to be affecting him. "It was amazing, really." He laughs, stroking my hair again. "I mean, if we were aiming to get it out of our systems, we sure as hell went out with a bang."

I nod against the pillow, reminding myself that's what we agreed. One and done, that's it. "Yep." I lick my lips and notice they're kiss-swollen. "Totally got it out of my system."

*As if.*

Dean looks at me for a long time, and I pray I was more convincing than I was when faking sleep. I wish I could read his mind as easily as he seems to read mine. Is he as cool under the surface as he appears to be?

He clears his throat, and I brace for him to say something about getting home. For him to clarify this was a one-time thing. Amazing and great, but we definitely shouldn't do it again.

We shouldn't, right?

"You've got a lightbulb burnt out up there."

"What?" I blink and realize he's pointing at the bar above the bathroom vanity. The light's on a sensor, which must mean Roughneck's in there drinking out of the toilet again.

I let that unromantic image fill my brain, doing my best to kill the silly glow infusing my whole body.

"It's been out since I moved in," I tell him. "I bought a spare bulb yesterday. Just haven't had time to put it in."

"I can get that for you."

He starts to move, but I put my hand on his chest. "No, I've got it. It's okay."

"I don't mind." He drops his chin down to kiss the tips of my fingers. "The maintenance guys are off tomorrow, so it'll be a couple days before we can get someone in here."

"I can change my own lightbulb, Dean." My voice comes out snappish, so I soften and try again. "I like doing my own chores."

He looks at me for a long moment, and I brace for an argument. Instead, he plants a soft kiss at my temple. "Whatever you want."

"Thanks."

What I want has nothing to do with lightbulbs and everything to do with Dean. I want to lie here forever in his arms. I want to find a way for this to be uncomplicated and normal, even though I know that can't happen.

For God's sake, he's the CEO at the company where I work. He's been in charge of everything from TV shows to zillion-dollar business deals. He's an oldest son, a Hollywood tycoon, a self-admitted control-freak. Every one of those details makes Dean Judson an excellent leader, but they also make him the wrong man for me.

He's watching me like he's trying to read my mind. The thought sends a shiver down my arms.

"You want dessert?" I don't know why I'm offering, since it's not like I'm going to get up and bake a batch of snickerdoodles. "I think I have some Ben & Jerry's in the freezer."

He laughs and sits up. "Tempting, but I'll pass. I should actually get going."

"Oh?" My brain teeters between 'thank God' and 'please stay here with me all night.' Between all that, I know it's best to usher him out. "I mean, yeah, we have to work early, right?"

"Right. Second interview with banking candidates. You still feeling good about the last candidate?"

"Absolutely." And now I'm talking shop while naked with the CEO. I take a few deep breaths to push back the rush of shame. "She has the strongest resumé, and I like that she's done some television work. I think she'd be great in the role."

"I agree." He kisses me again, softly on the lips. As my eyes flutter open, I see his silvery-hazel ones searching mine. "I'm glad we're on the same page."

"Me, too."

But as Dean gets up and dresses, casual and nonchalant as a guy who has no-strings flings all the time, I know we're nowhere near the same page. We're not even in the same library. He's just finished a short little tidy coffee table book while I'm diving deep into an epic romance novel. I know I need to nip this in the bud, but I'm not sure how.

"So, I'll see you tomorrow morning." I sit up, pulling the sheets over my breasts. "Want to meet in the coffee shop or the conference room?"

"Conference room," he says. "The PI wants to do another bug sweep later this week, so we've only got a couple days to make use of the conference room. We can spread out our notes and take a look at what we've got."

Pre-sex, I might have made a joke about the conference table and the TMI story we heard earlier today. Post-sex, I...well, I can't stop thinking about sex. Which is the opposite of what was supposed to happen.

"Great." I try a nonchalant hair toss, but I end up with a curl stuck in my mouth. I spit it out and clutch the sheets tighter around my breasts. "I'll meet you there."

"Sounds good."

"Fantastic."

I wonder if Dean hears the strain in my voice. If he knows this is way outside my comfort zone, and I'm not sure how to handle it.

Unfazed, he zips up his pants and bends to kiss me one more time. "Call me if you see any more balloon-covered snakes." He tugs on his shirt. "Or badgers or wolves or lizards or—"

"Okay, got it." I laugh as Roughneck jumps up on the bed, snuffling at my face until I scratch his ears. I rub him to keep myself from asking Dean to stay. To prevent me from blurting something dumb. "Have a good night."

"Good night, Vanessa." He grins at me a moment, then bounces back on the bed making Roughneck woof. "One more," he says, dropping a last kiss on my lips.

I kiss him back, making it last, making the memory imprint on my brain. If we can't do this again, I'm damn well making it count.

And then he's gone. I listen for the door to shut, then I look at my dog. "So that's it."

"Uff," says Roughneck and licks my face.

"Just the one time," I tell him, hoping I'll believe it. "That was enough."

My dog tilts his head to the side, accepting my words at face value. Or maybe calling bullshit, it's tough to tell.

I take a deep breath and swing my legs out of the bed. "We should go lock the door. There's creepy people out there who leave snakes on the porches of unsuspecting women."

Roughneck wags his tail, possibly understanding the word "go" and not much else. I slip out of bed and grab my robe off a hook by the door. Tiptoeing through the living room, I notice the blinds are wide open. I haven't closed them the last couple nights, but knowing someone was on my back porch sends me on a mission to shut every last one. Then I slam home the deadbolts and hustle back to bed.

Roughneck joins me, dragging his purple tiger. The naked patch around its neck is a little wider, and the remains of its stump tail is just a gummy wet nub.

He plunks it on the pillow beside me, then plants his big head down next to it and looks at me. I reach over and stroke the bare flesh around his neck. Will the fur ever grow back? I meant to ask Tia.

Some wounds don't ever heal completely. Sometimes, no

matter how you try to move beyond something, the old scars still show through.

As I trace a gentle finger over the bare ring on his neck, my dog sighs. "Me, too, buddy," I say. "Me, too."

***

So "one and done" didn't exactly happen.

I know, I know. *I know,* okay?

But really, it depends on how you see it mathematically. The first time we did it was this huge, mind-blowing jump from zero to one, which is like an infinite percentage increase. Then the second time—also amazing—we only increased the number of times by half, and the next was just an increase of one third.

Now I know that's a harmonic sequence that diverges and would get big eventually, but it's also important to consider how the guilt, the awkwardness, the hesitation—all those things are actually *decreasing*. Like, it was half as weird the second time, and half as weird again the time after that, and if you look at that series, it's monotonically decreasing toward zero. And guess what? The sum of that infinite series is only two!

In other words, the more we do it, the better it gets, the less guilty I feel about it, and we're still only approaching the prospect of doing it twice.

It's possible my math geek brain has gone overboard in justifying this fling with Dean. It's also possible I don't care at all. I like having sex with Dean, and I can't seem to stop doing it.

I'm mulling this when Dean strolls out of my bathroom buttoning his shirt cuffs. He's humming quietly and sporting sex-rumpled hair that looks like he spent an hour rubbing his head against my couch cushions.

That's exactly what happened, and I smile remembering how damn good it felt to have him moving between my thighs, hips thrusting as he—

"What are you so smiley about?" He grins and pulls me into his arms, planting a kiss behind my right ear.

"Your hair." I run my fingers through it, knowing that's not even a tiny fraction of what's racing through my mind right now. "You think anyone's noticing we're not in our offices right now?"

"Nope." He kisses me again, then steps back to grab his keys and wallet off my coffee table. "Are you kidding? Everyone's been working crazy hours. Gabe and Lauren were in the editing room until three a.m. Everyone knows you and I have been burning the midnight oil to get the budget nailed down."

Okay, so no one's likely to notice our Wednesday morning working breakfast that doesn't include breakfast. Or work. Or—

"You're fretting again." He smiles and leans in for another kiss. "I promise no one's thinking twice about whether we're at our desks right now. Hell, we both put in twelve-hour days all weekend."

"I know, you're right." That's honestly not what's bothering me. It's this growing sense that sleeping with Dean Judson has done the exact opposite of getting him out of my system. His smile, his body, his meticulous, beautiful brain. They're all I can think about lately.

Which isn't to say it's affecting my work. On the contrary, Dean and I work together like a well-oiled machine. Plans for Juniper Ridge are coming together perfectly, and I'm proud of the work we're doing.

"By the way, there's something I wanted to ask you." He sits on the edge of my sofa, shirt sleeves rolled to his elbows, and I catch myself wondering if that's a new thing. The Dean I met last month was never this casual. "It's about your screen time."

"My screen time?" I fumble to find myself in this conversation. "What, like how much I'm on my phone?"

He laughs and shakes his head. "Not what I meant. Also, not my place to judge."

My breath snags in my throat. How refreshing to date a guy who doesn't believe he has the right to dictate my life choices.

*You're not dating. Just boinking. And for a limited time.*

"I meant how much on-camera time you're required to put in once the show gets started," he continues like there's not a full conversation happening inside my scattered brain. "I've been thinking that if you're not comfortable being in the spotlight like that, we could revisit that part of your contract. Totally up to you, but I wanted to put it out there in case that's something you're worried about."

I swallow hard, absorbing the importance of his words. He's giving me a choice. He's considering my concerns, my complicated history with my mother and the showbiz limelight. Has any guy I've dated ever done that?

*You're not dating...*

"I'm good with it," I assure him. "I really am. I trust that everyone here will handle things with class and sensitivity."

"Good." Dean grins and stands up. "Gotta go. I have an eleven o'clock with a couple that wants to open a sporting goods shop in one of the retail spaces."

"Need another set of ears?"

"Thanks, but we've got it covered," he says. "Cooper's sitting in on it. He's really into the whole outdoorsy scene."

"Good luck." This time, I'm the one who kisses first. I pull him to me, pressing my lips to his as my body seeks out his warmth and strength.

When I let go, we're both breathing quicker. "Damn." Dean laughs and shakes his head, then makes a beeline for the door. "I'd better get out of here before we start round two."

More like round thirty-four, but who's counting? "I'll see you at the four o'clock meeting."

"Sounds good."

I listen for the sound of the door shutting, then take a shaky breath. What's happening here? Am I falling for Dean Judson, or just enjoying a quick fling? I'm honestly not sure. I know he makes me smile. I know he makes me feel amazing in a million different ways, but is that enough to trump the fact that he's the boss and I'm the last woman in the world who should date the guy in charge?

I distract myself for a while, straightening my clothes and running my fingers through my hair. Roughneck's snoozing in the corner, but I feel bad for ignoring him the last hour. I go to the cupboard and grab one of his favorite chicken jerky treats.

"You've been such a good boy," I tell him as he takes it gently from my hand.

Spying a paperback on the floor beside his bed, I pick it up and read him a chapter from my favorite Kennedy Ryan romance. We've just reached the end of chapter twelve when my doorbell chimes.

Roughneck perks up his ears and gives a hopeful little "uff."

I glance at my watch, startled to see it's already ten. "Your date is here," I tell him. "Ready for your walk with Lana?"

He hops up, wagging not just his stub tail, but his whole body as he prances to the door. He pauses and scoops up the toy basketball I got him yesterday, eager to present an offering to his lady love.

I follow him to the door, smoothing down my skirt to make sure I don't look like a hussy who just shagged Lana's brother on the sofa.

"Hey there," I say as I open the door. "He's ready for you."

Roughneck drops his basketball at her feet, earning a bright chirp of laughter from Lana. "Oh, that's very nice. What a good boy."

As she bends to pet him, I glance around my living room, surveying for signs of my morning tryst with Dean. There's nothing out of order, nothing to give away our guilty little secret. I suppose this is one upside to dating a guy who's enough of a control-freak to think of everything.

*You're not dating...*

"Is he a basketball fan now?" Lana's smiling as she straightens, and Roughneck picks up his ball again.

"What? Oh, Roughneck—I've been reading to him from Kennedy Ryan's *Long Shot*."

"That's a good one." She brushes a lock of honey hair off her face. "Good thing he's emulating the basketball aspect of the story and not the domestic violence one."

"He's a lover, not a fighter."

"The world needs more of that." Lana glances toward my bathroom. "Would you mind if I used your powder room? I should have gone before I came over, but—"

"No problem, be my guest." She's walking my dog for free; the least I can offer is some toilet paper. "I'll round up some doody bags." Wow, that was awkward. "For Roughneck," I clarify. "For your walk."

She laughs and heads for the bathroom. "I knew what you meant."

As she disappears through the door, I take a closer look at the living room. One couch cushion is a bit askew, so I straighten it and step back. There, that's good. Were those two coasters there before?

I'm pretty sure Lana hasn't memorized the placement of my coasters, so I order myself to step back and calm the hell down. The toilet flushes, and I hear water running in the bathroom. I step into the kitchen and try to look casual as Lana steps out with an odd little smile on her face.

"You want me to take this back to Dean?"

She holds up a leather wallet I recognize instantly. The DLJ monogram is a dead giveaway. *Crap.*

"Oh, um—yes. Yeah, thanks, that would be great." Heat rushes my cheeks, and I order myself not to sound guilty. "He came by to drop off the files for—"

"Relax, Vanessa." She smiles and pats my arm. "You know what my job was in Hollywood, right?"

"Public Relations?" I croak, not sure what this has to do with anything.

"That's one way to put it," she says smoothly, tucking the wallet into the pocket of her white capris before bending to hook the leash to Roughneck's harness. "Another way to put it is that I got paid to safeguard people's secrets. To make sure embarrassing things were never made public if that's what someone asked of me. You understand?"

I nod, grateful for her discretion. I should probably try harder to deny what she's assuming, but it feels good to let my guard down just a little.

Maybe that's what I'm doing with Dean. Why being with him strikes just the right chord in me. "Thank you," I murmur. "Thanks for everything."

"Don't mention it." With a smile, she moves past me through the kitchen, leaving me wondering just where this is headed. I should be careful. I should be concerned.

But as Lana skips out the door with my dog, all I can feel is happy.

# CHAPTER 13

**CONFESSIONAL 352.5**

Judson, Dean: (CEO, Juniper Ridge)

*Remember when we were kids and you guys used to break into my room and mess up all my stuff? Hiding my baseball glove, turning my books upside down, shit like that. Drove me bonkers. Huh? Yeah, I figured that's why you did it. I mean, I used to think it was just about pissing me off.*

*I still think that, but now I wonder if it wasn't about love, too. About knowing I needed to chill out sometimes so I didn't have a stroke before middle school.*

*No, goddamn it. Stop touching my mug.*

* * *

"Watch your step." I catch Vanessa's hand in mine, aware I'm not the best person to give advice on tromping through the woods at night.

Or in the daytime, for that matter. The Judson kids didn't exactly grow up roughing it.

But Vanessa just laughs and squeezes my hand. "Thanks. You

want to know another awesome thing about being out here after dark?"

"You mean aside from your promise to get naked?" A prospect I've thought about all week, to be honest. "I didn't think it got more awesome than that."

She laughs and stops walking so she can turn and face me. "The snakes that live in this area aren't nocturnal," she says, whispering even though we're all alone below the southern ridge. "It's too cold at night, so they're all tucked in their dens instead of lying around in the sunshine waiting to pounce."

I don't ask how she knows all this. If I've learned anything in the weeks I've known Vanessa, it's that she's smart as hell. If there's something she doesn't know, she researches the crap out of it until she's as knowledgeable as the leading experts on everything from culinary trends to the best brand of condom.

The latter is something we've tested pretty thoroughly these past couple weeks. What? I know it was meant to be just a one-time thing, but come on. The sex is amazing, we get along great, and our working relationship is solid as hell. I know I should worry about things spiraling. My feelings, the fact that I can't keep my hands off her—all of this is new to me.

But is it so wrong to want to see where this goes? To want Vanessa so much that I almost don't care that I'm losing control of the situation.

"So now what?" I'm whispering, too, which lends to the excitement of what we're doing out here in the woods. "This spot looks flat enough."

Laughing, she draws her body up against mine and kisses me until I see stars. "Eager, huh?" She kisses me again and draws back to look me in the eye. We flicked off our flashlights already, but the moon is bright enough to see the spark of delight in her eyes.

"I've gone thirty-two years without having sex in the woods," I say as I kiss my way down her neck. "I don't think I can wait another thirty seconds."

"Mmm, that feels good." She tilts her head back as I unbutton her shirt, moving my mouth over the spots I know make her moan like that. I've learned her body almost as well as my own, and I love knowing I can deliver this kind of pleasure.

I'm playing with fire, I know that. I've fucked up royally in the past. I've been a shitty boyfriend, a shitty fiancé, a shitty guy in general.

But don't I get some points for recognizing that? For wanting to do better this time?

"Dean." She murmurs my name like it's a prayer, like we're the only two people on earth. Out here under the stars, with crickets chirping in the distance, it feels like we might be.

I bury my face between her breasts, breathing her in. The flowery scent of her skin mingles with the earthy tang of the forest, and I'm dizzy before I know it. "You taste so good," I murmur, licking my way down her abdomen.

She gasps as I unhook her bra and toss it aside, covering her breasts with my hands. "Have I mentioned how much I love your breasts?"

"Once or twice." Her voice is high and airy as she turns in my arms so her spine curves against my chest. I groan as she grinds her ass against me. "Have I mentioned how much I love whoever invented hiking skirts?"

"I never knew that was a thing." But I'm grateful, especially as I flip hers up to discover nothing but a skimpy little thong between me and where I'm hoping to be. I slip the fabric aside, hissing out a breath as I find her slick and hot and ready for me.

"You'll have to thank Cooper for the skirt," she says. "Pretty clever to score all those product samples from the camping gear people."

"You'll have to stop thinking about my brother," I tease,

nipping the back of her neck as she arches her back to grind against me. “It’s throwing me off my stride.”

She laughs and presses into my hard-on, making me wish I had a hiking skirt of my own. I’d be inside her if I didn’t have this damn zipper.

“Your stride feels pretty perfect to me.” She tips forward and crosses her arms against the gnarled trunk of a pine tree, grinding against me through my jeans. “Are you going to stop teasing soon and fuck me?”

“Now who’s eager?” I’m grinning as I unzip my fly and shove my jeans around my hips. The condom is already in my hand, and within seconds I’ve rolled it on and I’m sliding inside her. “Oh, fuck.”

It’s like this every time, slick and tight and so mind-blowingly great it takes my breath away. Actually, that’s not true.

As Vanessa cries out, and I thrust into her again, I realize it’s getting better. Better than it was our first or second or twelfth time. Better than anything I’ve felt in my life.

*That doesn’t have to mean anything.*

But it does.

I know it does; I’ve known it for days. This thing we’re doing, it’s so much more than sex. I don’t know what the hell it is, and that should definitely scare me.

The thing is, it doesn’t. When I’m with her, I feel safe and whole and hopeful I can crawl from the wreckage of my last relationship and just be myself. I’ve never done that before, not ever. I’ve never been comfortable enough to let my guard down, to be at ease in a relationship and in my own skin.

Vanessa moans again, and I can tell she’s getting close. I’m almost there myself, and I grip her hips tighter to thrust hard and fast the way she likes it.

“Don’t stop,” she pants. “Dean, *oh God*.”

“That’s it,” I coax as she slips her fingers between her thighs to rub her clit. I love how she does that. How she's confident and in control enough to get herself there.

My ego reminds me that I've got a role in this, too, so I tilt my hips to hit the spot that makes her cry out and clench around me.

"Yes!" She screams the word as she drags her nails down the tree trunk. A flock of night birds scatters as Vanessa clenches and cries out and comes apart in my arms.

I'm three seconds behind her, thrusting and pumping and losing myself inside her. My God, it's unreal. These feelings, the pleasure, this total loss of control.

I never knew it could be like this.

When we both catch our breath, Vanessa straightens and turns. Grinning as she tugs her skirt down, she stretches up to kiss me. "Check that one off your bucket list."

"That was…whoa." Way to sound like a damn caveman.

Vanessa just laughs and smacks my ass. "You're officially an outdoorsman now."

I get rid of the condom, tucking it in one of Roughneck's doody bags because I'm not an asshole who leaves garbage in the forest. Not even if I own the forest.

When I straighten back up, Vanessa's staring up into the tree with a frown. "Huh."

"What?" I look up, and there it is. Her bra, pink and lacy and dangling fifteen feet off the ground.

Vanessa squeezes my bicep. "Guess you don't know your own strength, Judson."

"That's kind of impressive." I glance around for a fallen limb, calculating how long it should be to snag the bra out of the tree.

But Vanessa's way ahead of me. She's already striding toward the trunk, grabbing one of the lowest branches to hoist herself up. "You know what my mother said when she caught me climbing the oak tree in our backyard?"

I stare at her, mesmerized by the glow of her breasts in the moonlight. "Maybe you shouldn't do that topless?"

She laughs and climbs higher, stretching up to reach the next branch. "No, but close. She said it wasn't ladylike. That men feel uncomfortable around women who engage in unfeminine pursuits."

Watching Vanessa—this woman, this marvel of nature—climbing higher into the evergreen like she's done this a thousand times, I'm positive I've never seen a more perfect example of powerful feminine grace. I open my mouth to tell her to be careful, then shut it again. She doesn't need me to manage her.

She's doing just fine on her own.

"How old were you?" I ask, sucking in a breath as her foot slips just a little.

But she catches herself and draws her body up onto the next branch. "Eight," she says. "Can you imagine? Talking to your eight-year-old daughter about landing a husband?"

I shake my head, too angry to say anything right away. As I watch Vanessa snag her bra off the limb, a wave of admiration washes away my fury, leaving something that feels alarmingly like love.

But no, it can't be that. We're just fooling around here. We can't be serious.

"Crazy." I shake my head, hoping she thinks I'm talking about her mother. Hoping she can't read my mind, can't hear the words clanging around in there.

I'm falling for Vanessa Vincent.

And even though that's the wildest thing I've ever done, I can't help smiling. Can't help stepping forward to catch her by the waist as she descends. She laughs, sliding down my body as I lower her to the ground.

As she tips her head back to kiss me, I wonder how the hell I made it this far in life without having sex in the woods.

How I thought I was happy before I met Vanessa.

# CHAPTER 14

**CONFESSIONAL 367**

Vincent, Vanessa: (CFO, Juniper Ridge)

*You know what my mom used to call me? A free spirit. No, it wasn't a good thing. I know it might be for some people, but trust me. The way she said it was like "Satan" or "calories" or "polyester." I guess to her, that was the worst thing I could be. Part of me wanted to rebel, to go out and climb mountains and howl at the moon. Most of the time, though...well, I just want to feel safe. Loved. Understood.*

*Um, can you stop recording? Yeah, just scratch the whole thing. That'd be great.*

* * *

Two days later, I walk into the coffee shop with my nerves a jangled mess. Colleen's behind the counter and flashes me a broad smile.

"Hey, Vanessa," she calls. "What's shakin'?"

"Not a whole lot."

Just my hands at the prospect of seeing Dean, which is dumb. We've slept together dozens of times since that first night at my place. I shouldn't be this quivery in my excitement about a stupid breakfast meeting.

So much for getting it out of my system.

"You meeting someone, or taking it to go?" Colleen sets her laptop on the counter and stretches, her long gray braid swinging over her shoulder. "I'm getting pretty good at making those designs in the foam. Earlier I made a shamrock for Lana."

"That was not a shamrock." Patti emerges from the back room wiping her hands on a dish towel. "It was absolutely a penis."

Colleen grins at her wife. "Admittedly it's been a few decades since I've seen one, but that didn't look like any penis I've ever met."

All this talk of penises is bringing my thoughts of Dean to a head, but I try not to let it show. I rest my palms on the counter, scanning the chalkboard menu behind them. "Do I want a vanilla latte or cardamom?"

"Cardamom," Colleen says without hesitation. "You've had the vanilla three days in a row. Time to try something new."

"Good point." I try not to read too much into that. It's not like Colleen has any idea about my habit of repeating mistakes. Not that my lattes have been poor choices, but men...

*Stop thinking about men.*

Besides, Dean's not showing signs of being controlling. Great in bed, yes. Sweet and attentive and—

"Can I make that a double?" I ask, dragging a twenty out of my wallet. "And whatever flavor of muffin you've got today."

"Peach rhubarb," Patti offers helpfully, sliding one onto a plate for me. "Did we tell you we spotted Francine again? And she had a friend with her."

"No way! That's awesome."

Francine is one of several Sierra Red Foxes they've been

monitoring for the Department of Fish and Wildlife. The species has teetered on the edge of extinction for years, so the sightings here are a big deal.

Colleen cranks some levers on the latte machine. "We watched them on the wildlife cam just down from the southern ridgeline. Must have been around eight, maybe eight-thirty a couple nights ago."

From the corner of my eye, I see Patti give Colleen a warning look. It takes me a moment to get it.

"The southern ridge?" My voice sounds weirdly high, and I concentrate very hard on scratching a dot of chocolate off my purse strap.

"Yep, maybe a couple hundred yards down." Colleen finishes my drink and sets it on the counter. "The Department of Fish and Wildlife has five different wildlife cams in the area."

Heat floods my face. "Oh my God. You—you saw—um—?" I don't say it out loud, just in case. But it's clear from the look they exchange that Dean and I didn't nail the privacy aspect of our outdoor hookup.

I close my eyes, wishing I'd just kept my mouth shut when Dean confessed an outdoor tryst was high on his bucket list of unfulfilled sexual fantasies. But come on, it was amazing.

So amazing I start to smile as I open my eyes again and catch Patti studying me with sympathy. "You okay?" she asks.

I nod as another wave of embarrassment washes through me. "Ugh, I'm just—*ugh*. Sorry."

Colleen only laughs and messes with some levers on the espresso machine. "Nothing we haven't seen before, girl."

"Breathe, sweetie." Patti adds a second muffin to my plate. "We won't tell anyone."

"Just wanted you to be aware," Colleen adds. "Our lips are sealed if you'd rather not tell D—"

"Tell *him*," Patti whispers, throwing me a wink. "God knows it's going to be tough enough finding privacy in a place like this."

Isn't that the truth. When I signed on for this job, I never in a million years thought that would be an issue. How was I supposed to know I'd end up banging the CEO?

"I'm so embarrassed." I pick an edge off a muffin and glance behind me to make sure Dean's not early. No sign of him, though I'm just now noticing Mari in the corner. I throw her a friendly wave, but she's got her face buried in her laptop and doesn't see me.

I turn back to face Colleen and Patti. "Thank you for being discreet."

"Not a problem." Patti smiles and turns back toward the kitchen. "God knows we remember what it's like to be young and crazy in love."

"Or not in love." Colleen regards me with a serious look. "None of our business what you two have going on."

"Thanks." I nibble my muffin as Patti wanders into the back room and Colleen starts ringing up my purchase.

As she hands me my change, her expression turns serious again. "By the way, there was another hacking attempt."

I freeze. "Another?"

"Yeah," she says. "I sent Dean an email about it but figured you'd want to know."

"Thanks." I'm not sure what he's told her about the snake or postcard or any other incidents. "Did the hacker get through?"

"Nah, we were able to block it." She shakes her head. "Whoever this guy is, he's getting sneakier."

I sip my latte, wishing I had something to add to the conversation. Something besides guilt that I could somehow be behind this. "What do you think is going on?"

Colleen shrugs and leans back against the counter. "Beats me. I'm no cop."

"Surely you have a theory."

She takes her time considering that. "I know a lot of folks out here weren't happy about a bunch of Hollywood elites swooping in and buying a bunch of prime acreage. Especially for a reality TV show."

"You think that's it?" The theory ebbs my guilt just a little. "What about some of the cult people? Maybe they're behind it."

"Could be." She shrugs again. "Maybe the new PI will have some insights."

"Lieutenant Lovelin?" I assume that's who she means, though a PI and a police chief are hardly the same thing. "She's great, isn't she?"

Colleen anchors a lid on my mug and sets it on the counter. "She's terrific, but I meant the PI. The new guy Dean hired after what happened out at your place."

She's looking at me like I'm supposed to know about this, so I do my best imitation of someone with a clue. "Oh. Yeah, of course." I pick up my drink and take a sip, burning my tongue. "Well, I'm sure someone will get to the bottom of it."

"Hopefully."

Grabbing my plate and mug, I turn and head for the table Dean and I have used for our last couple meetings. I'm halfway there when Mari glances up from her laptop. She's wearing yoga pants and a hoodie sweatshirt, and I'm instantly jealous of how comfy she looks.

"Hey, Vanessa." She smiles and nudges her glasses up her nose. "Settling in okay?"

"Great," I tell her. "We've got most of the candidates narrowed down on the finance side of things."

"Wonderful." She leans back in her chair as her gaze sweeps over me. "I actually meant outside of work. This must be a big change, uprooting your life and having to be on camera. That's on top of the stress of what happened the other night."

For a second I think she means sex in the woods with her brother, and it takes my brain a second to catch up. "Oh, you mean the snake."

Mari folds her hands on the table beside her laptop, studying me with bookish intensity. "I can only imagine how triggering it must be to have someone pinpoint your phobias like that. I was chatting with Oprah a couple years ago and—this was on the air, by the way, so I'm not breaching confidentiality—"

"Of course," I manage, taken aback by how casual she's being about a conversation with television royalty.

"Anyway, Oprah also suffers from globophobia," Mari continues. "She traces it back to childhood."

"Really? I had no idea."

Mari's sitting straight in her chair, in full-on shrink mode now. "In her case, the fear is rooted in the sound of balloons popping and the fact that it triggers thoughts of gunfire." She tilts her head to study me. "I don't suppose that's a factor for you? Because if it is, there are strategies we can discuss to alleviate some of your fears."

"That's very kind." It really is, and I sense she's not just speaking as a therapist. That she's someone who could become a close friend. "I can't say I've had any exposure to gunfire," I admit. "But I don't like surprises."

"Ah, I see."

I wonder if she does. If she sees everything, not just my fears. If she can tell by looking at me that I'm sleeping with her brother, and that it's gone way beyond the plan of having sex once to get it out of our systems. Would she tell me in cautious, clinical terms what an abysmally bad idea it is?

I don't need a shrink to tell me that. *I* know it.

But somehow, I can't stop myself from blurting the question. "Is it true about getting closure? About, um...ways to get someone out of your system by being intimate with that person." I bite my lip as heat rushes my face. "I'm asking for a friend."

Mari leans forward in her chair. "Have a seat." She says the words plainly, kindly, with a tone I find myself obeying without question.

Sinking down into the metal and wood chair, I glance around

the coffee shop. Colleen and Patti must be in the back room, and Dean's not due for ten minutes.

"I'm sorry," I say again, keeping my voice low. "I tried Googling it, but I didn't find much, and—anyway, I just wondered. You told me at orientation that I could ask personal questions, so—" I shrug, aware that I may have just stuck my foot in it.

But Mari regards me with a calm, professional expression. "Anything you say to me is confidential," she says. "I do have to warn you that conflict of interest precludes me from serving as your therapist, but I can certainly discuss the issue in general terms."

"I understand." I also notice she saw right through my bullshit about asking for a friend.

I sip my latte, grateful Colleen suggested the cardamom. It has a complex citrusy, minty spice to it, which is a nice change from vanilla. "I mean, I get that this show is partly about people hooking up," I add. "I understand that's part of the social experiment."

"Absolutely." Mari studies me for a few beats. "What do you think changed from when you applied for the position?" Her voice is achingly kind, and any defensiveness I'm feeling dissolves like a sugar cube in hot tea. "As I recall, you indicated that you would prefer to staple your eyebrows to the carpet than find yourself in a romantic relationship."

"I did write that, didn't I?" God, I'm an idiot. Oh, and also—"It's not a relationship."

She doesn't say anything to that. Just looks at me with one of those wise, thoughtful expressions shrinks are so good at. It occurs to me I haven't actually said Dean's name. Does she know we're involved, or does she think we're talking about some random guy?

"Vanessa." She crosses her legs, never breaking eye contact. "There's nothing wrong with two consenting adults engaging in mutually fulfilling physical contact, assuming they've both agreed to those terms." She pauses, brow furrowing. "You're consenting, right?"

"Enthusiastically." I wince. "Yes. I'm consenting."

Mari doesn't blink. "There's clearly something you're getting from the arrangement. It might behoove you to explore what that is, and whether you're truly comfortable with whatever it might be costing you in the bigger picture. Perhaps the trade-off is worth it, if you're ultimately having your needs met."

"Right." She has a point, but all I can think about is having my needs met. About the things I'm getting out of the arrangement.

*Multiple orgasms.*

*The best sex of my life.*

*The pleasure of touching the hottest, sexiest man I've ever—*

"Okay," I say, pretty sure I shouldn't be thinking these things about Dean with his sister sitting across from me. "I guess I can explore that."

"That's a terrific idea."

I love how she frames it like I'm the brilliant one, when all I've done is think dirty thoughts about her brother.

She tugs a pen out of her bun, and I expect her hair to tumble down around her shoulders. But no, she's got two more pens in there, plus maybe a chopstick?

"I'm writing down the name of another therapist who's top-notch," she says. "He's in LA, but he does online appointments. I'd be happy to make an introduction if you're interested."

"Thanks. I'll think about it." I pocket the card and wonder if I'll ever use it. "Thank you, Mari. I guess I'm feeling a little lost not talking to my sister every night, you know?"

It might be my imagination, but I swear she flinches just the tiniest bit. "Of course," she says. "Some of us have been talking about doing regular girls' nights. Poker or book club or something like that. I can let you know if you're interested."

"That would be great. Thank you."

"Don't mention it."

The door chimes, and I look up to see Dean striding through. God, he's hot. Dark jeans and a blue and white button-down with the top couple buttons unhooked. My face heats up as I remember what it feels like to press my nose into that spot, and I don't realize Mari's spoken until she puts her hand on my arm.

"Hey." Her voice is low and Dean's out of earshot at the espresso bar, but I lean forward anyway. "There's no shame in changing your mind. In letting relationships flow where they need to. Just be wary of letting them flow into old patterns."

"All right, I will." I want to, anyway. "Thanks, Mari."

"Don't mention it."

I get up and hustle over to the table Dean and I have occupied for our last couple meetings. He's already set his laptop on it, so I put down my coffee and the muffin plate and drop into the opposite chair.

Dean appears moments later, a cup of coffee gripped in one massive hand. "Damn, that looks delicious."

I blink up at him, conscious of his eyes skimming my legs. No, not my legs. The muffin perched on the plate at the edge of our table.

"Want one?" I nudge the plate closer. "They gave me two, but I'm really not that hungry."

"You sure?"

"Positive. Help yourself."

"Thanks." He picks up the second muffin and takes a bite, groaning with pleasure. My skin prickles with arousal as my body identifies the sound as something else entirely.

*Down, girl.*

I glance over at Mari, who's gone back to typing on her laptop. Colleen's out of earshot, but I still lean forward and keep my voice low as I grab Dean's arm.

"Colleen and Patti saw us having sex, and Lana found your

wallet in my bathroom, and also Mari might know we're sleeping together."

Dean stares at me as he swallows a bite of muffin. "Good morning to you, too."

"Sorry." I take my hand back and pry the top off my latte, frowning down at the design. After a few sips, it looks less like a penis and more a misshapen airplane.

"It's all right, isn't it?" he asks. "We're both adults. Not like anyone's going to judge us for it."

"Judge *you*, maybe." I take a slow sip of my drink, stalling as I gather my thoughts. "I'm worried people won't take me seriously if they think I'm sleeping with the boss."

It's not the only thing I'm worried about, but we'll start there.

Dean watches me, finger tracing the rim of his favorite mug. "You're living on the set of a reality show devoted to people pairing up," he says slowly. "Isn't stuff like this to be expected?"

Again, he's missing the point. "They'll assume I'm sleeping with you for some kind of career advancement."

He frowns. "Who's this mysterious they? Tell me, and I'll handle it."

I bite my lip, hating how the whole master-and-commander thing turns me on. "I don't need you to handle it," I tell him. "Besides, you can't handle everyone. What about viewers when the show starts airing?"

"What about them?"

"Come on." I sip my drink again. "Everyone knows people watch reality shows to judge the participants."

"Ouch."

"But true, right?"

He doesn't say anything right away. "You don't seem like someone who'd care what strangers think of you."

"I don't." I pick up my drink and blow on it, steam billowing around me. "I care what my colleagues think. In this case, that's your family. And I care what my friends think, and right now, the cast—the *community members* who've signed on so far—are the closest thing I have to friends."

"I see."

I'm not sure he does, but at least he looks like he's considering it. He takes a slow sip of his coffee and glances out the window. "Is the biggest problem that we work together, or that you just don't see anything long-term with us?

Wow. "Anyone ever tell you you're alarmingly blunt?"

"All the time." He gives me a smile that doesn't totally reach his eyes, but I don't get the sense he'd be upset by any answer I might give.

I consider the question a while. "I'm also judging myself, okay?" I sigh and set my cup down on the table. "I came in here determined to take my work seriously and put my love life on the back burner. Here I am only a few weeks in, and I'm boning the boss."

"Okay, you need to stop calling me the boss." He leans closer, hazel eyes flashing. "Goliath or He-Man or—"

"Dean, I'm serious." I'm also laughing, which probably undermines my seriousness. "What are we doing here?"

"We're having breakfast and a business meeting." He leans back in his chair and picks up his muffin. "We can bust out some spreadsheets if it'll make you feel better."

"I mean what are we doing in the grand scheme of things."

He gives that some thought. "Well, we're having the most amazing sex I've ever had in my life. How's that?"

*That* is a compliment that fills me to bursting with all kinds of good vibes. As heat rushes my cheeks, I fight to keep myself from grinning like a big dork. "But what happens when it all blows up? Won't that make our working relationship awkward?"

"Not if we don't let it." He polishes off his muffin and dusts the crumbs off his hands. "Vanessa, I'm having fun with you. I love spending time together in and out of the office. But if that's not working for you, I can accept your decision. It won't change anything between us on a professional level."

Okay, that's...not what I want. Is it?

Maybe that's not the part I should focus on. "You'd do that?" I ask.

"Of course," he says. "I wouldn't like it, but if you called it quits, I'm confident it wouldn't affect our working relationship one bit."

How can he be so confident?

Or maybe the better question is how can I *not* be?

"Maybe you're right." I pick up my muffin and take a bite. The tanginess of the rhubarb and the sweetness of the peach are such a delicious contrast that I get lost in thought for a moment.

"That." His voice is gruff and familiar. "That right there."

I blink. "What?"

"That look." He leans close, even though Mari and Colleen are far out of earshot and minding their own business. "It's the look you get right before you come, and it's my favorite thing in the whole world."

"Dean." I pick up my latte to hide the heat in my cheeks. "I thought you said we were in a business meeting."

"We are." He grins. "We're multi-taskers, aren't we?"

It's one of many things we have in common. I'm about to say something sarcastic about that when the door chimes and Cooper strides in. His brow is furrowed, and even though I don't know him well, I can tell he's upset. Hands clenched at his sides, he scans the coffee shop. The instant his gaze lands on Dean, he makes a beeline for our table.

"Bad news," he announces with no preamble.

Dean frowns with his mug raised halfway to his lips. "Is there some kind of conspiracy to rain on my morning?

Ignoring him, Cooper waves to Mari. "You're going to want to hear this, too."

"Oh?" She looks up from her laptop and frowns. "What happened?"

She doesn't wait for an answer. Just stands up and walks to our table, her cozy-looking slippers tapping the floor. The second she sits down, Cooper rakes his fingers through his hair.

"Someone called the County on us," he says. "Our filming permits have been denied."

Dean's expression is stony. "That's not possible."

"Oh, but it is." Cooper gives a disgusted grunt. "I just got off the phone with the head of the department. Apparently, they received an anonymous tip."

"What kind of tip?" Mari glances from one brother to the other. "I thought we nailed down the proper legal clearance months ago."

"We did," Dean growls. "I handled it personally."

"Somehow, it's been un-handled," Cooper says. "The County is sending over the report, but apparently it has something to do with code violations."

Mari looks personally affronted. "We're following codes to a tee. This is ridiculous."

"I don't know, Mar." Cooper throws up his hands. "Look, it's becoming pretty clear someone doesn't want us here."

"But who?" Mari looks at Dean. "This is asinine. We've had focus groups with neighbors. The police have profiled former cult members and assured us they don't see any cause for concern. For crying out loud, who else would do something like this?"

Dean's not looking at me, but the weight of the question weighs on my shoulders. The postcard, the balloon snake—it seems so clear this isn't about the Judson family.

It's about me.

"What's our recourse?" I lick my lips, stalling for time. "Can we appeal or pay fines or something?"

Three pairs of Judson eyes swing toward me, but it's Dean

who speaks first. "I'll handle it." He looks from me to Mari to Cooper and back again, radiating confidence with every moment of eye contact. "I'll take care of this, okay? Trust me."

A shiver ripples up my arms, but I nod because that's what Cooper and Mari are doing.

But deep down, I know it's not that simple. Deep down, I wonder if I'm the last thing in the world Dean Judson needs right now.

If there's more than one reason we shouldn't be together.

# CHAPTER 15

**CONFESSIONAL 371.5**

JUDSON, DEAN: (CEO, JUNIPER RIDGE)

*DID I EVER TELL YOU WHAT THEY CALLED ME AT THE FIRST STUDIO I WORKED FOR? MISTER FIX-IT. NO, IT HAD NOTHING TO DO WITH REPAIRING SHIT. IT'S THAT SOMETHING WOULD GO WRONG—A SPONSOR PULLING OUT OR A PROBLEM WITH THE VENUE OR WHATEVER—AND EVERYONE WOULD LOOK TO ME. LIKE THEY THOUGHT I HAD SOME KIND OF MAGICAL POWER TO SOLVE IT.*

*THE THING IS, I USUALLY DID. PROBABLY NINETY-EIGHT PERCENT OF THE TIME, I DID. THAT OTHER TWO PERCENT, THOUGH...*[SCOWLING] *YEAH, I'M NOT PERFECT. WHO THE FUCK IS?*

* * *

That evening, sitting on my back deck with crickets chirping in the field and a cold beer in my hand, I can't stop thinking about Vanessa.

It's nothing new since we started sleeping together, which I realize was supposed to be a one-time thing. But come on, that's like having one taste of a perfect Wagyu ribeye with a 2008

Screaming Eagle Cabernet and then saying, "no more, thanks, I'm good." Who does that?

Not me, which is currently the least of my problems.

I spent two hours on the phone with County officials, trying to sort out the bullshit with our filming permits. In the end, I got a tentative okay to continue what we're doing.

"You're not in the clear, yet," the woman on the phone informed me. "There's still an appeals process we'll need to go through. And a thorough review of—"

"I'll handle it," I told her. "Whatever hoops you need me to jump through, I'll take care of it."

"Hmph," she said and hung up.

Now I'm on my back deck, clutching one of the sample beers we got from a brewer we interviewed late this afternoon. I take a sip, savoring the dark, malty froth of the porter. It's the creation of a guy named Griffin Walsh, a brewer out of Colorado. He's got great plans for opening a brewery right here at Juniper Ridge. Great beer, too.

I rest the bottle on the arm of my Adirondack chair and gaze out over the sunset. So many colors, orange and pink and red and even bright magenta right at the edge of the mountains. I wish Vanessa were here to enjoy it with me. I'm supposed to head to her place later, but for now I'm enjoying this rare breath of quiet. I haven't been alone much since moving to Oregon, and it's a nice treat.

As though summoned by that thought, my phone pings with an incoming text. I pick it up, heart ticking excitedly at the thought of seeing Vanessa's name on the screen.

It's not Vanessa. It's Andrea.

ANDREA: Hey, Dean. Any chance you're free to talk?

. . .

HELL. I take another sip of beer and sigh. I could pretend I haven't seen it. Just act like I don't have my phone glued to my hand at all times.

But Andrea knows me better than that. She once took me to task for checking my phone during our anniversary dinner, which I know now was a dick move. At any rate, she knows I have a tough time disconnecting, so she'll use that to her advantage. She'll keep texting until I respond.

ME: What do we need to talk about?

THERE, that's plenty blunt. Hopefully enough that she'll take the hint. I start to set the phone down, but there's already a message coming in.

ANDREA: I'm moving to Oregon. Please call.

WHAT THE—

I stare at the screen, hoping I've read it wrong.

**I'M MOVING TO OREGON. Please call.**

SHE CAN'T BE SERIOUS. Andrea was born and raised in Hollywood. She's been part of that world her whole life. No way could she leave that behind for this quiet, sleepy part of the Pacific Northwest.

I'm dialing her number before I have a chance to process that this is exactly what she wants. I'm sure Mari would have a name for whatever psychological phenomenon it is, but I'm too annoyed to care.

"Dean." Andrea's voice is soft and sweet on the other end of the line. "How are you doing, hon?"

I brace for my body to respond to the term of endearment. My only response is irritation. "What are you talking about? What is this about moving to Oregon?"

"Oh, that." She gives a musical little laugh. "Yes, well, there's a cute little ranch that came up for sale near Prineville. I've been wanting to find myself some quiet retreat, away from the cameras and gossip rags and—"

"You'd hate it there," I blurt before she gets the words out. "Trust me, Central Oregon's too small for you. It's farms and ranches and not a Chanel boutique in sight."

That should be enough to scare her off, but Andrea only laughs. "I'm not as shallow as you think, Dean."

"I never said you were." I pinch the bridge of my nose, eager to have this conversation over. "You've never *not* lived in a city."

"Please." She makes a scoffing sound. "Besides, Portland's not that far."

"Three-and-a-half hours' drive each way." Longer on snowy roads in winter. "And even Portland's not like the cities you're used to. Trust me, this isn't your scene."

"Don't you think I'd be the best judge of that?"

Her tone is mild and almost flirty, which means my gruffness isn't getting through. "No," I grunt. "I don't."

"There's the Dean I know and love." She laughs again, and the sound is starting to annoy me. "You always think you know what's best for everyone. It's sweet, actually."

Her praise leaves a sour taste on the back of my tongue. I

swallow and try another tack. "Look, I don't own the state of Oregon. If you want to come check it out, be my guest. I'm just telling you as a courtesy that this isn't your kind of place."

Andrea scoffs. "Is that what you're telling all the castmates on your show?"

"The ones who won't love it here, you bet." I clear my throat. "I believe in being honest."

*Unlike some people.*

If she hears my unspoken accusation, she doesn't let on. "Oh, Dean. You haven't changed a bit. Another thing I love about you."

"Great." If she's fishing for a compliment, it's not happening. "Do what you want, Andrea. But I've moved on with my life, and I hope you're doing the same."

There's a long pause, followed by a deep breath. "Dean, I just want to say again that I'm sorry."

Some of the tension leaks from my shoulders. I'm not angry anymore. That's when I realize it. I'm not sad, either. I'm just... over it.

"I forgive you," I tell her. "I'm sorry, too."

"For what?"

"For being a self-absorbed dick. For working too much and ignoring you. I wasn't a great fiancé."

"Oh, Dean." Tears choke her voice, and I think that's my cue to end the call.

"So, yeah." I clear my throat. "I guess that's it."

*Closure.* Funny how it feels nothing like the closure I tried for with Vanessa. Every moment with her, every shared breath or sigh, it feels like a beginning. Before I know it, I'm grinning like a fool.

"You're right," Andrea says, and I remember I'm still on the phone with her. "LA brought out the worst in both of us."

"Yeah. I'm in a better place now."

Andrea laughs. "Well see? Now you've convinced me I really do want to see Oregon."

I sigh. "I won't stop you. Just please don't make any rash moves."

"Like ending our relationship over text."

*Ouch.* Ouch, but not incorrect. "I'm sorry again about that."

"I shouldn't have said that." Her voice softens. "It was a cheap shot."

Maybe, but I don't care anymore. I truly don't. "It was nice talking with you." It wasn't, but I'm being polite.

"Same. Really nice. Thank you for everything, Dean."

"I'll see you around."

I hang up the phone and stare at it a few beats. It's not like that's the first time we've spoken since the split.

But it's the first time I haven't felt even the tiniest pinch of "what if?" Of wondering what might have happened if I'd stayed in LA or she'd stayed faithful or I hadn't been such a self-absorbed prick. I wish her the best, but I honestly don't care what she's doing with her life. That's really fucking freeing.

I don't know how long I stare at my phone before I hear voices. My ears prick up, and it takes me a second to recognize my brothers bickering at the front of my house.

"Well, he must not have seen it yet, dumbshit."

"Which means he's not home, *dumbshit*."

"Jesus, Gabe—don't touch it."

"I wasn't touching it. Just getting a closer look."

Even from the other side of the house, I hear Cooper's grunt of disgust. "Where the hell is he, anyway?"

"Back here." I shout loud enough for them to hear me. I'm pretty sure they're on my front porch, and I try to recall if I left the door unlocked. No, wait. I didn't go inside, did I? Just walked around to my back porch to watch the sunset in silence. I already had my beer, so there was no reason to hit the kitchen first.

My brothers aren't saying anything, so I shout again. "Gabe? Coop? I'm in back."

There's another silence, then footsteps. I turn to see both of them walking around the edge of the cabin. I'm expecting laughter, maybe one of them throwing an elbow at the other.

But I'm not expecting the grim expressions. I sit up as they trudge up the steps to the deck like it's some kind of death march. "What is it?" I look from Gabe to Coop and back again. "What the hell is wrong?"

"Dude." Gabe's trademark brown eyes are wide and a little stunned. "What the fuck?"

I frown. "Can you be more specific?"

"See?" Cooper gives him a look. "I told you he wouldn't leave it like that."

Gabe shakes his head and looks at me. "Did you go in the back door or something?"

"I haven't been inside." I gesture to the sunset with my beer bottle. "I didn't want to miss that. Now what the hell are you talking about?"

Gabe stares at me. "How long have you been back here?"

"No idea." I glance at my watch, struggling to ignore the growing unease in the pit of my stomach. "Twenty minutes or so."

"Come on." Cooper jerks a thumb toward the front of the cabin. "You need to see this."

Neither of them wait for my reply. They just turn and march back around the side of my house. I consider not following. They're acting like weirdos, and it'd be just like them to play some kind of prank.

But something tells me they're not messing around. Standing up, I set my beer on the deck rail and follow after them, pushing back the wave of unease in my gut.

As I round the corner, I see them on the lawn beneath my front steps. They're bickering again, and Cooper's pointing at the front door.

"Don't you think we need to call the police?" he's saying.

"That's his call," Gabe argues. "It's his damn house. Maybe it's some kind of inside joke with him and Vanessa."

It's Vanessa's name that gets me moving. I practically sprint to the edge of the porch where they're standing. "Call the police for what?"

Cooper points to the front door. "That."

As my gaze follows his finger, the blood slowly drains from my body. "Holy shit."

My brain takes a few beats to process what I'm seeing. There, in my front door, is a large knife. Big and sharp with a dark wood handle and a shiny blade, it looks a lot like the chef's knife I use in my kitchen. It's jarring to see it anchored in the wood of my door, but that's not the worst part.

I blink, trying to refocus my eyes. "Vanessa. That's a photo of Vanessa."

"Yeah." Cooper's voice is soft as he shuffles closer to me. "I got a good look at it when I went to knock."

"The dumb fuck actually touched the doorknob." Gabe sidles closer, looking grim. "Hopefully that doesn't screw with fingerprints."

But I already know there won't be prints. Just like there weren't any on the snake or the balloons or the postcard. Just like Colleen can't figure out who the hell is screwing with our website. Just like County officials can't seem to trace that anonymous tip.

I hate the feeling of helplessness that blasts through me. I hate it more than anything.

"I'm sure whoever did this wore gloves." I glance from brother to brother. "You didn't call the cops?"

Gabe shakes his head. "We waited for you."

I take a few steps closer, trying for a better look at the photo. Unlike the picture of teenage Vanessa, this one's recent. I can't tell if it's candid, but it's definitely a professional shot. I take one more step, frowning. Something's off.

It comes to me in a rush. "She doesn't have a dimple."

"What?" Gabe steps up beside me and stares at the photo. "What are you talking about? She's got a dimple right there."

"Right, but Vanessa doesn't." I've studied her face awake and in sleep, happy and sad. I know that face like the back of my hand, and this isn't it. "That's not Vanessa."

"The hell it's not." Cooper joins us at the door, looking at me like I'm nuts. "That's definitely her."

"It's her sister," I insist. Not that I've met her sister, but I'm sure that's not Vanessa. "She has a twin, Valerie. That's gotta be her."

Both brothers are staring at me now, and I can't tell if it's respect or confusion. "I forgot she had a twin," Gabe says.

I study the photo again. A faint wind rustles the trees behind us, making the knife sway in the door. A shiver runs down my spine.

"Dude." Cooper shakes his head. "We figured you had something going with her, but that's next-level stuff."

I glare at him. "Identifying whether it's her in a photo is next-level?"

Gabe shrugs. "Seems pretty serious to me."

"It's cool," Cooper says. "Happy for you, man."

I don't have time to follow that train of thought. I turn back to the picture, struggling to piece it together. Whoever did this drove the knife straight through the middle of her face. The tip spears her forehead, and even knowing it's not Vanessa, I'm flooded with rage.

And fear, though I don't want to admit it.

"Should we get Vanessa over here?" Cooper asks. "Maybe she'd know who'd do this. She could at least tell us where that photo came from."

"No."

It's not 'til my brothers flinch that I realize how harshly I've said it. But I can't let them terrorize Vanessa with this. It's one thing to get a postcard in the mail or a creepy reptilian gift on the back porch. It's another to see a knife between your sister's eyes.

Eyes that look just like Vanessa's. *God.* If I hadn't spent so much time with her, I'd never have known the difference.

"I'll handle it." I tear my gaze off the photo and look from Gabe to Cooper. "I'll take care of everything."

Gabe's brow furrows. "You sure? We should at least let the PI know—"

"I've got this." I slip my phone out of my pocket and hit the home button. "I'll reach out to Lieutenant Lovelin right now."

My brothers exchange a look, then shrug. "All right." Gabe glances at Cooper. "We were going to invite you back to the lodge. That brewery guy left a couple extra cases of beer."

"And ginger ale," Cooper says before I can get on his case. "He brews it himself."

Gabe shoves his hands in his pockets. "Figured you'd be up for a guys' night in."

"Can I take a raincheck?" I glance back at the knife in my door, and my gut churns again. "Tomorrow, maybe."

I don't mention I've got plans tonight. Vanessa had a phone date with her sister, but that should wrap up soon. I'm just waiting for her call to come over.

The thought of seeing her again eases the discomfort in the pit of my stomach.

Gabe's studying me, frowning. "You're sure you're okay?"

"Positive." I hold up the phone, which is cued up to call Amy Lovelin. "I've got this covered."

Cooper shrugs. "All right, but don't blame us if you miss out on the ginger ale."

Gabe laughs and turns to go. "Don't worry, we'll save you one. Maybe two, if you're not an asshole."

Cooper cracks up and falls into step with Gabe. "If that's the criteria, he's not getting any."

I watch them walk away, the fading sun spotlighting them

from behind. I don't say it often enough, but my brothers are good guys. Annoying sometimes, but smart and kind and funny as hell. There's no one else I'd trust to join me in a business venture like this, except obviously my sisters.

Maybe I should think about letting go a little more. Trusting them to handle things on their own.

*No way. It's your job to protect them. To keep them all safe.*

I push the thought from my head and hit speed dial for Lieutenant Lovelin. She picks up on the second ring. "Hey, Dean," she says. "Everything okay out there?"

I stare at my front door, at the knife embedded in a face that looks so much like Vanessa's. A shudder ripples through me, and I have to pause and catch my breath.

"There's something I'd like you to see."

She's quiet for a few beats. "You're not in danger, are you?"

I don't think so, but the knife gives me the creeps. "Probably not."

"Dean?" Her voice tips up in concern. "Do I need to get a team out there?"

"Nothing that urgent." The last thing I need is to have the place swarming with cops. "Just—could you come right away?"

"Sure thing," she says. "I'm maybe ten minutes out."

I consider Vanessa's observation about Amy being nearby the last time something happened. I never found it suspicious before, but anything's possible. "You're close, then?"

"Just visiting Tia," she says, and my edginess doesn't subside. "It's my day off, so I'll be in my personal car instead of the police cruiser if that's okay."

"That's fine." Better, actually.

I stare at the photo, wanting more than anything to rip that knife from the face that's so achingly familiar. I turn away, not comfortable looking anymore. Not able to bear the thought that I wasn't there to stop whoever did this.

"Hey, Amy?"

"Yessir?"

"Could I ask you to keep this to yourself for now?"

Again with the long pause. "This call, you mean?"

"Yeah, and the details of what I'll be showing you." Maybe that's not allowed, but hopefully it is. She's officially on the Juniper Ridge payroll, even if she's got another week left at her cop job. "I'm not asking you to cover up anything illegal," I add quickly. "Just…trying to prevent panic."

I don't say it's Vanessa's panic that worries me. I'd like to spare her that if I could.

Amy's pause drags out so long this time that I'm sure we've dropped the call.

"I'll be right there," she says, and hangs up before I can say anything else.

I shove the phone back in my pocket and look out at the mountains. The sun's completely down now, the color faded from the horizon.

As I glance one last time at the photo, a shiver jerks down my spine.

# CHAPTER 16

**CONFESSIONAL 388.5**

Vincent, Vanessa: (CFO, Juniper Ridge)

*Trust. Yeah, that's kind of a big deal to me. When you're a twin —I mean, assuming you're close twins—you have this built-in support system. You know someone has your back no matter what. That you can tell her everything and she won't judge. Having that kind of trust is huge. I don't know, maybe I've unconsciously been looking for that in all my relationships. That's why it's so huge when I do start to trust someone. When I let my guard down and start to think hey, this could be it. This might be someone I could count on. It's scary and exhilarating and terrifying and crazy and scary and exciting all at once. Did I already say scary?*

* * *

"You're kidding me." My sister's outrage is palpable from 5,200 miles away. "What are they going to do if they can't get the permits?"

"Dean says he's handling it." Saying that fills me with equal parts pride and frustration. "He invited the County officials out to do another inspection."

"Is it really that simple?"

"Probably not. But Dean seemed confident he can make this go away."

Valerie laughs, remarkably cheerful for as early as it is in Paris. "You always fall for the confident boys, don't you, Ness?"

My gut churns just a little. "Dean's not like Raleigh." Or Bradley. Or Colton. Or my mother. Or—

"I didn't say he was like Raleigh," she says. "Speaking of which, I had a text from him."

"A text? About what?" I'm surprised he still has her number.

"He asked about you, actually. Wanted to know where you're working, how you're doing, all that."

A niggle of unease moves through me. "When was this?"

"I don't know, maybe a week ago? I didn't tell him, don't worry. Why?"

"Nothing. It's no big deal."

My sister pauses. "I'm glad you have Dean now."

"I wouldn't say I *have* him, exactly—"

"You're into him, right?"

"Right, but—"

"You respect him. He makes you laugh. What did you call him? Smart and clever and kind."

"Sure, but that doesn't mean—"

"And he's amazing in bed."

I sigh and scratch my dog's head. "It's hardly a basis for a relationship, is it?"

Valerie takes her time answering. "That depends. Are you asking because you want me to agree with you, or disagree with you?"

This is the thing about having a twin. You can't get away with lying to yourself. Not ever. "I don't know." I rub the bald spot under my dog's chin. "I feel a little foolish."

"About what?"

"I made such a big deal about not wanting a relationship. For crying out loud, I put it in my job application."

"So?"

"So that makes me pretty flaky, doesn't it?"

"It makes you human, Nessie. People are allowed to change their minds. It's growth, not a character flaw."

I wish I had my sister's confidence. "Maybe." I glance at my watch and smile. "He's coming over tonight."

"Oh yeah? Maybe if we switch to FaceTime, I can meet him."

"No." Then again, I've met his siblings. Would it really be that weird? "Okay, maybe."

"Really?" Val laughs. "I was kidding, but this is awesome. This is fantastic. This is—"

"Why are you so excited about meeting a guy I'm sleeping with?"

"Because you never just introduce me to guys you're sleeping with. Which means this is serious."

"I don't know about serious…"

She does have a point though. I wouldn't consider introducing anyone else to Val, but with Dean, I feel safe. I want my sister to see him, and I want him to meet her, too.

"Okay, hang on." I pull the phone from my ear and pull up Dean's name in my contacts. Before I can second guess myself, I fire off a text.

> ME: Still chatting with Val, but do you want to come over anyway? She'd like to say hi.

I STARE AT THE WORDS, hoping they don't sound too forward. Given the personal nature of this business, it's not that weird to introduce a colleague to my twin. It doesn't necessarily mean this is a relationship or that I'm taking this seriously or expecting anything like—

DEAN: Sounds good. Be right there.

A FLUTTER of joy tickles my chest. I put the phone back to my ear. "Okay, I'm switching to Facetime. He'll be here in a sec."

"Oh my God, I can't wait." I can practically hear my sister bouncing in her chair, and ten seconds later, I'm seeing it.

As her face fills the frame, my chest fills with a deep fondness blended with melancholy. "You look beautiful." I soak up the view of her face, which is filled with exactly the kind of radiance you expect from a newlywed. "Did you get highlights?"

She touches her hair. "No, just spending more time in the sun. You look good, too." She laughs, and this time I can see her dimples. "It's all that good sex, isn't it?"

"No comment." I can't stop grinning. "Should I go put on lipstick before he gets here?"

"You're perfect." She leans forward, peering closer at the screen. "Hang on, you've got something on your chin. Marker or something."

I draw a hand up and brush something sticky at the edge of my jaw. "Chocolate," I tell her. "I made brownies."

"Brownies?" She laughs. "You must have it bad if you're baking."

"Shut up." That's the best retort I can manage before there's a knock at the door.

Roughneck gives a happy "uff" and jumps off the couch. I

follow after him, holding the phone so my sister can see. "I'm nervous," I whisper. "Why do I feel nervous?"

Val doesn't hesitate. "Because you care."

She's right, though I hate to admit it. "Okay, here we go." My heart rams itself into my throat as I open the door.

"Hey, Dean." I step aside to let him in, holding the phone up to give my sister a good look. "Valerie, meet Dean. Dean, meet Valerie."

"Valerie." He peers at the screen, then does a double take. "Wow. You really do look alike."

She laughs, dimples flashing. "It's great to finally meet you."

"Same." Dean slips an arm around my waist and pulls me close. "Don't hold it against me if I kiss your sister, okay?"

"I hope you're talking to Val and not me," I tease as his lips draw close to mine.

"Oooh, this is fun." Val claps as Dean lands a soft kiss on my lips and draws back. "Nice chemistry, you two," she adds.

"Thanks." My cheeks feel hot, but it's not from embarrassment. I get like this anytime Dean touches me.

He swings his gaze back to my phone, looking a bit sheepish. "Sorry. I missed her."

"So do I," Val says, "but I doubt she'd grin like that if I walked through the door."

"Not true." I adjust the phone so I can see her face, though now Dean's not in the frame. "You don't usually greet me like that."

"This is true." Val waves a hand. "Give the phone to Dean. He's got longer arms so I can see both of you at once."

"Glad I'm good for something." Dean takes the phone and holds it up for both of us to see. "Better?"

"Much. Thank you."

Val takes him in, and I know what she's thinking. She's waiting for one of the lewd jokes we've been peppered with since we were teens. The kind of shit guys say about seeing us kiss or making a twin sister sandwich. Our whole lives it's been a litmus test, a chance to weed the jerks from guys with real potential.

Dean only smiles. "How are you liking Paris, Valerie?"

"It's wonderful. This is the longest I've stayed in one spot since I started traveling."

"You're there a few more months?"

"Until October." She grins. "You two should totally come visit."

He looks at me and I hold my breath, hoping she hasn't been too presumptuous. "That sounds great," he says. "Paris is beautiful in the fall. Maybe after the show gets going."

I'm not sure how to take that. Is he making conversation, or is he really thinking long-term? Thinking we'd be at the point of making travel plans together in a few months.

"Let's go to the couch," I suggest. "It's cozier in there, and then Roughneck can be part of the conversation."

"Perfect," Val says, beaming. "Did you read him that book I sent about dog heroes?"

"It's his favorite," I assure her. "I show him the pictures every time I read it."

Dean grins. "I even read him a chapter. The one about the dog who saved his mistress from an intruder?"

"I love it," Val says, clapping her hands together.

We're passing through the kitchen and Dean inhales deeply. "Valerie, if you were here, I'd definitely offer you some of whatever smells so good." He shoots me a hopeful grin. "What is that, anyway?"

"Brownies," I tell him. "They've got a couple minutes left, but you can have one as soon as they're out."

He clutches his chest and pretends to swoon. "Is it too soon to ask you to marry me?"

I know he's joking, but I can't help the rush of heat to my face. Can't help thinking how different he seems from the guy I met when I first arrived. He's loosened up a little, joking more than he ever used to. Maybe Oregon agrees with him.

Or maybe, just maybe, it has something to do with me.

Joy fills my chest cavity as we settle together on the sofa. On the phone screen, I see Val assessing our connection. I know her well enough to see approval lighting her face. "Okay, can I just say it's really weird to be talking to Dean Judson?"

"Weird how?" He looks genuinely curious, and I cross my fingers Val doesn't launch into her story about the locker posters.

"Just that we grew up seeing you in magazines, and here you are."

"Uff," says Roughneck, almost like he's agreeing. Dropping the purple tiger at Dean's feet, he hops up beside him and lays his head on Dean's thigh.

"Looks like you're dog-approved," my sister observes. "That's important."

"Absolutely." Dean softly scratches the bald patch around my dog's neck, keeping his eyes fixed on the phone screen. "It's kinda cool seeing the differences between you two."

Val quirks an eyebrow. "How do you mean?"

"Well, Vanessa's got those three little freckles next to her eye." He pauses to point them out, and my skin starts tingling all over again. "And Valerie has dimples."

"Damn." My sister feigns another round of applause. "It usually takes ages for people to notice that."

"If they ever do," I agree. "Plenty don't."

Dean plants a soft kiss on my temple. "I pay attention."

"No kidding." Aside from being a generally awesome trait, it's also what makes him fabulous in bed. As I bite my tongue to keep from saying that out loud, the oven dings.

"Want me to get that?" he asks.

I laugh. "You're just eager to get your hands on my brownies."

"That's true." He throws me a wink. "But first, I'd like dessert."

Valerie cracks up as he hands the phone back to me. "Want milk?" he asks.

"Yes, please."

"On it."

He's barely out of earshot when Val makes bug eyes at me. "Oh my God," she hiss-whispers. "He's even hotter in person."

"This isn't in person."

"You know what I mean. Not on TV or in magazines or whatever. And the way he looks at you before he kisses you. He's not just fooling around, Ness."

I fumble with the volume, struggling to turn it down while wanting desperately for her to continue. "You can't really tell all that over the phone."

"Damn right I can," she insists. "I can read it on your face, too. You're smitten."

I consider arguing, but what's the point?

"Yeah," I admit, glancing toward the kitchen where Dean is humming what sounds like Beyoncé's "Crazy in Love" as he cuts up brownies. "I guess I am pretty smitten."

"Put him back on," she demands. "I want to ask him questions. Make sure he's worthy of you and all that."

"What's that?" I rub my hand over the phone's camera, making crackly noises with my mouth. "We must have a bad connection or something. If I lose you—"

"Shut up, dork." Val's laughing as her husband slips into the frame behind her.

Josh kisses her temple and hands her a cup of coffee. "Hey, Ness," he says. "Special delivery latte. Sorry I can't bring you one."

"That's okay. I'm getting brownies."

"Atta girl."

My heart feels so full. I love that my sister and I both have good men who bring us drinks and brownies and smile at us like we hung the damn moon. I know it's early days with Dean, but it just feels right. I trust him, and I'm pretty sure he trusts me. I've never had that before, not really.

When I glance back at Val, the look on her face is pure love. She whispers something to Josh as he walks away, and my heart catches in my throat as he trails a hand along her arm. It's like he can't bear to stop touching her, and I suddenly want that more than I've ever wanted anything in my life.

As I glance back toward the kitchen, Dean looks up. Grinning, he throws me a wink and mouths two simple words:

*You're beautiful.*

God. Could I be falling in love with him?

I shift my gaze back to the phone and see Valerie assessing me. "I've never seen you this happy, Ness," she murmurs. "Whatever you're doing, keep it up."

"I'll try."

She smiles and sips the wine Josh brought her. "I should go get ready. It's our one month anniversary, so I'm shopping for a dress to wear to dinner."

"A romantic anniversary dinner in Paris. Sounds amazing."

"Say goodbye to Dean for me." She smiles and lowers her voice to barely a whisper. "I really like him."

"Me, too."

"I'm glad it's more than a fling." Her words tilt up in an unspoken question, so I answer without thinking.

"Maybe?" I glance toward the kitchen, where Dean's still humming as he piles brownies on a plate. "I'm glad I have your approval, though. That means a lot."

She laughs. "Like you've ever needed my approval. You just need to trust yourself."

I have to swallow a couple times to get rid of the lump in my throat. "Thanks. I'll try."

We say our goodbyes and hang up as Dean walks back into the room carrying a plate with brownies and a big glass of milk. "Shoot, did I miss her?"

"She had to go, but she said goodbye. Also, she approves of you."

I say it with a teasing tone, but Dean's whole face lights up. "Yeah? That's huge. The sibling approval thing, I mean."

I pluck a brownie off the plate and take a bite. It's a little too hot and falling apart, but I scarf it down anyway and reach for the milk. "What do your siblings know?"

"About us, you mean?" He shrugs. "They all know we're seeing each other."

"All of them?" I swallow. "Even your brothers?"

"Yep. Everyone approves."

I wait for more, not sure what else I'm expecting. "So they don't see any sort of conflict with our work relationship?"

"Nope." He pops a bite of brownie in his mouth and grins. "They're nuts about you, and they see I'm happy. That's pretty much all they need to know."

"Huh." Could it really be that simple? My sister approves. His brothers and sisters approve. I know it's not what I planned when I took this job, but maybe changing my mind isn't the worst thing. Maybe I could learn to think of it as growth, rather than flakiness.

"What's going on in that beautiful brain of yours?" He grabs another brownie off the plate.

"Just wondering how to think about this," I say slowly. "What we're doing together, I mean."

He stares at me blankly for a second, and I realize I've just spit out a big mouthful of nothing.

*Be brave. Be specific. Be clear.*

Dean smiles. "Did I just watch you give yourself a silent pep talk?"

"What?"

"Your lips moved a little." He cocks his head. "I'm not sure, but I think you told yourself 'bean bake, beet pacific, bee click.'"

And now I'm laughing. "What the hell kind of pep talk is that?"

"Beats me." He licks brownie off his thumb, then his forefinger. "You're the one giving it."

I take a deep breath. "This is me being brave, Dean. This is me telling you that I know I told you I didn't want a relationship, but these last few weeks have changed my mind. Changed *me*. I like you a lot, but more than that, I trust you."

"Wow." He reaches out and tucks a strand of hair behind my ear. "That's huge."

The fact that he knows what a big deal it is means so much to me. "Right. It is."

He laces his fingers through mine and smiles. "Thank you. I feel the same. I know I kinda fucked up my last relationship, and I own that. But being with you—it makes me want to be a better guy. To do better with you because you deserve it. You deserve everything, Vanessa."

These are not romantic declarations like the kind you'd see in movies. They're the words of two mistrustful people putting their hearts and vulnerabilities on the line, and that means so much more to me than flowery words could.

"So we're on the same page," I say. "We're dating. In a relationship. Whatever you want to call it."

Dean grins and squeezes my fingers. "Boyfriend and girlfriend?"

"Ew. That sounds like elementary school."

"I see. So you'll probably nix 'schmoopies' or 'baes,' right?"

"Affirmative." I'm fighting to hold back a smile.

Dean leans back against the couch, throwing an arm around me like it's the most natural thing in the world. "Let's see, there's 'bed buddies,' but that's a little too focused on the sex. We're more than that, yes?"

"Yes." I nod in case I wasn't clear enough. "Definitely, yes."

"Okay, hmm." He pretends to think. "Partners?"

"Makes it sound like we're in business together."

"Technically, we are, but I get your point." He pulls me closer and I burrow against the warmth of his chest. "I'm thinking 'companions' is a little too geared toward old people."

"Same with 'lady friend' or 'gentleman friend.'"

"And 'lovers' is pretty oogie."

"For sure." Talk about TMI.

"What about 'significant others'?" he tries.

I consider that for a bit. "That could work, but it sounds a little detached. Like we go to a restaurant and one of us is all, 'my significant other is just parking the car.'"

"You're right, that won't do." He scratches his chin. "We're running out of options here."

I circle a hand on his chest as I circle back through the words we've tried. On second thought…

"Maybe boyfriend and girlfriend isn't so bad." I bite my lip. "If you're ready to go there, I mean."

Dean grins like I've offered a hand job and a ham sandwich. "I'm ready if you are."

"I am." I can't believe it, but I am.

"Well, in that case, there's something else I'm ready for."

"Oh?" I know what he means from the glint in his eye, but I pretend not to get it. "You want more brownies?"

"I want something sweet, but not brownies." He slips a thumb under my chin and tips my head up to kiss me. It starts out slow and sweet, his tongue brushing mine with the taste of chocolate and heat.

By the time he draws back, I'm panting and clutching at the front of his shirt.

"What do you say we go consummate this official relationship?"

I lean up to kiss him again, breathless with anticipation. "Sounds like a plan."

* * *

WHEN I WAKE the next morning, Dean's beside me. That's new.

"Morning," he murmurs, rolling over to kiss me softly.

"You didn't go home." It's such an unexpected thrill that I can't keep from smiling. "Usually you slip out to go exercise or work or whatever you do at your place."

He laughs and kisses me again. "Figured being in an official relationship calls for a sleepover." Throwing his legs out of bed, he stands up and starts pulling on his jeans. "I should get back, though. I like showering at my place."

"Oh?" I prop my chin on my hand as Roughneck jumps up to occupy Dean's warm spot on the bed. "You have better water pressure or something?"

"I don't know about that, but I'm kinda picky about toothpaste and razors and shower gel. Breakfast, too. Like I always have an omelet with two eggs, peppers, mushrooms, swiss cheese, and a little bit of bacon." He makes a face. "Sorry, I know it's lame. I'm sure I could make do with whatever you have here, but—"

"No, I get it. I'm picky, too." Picky enough to finally hold out for a guy who ticks all my boxes. I still can't believe I'm in a relationship.

Dean leans down and kisses me. "I love that smile. It means you're thinking happy thoughts. Or maybe dirty thoughts."

I grin. "Maybe both."

He laughs and finishes finger-combing his hair. "I might be a couple minutes late getting to the office. Gotta take care of some busywork."

"Need help?"

"Nah, I've got it." He starts for the door, then pauses. "Thank you, Vanessa."

"For banging you silly?"

Dean laughs. "For that, yes. But also for giving us a chance."

"You're welcome." I can't contain the smile tugging the edges of my mouth. "Thanks for being patient with me."

"You're worth the wait."

Blowing me a kiss, he slips out of the room. When I hear the front door shut, I get up and throw the lock before heading to the shower.

I take my time getting ready, noticing the extra flush in my cheeks that might be beard burn. Or maybe it's just happiness. Even if I failed at my goal to stay single, I failed in the most spectacularly delicious way with a guy who's amazing.

More importantly, I trust him. I trust him to let me stand on my own two feet and be the person I'm meant to be. Have I ever been with anyone like that? My brain scans the rolodex of men I've dated. Nope, no one comes close.

But it's less about them and more about me finally learning to make good choices. That's the best part of all this.

Since my morning is off to such a sunny start, I pull on my favorite champagne-colored dress that Val says makes my eyes sparkle. Leaving my hair loose the way Dean likes it, I throw together a quick breakfast scramble with egg whites and tomatoes to save me from spending money and calories at the coffee shop. I even make my own coffee in a reusable mug that Lana gave me yesterday.

*I DON'T CARE who dies in a movie as long as the dog lives.*

I'M SMILING about it as I walk the sun-dappled cinder path to the lodge. It's a quarter to nine, and the June sunshine bathes the basalt cliffs in a red-gold glow. Even the junipers look brighter this morning, with tufts of blue berries bouncing on the breeze. I reach the main lodge and push through the side door off the corridor to my office. I'm halfway down the hall when Cooper's voice rings from the doorway next to mine.

"Maybe he didn't know it isn't her in the picture," he says. "Could be he got the wrong twin by mistake."

I freeze at the edge of his door. Twin? We make up three percent of the world's population but come on. He has to be talking about me.

Heartbeat thudding in my ears, I take a small step forward. I'm not trying to spy. I legit have to pass by to reach my office, but yeah, I'm curious who he's talking to.

Cooper has his back to the door, and Amy Lovelin stands facing him with arms folded over her chest. She's not in her cop clothes and looks sharp in slim black jeans and a white button-down with the sleeves rolled to the elbows. Her inner cop must sense me there, because she looks up and frowns.

"Vanessa. Hey."

Cooper whirls around, mask slipping into place just a few seconds after I register surprise in his eyes. "Morning, Vanessa. You're early."

I glance at my watch. It's ten minutes to nine, but that's nothing new. "Were you guys talking about the postcard or something?"

Cooper opens his mouth to answer, but Amy beats him to it. "We were discussing the attacks on Juniper Ridge and how the assailant seems zeroed in on you specifically."

Interesting. Is it just me, or did she not really answer the question?

Cooper looks uneasy, and his posture's ramrod straight instead of slouchy like normal. He studies me like he's searching for words. "Have you seen Dean this morning?"

"About an hour ago." I decide to leave it at that and not mention he spent the night at my place. "How come?"

"Just curious if he said anything about...anything."

Huh? "About what?"

Amy clears her throat. "Are you doing all right, Vanessa? No new threats or anything unusual happening?"

Okay, now they're creeping me out. Something's niggling the back of my brain, something I can't quite grab.

It hits me like a sucker punch. "Wait. You said something about getting the wrong twin. Did something happen to Valerie? Is she in trouble or hurt or—"

"No!" Amy steps forward, shouldering past Cooper. "Your sister is safe and healthy in Paris right now."

My mouth goes dry. "How did you know my sister's in Paris?"

She doesn't miss a beat. "Dean's kept me apprised of all relevant details." Her expression is perfect cop-neutral, but something in her eyes tells me there's more to the story. Why would Dean need to share where my sister lives?

Cooper's brow is furrowed, and he keeps throwing glances at Amy. "Is Dean on his way in?"

"I—yeah, sometime in the next hour." Why the hell is no one being straight with me? I try again. "What's going on here?" My voice comes out squeaky and I hate it. "What aren't you telling me?"

Cooper turns to Amy, his expression vaguely annoyed. "Let me guess—he asked you not to say anything?"

Amy doesn't answer, but I see her jaw clench. Otherwise, her expression is completely unreadable. "I'm not at liberty to discuss details of a pending investigation."

She meets my gaze and holds it, eyes softening with unspoken apology. For what?

Cooper drags his fingers through his hair. "Goddammit. This is just like him."

"What?" I'm still trying to understand what's happening.

He heaves a sigh. "Look, Dean's in charge. I'm sure he has reasons for—for whatever it is he's doing."

A sick feeling puddles in the pit of my stomach. I curl my fingers into my palms and step forward, hoping they can't see my hands shaking. "Tell me." I take another step into the office. "Whatever this is involves me, right?"

Amy shifts from one leg to the other, and I realize there's a holster on her hip. A gun, she's wearing a gun. Is that odd? I've never noticed it before.

"Look, Dean should be in shortly," she says. "I'm sure he can explain everything—"

"Last night," Cooper says, taking a step toward me. "Gabe and I got to Dean's place around eight."

"Cooper." There's a warning note in Amy's voice.

"What? He didn't order me to keep my mouth shut. I'm not going to stand here and bullshit her."

"I appreciate that," I say faintly, pretty sure whatever he's about to tell me could open a can of squirmy sibling worms.

Cooper reads my mind. "It's fine. Dean might be the bossy big brother, but he's sure as fuck not *my* boss. I'm supposed to speak up when I think he's being a dumbass."

"That's in your job description?" I'm trying for lighthearted, but my voice cracks on the last syllable.

"Yeah." Cooper offers a smile that's achingly kind. "Anyway, Gabe and I got to Dean's place last night and there was a photo stuck on the door. A photo with a knife through it."

My knees start to buckle. I grab the edge of the desk and fight to keep my voice even. "Another photo of me?"

Even as I say the words, I know that's not it. Not all of it, anyway. "That's what we thought," he says. "But it wasn't you. Dean figured that out pretty quick."

The other shoe drops, and I force myself to swallow a few times before speaking. "My sister. It was a photo of Val, wasn't it?"

Amy stares at me, not saying anything. If I weren't staring right at her, I'd never notice the tiniest tilt of her head. Maybe a nod, or maybe I imagine it.

But I'm not imagining the flood of nausea swirling in my gut.

As I grip the desk tighter, Amy's gaze flicks over my shoulder, then flashes with alarm. I know without turning who's behind me. I can feel his presence, smell the grassy, woodsy scent of his shampoo.

Slowly, I pivot. As Dean's hazel eyes lock with mine, I see him register what's happened. Maybe he heard, or maybe he can tell by the stricken look on my face.

How could he spend the night with me and not say a word? How could he sit there on my couch making small talk with my sister and never think to share that someone stuck a knife through her picture and tacked it to his door?

I order myself to take a few breaths before speaking. "Were you going to tell me?" My words come out hoarse and weak, so I straighten my spine and try again. "About the new threat? That it involves my sister now, too?"

He doesn't say anything right away. Doesn't deny it or play dumb, which I'd appreciate if I weren't seriously struggling not to pick up Cooper's paperweight and throw it at him.

Finally, Dean sighs. "Vanessa, it's not that big a deal."

"Not. That. Big. A. Deal." I say the words slowly, enunciating each one in case I've misunderstood. "Really? So if I found a photo of Cooper or Mari or Lana stuck to *my* front door with a knife through it, you wouldn't think that's something I should tell you?"

He winces, and I'm not sure if it's the mental picture I just painted or the way my voice has risen to an almost-shriek. A door clicks behind me, and I'm guessing Cooper and Amy just slipped out the side door to give us privacy.

I don't turn and look. I keep my eyes fixed on Dean, hoping he has some explanation. Some good reason for keeping me in the dark. For controlling the narrative in a way that shuts me out completely.

"I'm taking care of it, Vanessa," he says slowly. "I didn't want you to panic and do anything crazy."

My teeth grind together as I stare at him. "Is there something you've observed that makes you think I'm prone to panicky, crazy outbursts?" I'm trying for sarcasm, but it comes out sounding like a real question.

That's when I realize that I really want the answer. I need to know if that's what he thinks of me.

My mother's voice rings in my head, drowning out the thud of my heartbeat.

*You're too irrational, Vanessa. You'll never have a head for business if you can't stop reacting to things. Just find a husband and settle down. It's the best thing for you.*

Dean's not answering, so I try again. "Seriously, Dean—if you think I'm not levelheaded enough to handle basic information about me and my family, then I can't imagine you think I'm levelheaded enough to handle accounting for a multi-million-dollar development."

A muscle twitches beside his eye, and I realize I've hit a nerve. I'm not sure which one, but there's definitely something else he's not telling me.

He also hasn't answered the question.

"That's not the issue." He takes a deep breath and flicks a hand down the hall. "Can we please go into my office and discuss this there?"

"No." My retort snaps out clipped and tense, but I'm tired of being handled. Tired of letting someone else decide where I go, what I do, what I *know*. "We can talk right here, Dean. I'm not letting you lure me behind closed doors so you can feed me platitudes or throw me off with those goddamn bedroom eyes."

"Bedroom eyes?" He looks genuinely startled. "See, this is what I was afraid of. You're blowing things out of proportion. I can handle all of this with a few phone calls. I swear, Vanessa—I have this under control."

"No, Dean. You don't." My hands have started shaking, so I clench them at my sides, fingers curled into my palms. "I'm not a thing to be 'controlled' or 'handled.' This is my life we're talking about. My *family*."

He sighs like I'm twisting his words around, but he's the one who keeps saying shit he knows will make my blood boil. He knows about my mother. He knows about every guy I've dated who's treated me like a goddamn doll to be propped up in a corner.

I thought he was different.

"This isn't about controlling you," he says. "It's about *protecting* you. When I saw you with that knife through your head—that moment before I realized it wasn't you—I lost it, okay? All I could think about was keeping you safe."

I know I should be flattered. I should be touched he's sweet enough to care.

But all that is secondary to the fact that he thinks he has the right to manage and manipulate my reality. My *life*. "I thought you said it wasn't a big deal," I say. "A minute ago, you downplayed it as no big deal. Now it's about protecting me?"

"Goddamn it." He thumps a fist against the wall. "I'm trying to tell you that I care about you."

"By keeping me in the dark?" I shake my head slowly. "I've had enough of that kind of caring to last a lifetime, thanks."

He makes a noise that's not quite words. More like exasperation. If I'm expecting him to apologize or back down, it's not happening. "I'm the CEO," he says. "It's my job to look out for everyone. To ensure the safety of my staff and community members and family and everyone I care about."

I can't decide whether I want to hug him or slug him in the arm. "That's an awfully big burden to pile on one person's shoulders."

"No kidding."

"So, don't!" I throw my hands in the air, exasperated all over again. "Let other people in, Dean. You have a team here. Smart, capable people, including me. Let us be part of things, especially when it involves us."

I'm probably overstepping. This is about him and me, not his siblings and the whole crew. But dammit, I'm tired of having my engine throttled at every turn.

Shaking his head, Dean stuffs his hands in his pockets. "I've got it under control, okay? My PI knows a guy in the Paris field office who's keeping an eye on your sister. And your bodyguard should be here by lunchtime today."

"My bodyguard?" I blink at him. "Were you planning to tell me? Or were you just going to have some guy trailing me around the compound like a creepy stray dog?"

He doesn't answer, but I see his jaw clench and unclench. That's answer enough for me.

"I see." So, he did plan to keep me in the dark. "Don't you think that's the sort of thing to share with me? If I'm under surveillance—if my sister's under surveillance or possibly in danger—"

"She's not in danger."

"You don't know that!" Fear and fury makes my voice quiver, and I order myself to breathe. To dial it back and focus on facts. "What have you learned?" I ask. "The knife, were there any prints?"

He hesitates. "No prints. Not on the knife, and not on the photograph."

Big shocker there. Like we've said all along, this guy is a master at not getting caught. "What else? What aren't you telling me?"

Again with the hesitation. He stares at me for ten, fifteen seconds without saying a word. Then he slips a hand into his pocket and pulls out his phone. As I watch, he taps the screen a few times, then hands it over.

"Why are you—oh." I feel the blood drain from my face as I

stare at the screen. My fingers tingle as I stare at the insignia of the American Institute of Certified Public Accountants.

It's a copy of a complaint. A complaint filed the day after I took the CPA exam. I know the words by heart, but I force myself to read them again anyway.

*Suspicion of misconduct.*

*Candidate accused of concealing notes.*

*Full investigation to include...*

I hand the phone back. I don't need to read any more. "Where did you get that?"

Dean shoves the phone back in his pocket, never breaking eye contact. "It showed up in my email. Anonymous sender."

"When?"

He hesitates. "Last night. After you'd gone to bed."

I stare at him, waiting for him to ask me about it. Waiting for him to tell me he didn't see the email until just now. Or that he had a good reason for not asking me about it last night. Or this morning when we woke up together or he kissed me goodbye or—

"I've already talked with Lana," he says, and my jaw falls open.

"What?"

"Her specialty is crisis management and image control. She knows how to get on top of this sort of thing before it can do damage. I have a meeting with her at—"

"Wait, what?" I stare at him. "You get an anonymous email suggesting I cheated on the CPA exam, and your first conversation isn't with *me*?"

He closes his eyes for a few seconds. "With a TV show that's shopping for sponsors, we need to control potential scandals. To get out ahead of it so—"

"I don't believe this." I blink hard, surprised to realize my eyes are watering. "You could have asked me about it. Hell, you could have called the AICPA."

I'd have been pissed about that, too, but *Lana*? She's the

closest friend I've made at Juniper Ridge, and Dean just told her I'm a cheat.

The lump in my throat is now a cannonball. I can't speak. I can't even wrap my head around the turn this has taken.

"Cheating's nothing to mess around with." Dean's jaw clenches, and I know he's not talking about how things play on TV. This is personal, I can see that. "We need to take it seriously."

"I take it pretty damn seriously myself." The rancid stew of hurt and fury is bubbling in my gut. "More seriously than you, considering this is *my life* we're talking about here."

"Look, Vanessa." He takes a step toward me, then stops. "The fact that that this email doesn't faze me—that I can put the whole thing aside—doesn't that tell you how I feel about you?"

I gape at him. "You expect me to be *flattered* by this?"

He closes his eyes again, dragging a hand through his hair. "This is not how this is supposed to go."

"Because it's not your narrative to control!" I'm shouting again, and I hate that. My only comfort is that his eyes are still closed, so he can't see the tear slip down my cheek.

Another one falls, and I dash it away. He hasn't asked a single question. Hasn't given me a chance to explain or defend myself or offer one tiny shred of input on my own situation.

I take a step back and Dean opens his eyes. "Where are you going?"

"Leaving."

"I can see that." He frowns. "Vanessa, I can fix this."

"I'm not asking you to fix anything, Dean!" I take another step back. And another, until I've put a few feet between us. "I thought you were different."

Dean's brow furrows. "What's that supposed to mean?"

I shake my head slowly as my gut roils with nausea. I take another step back, widening a gap that I know can't be bridged.

"I won't tolerate someone who treats me like a situation to be managed." I manage to keep the quiver out of my voice, surprising myself with the force of my own words. "That's an absolute for me, Dean."

He sighs like I'm being unreasonable. "I don't want you to worry about this. Let me take care of this. *Please*. I can handle it, I swear."

"I didn't ask you to."

As a matter of fact, I asked him not to. It's the one thing I was clear about. I don't want his money or his fame or his strong, steady hand maneuvering the chess pieces of my life.

I want his respect.

Clearly, that was too much to ask.

He takes a deep breath. "What do you want me to say?"

I stare at him. There's so much I want to say, but he hasn't given me the chance. Looking at him now, I realize he never will.

So, I say the only thing I *can* say.

"Goodbye, Dean."

Then I turn and walk away.

# CHAPTER 17

**CONFESSIONAL 401**

JUDSON, DEAN: (CEO, JUNIPER RIDGE)

*WHEN YOU'VE GOT A SISTER WHO'S A SHRINK, YOU LEARN A LOT OF SELF-HELP JARGON. STUFF LIKE 'GROWTH OPPORTUNITY' AND 'PROBLEM SOLVING.' I'VE TRIED LIKE HELL TO TREAT EVERY FUCKUP LIKE A CHANCE TO DO BETTER. TO BE BETTER. I LIKE TO THINK I'VE DONE THAT. THAT I'VE MANAGED TO LEARN FROM WHERE I'VE SCREWED UP SO I DON'T DO IT AGAIN.*

*IT'S POSSIBLE I LEARNED THE WRONG LESSONS.*

* * *

I should go after her. That's what a good boyfriend would do, a good business leader.

But I'm neither of those things, so I watch her walk away. As my eyes trail Vanessa's lovely, familiar form in a dress the color of champagne, I hate myself with every step she takes.

I don't know how long I stand there before I hear Cooper's voice. "You okay?"

I turn to see he's slipped back into his office. Lieutenant Lovelin is nowhere to be seen, and I'm glad about that.

I take a step through Coop's doorway and shove my hands in my pockets. "Yeah. I'm fine."

He kicks the door closed behind us and leans against the wall. "You don't look so good."

I ignore the jab and look down at his desk. It's covered in a mess of papers and cables, and inexplicably, a pile of Legos. "How much of that conversation did you hear?"

"Enough," he says. "You were pretty loud."

Such a Cooper answer. I meet his eyes, my baby brother who's a half inch taller than me. I hate that.

But not as much as I hate the feeling in my gut right now. "You caught the stuff about cheating?"

Cooper nods. "The CPA exam, huh? Seems like the kind of thing you'd catch in a background check."

"I don't understand." I drag my hands through my hair, trying to figure out where I went wrong. "Mari handled the checks, and I even did a second one to be safe. Got a copy of her CPA license. Called her references. Had the PI do some digging. Nothing ever came up."

My brother studies me for several long seconds. "May I see it?"

"The email?" I slip out my phone and cue it up to the email, then pass it over without a word.

Coop's eyes sweep over the screen, his brow furrowing as he takes it in. I can picture the words in my head, and my gut sinks all over again like it did the instant I saw it in my inbox.

I'd kissed her goodnight, long, and slow, and sweet. And then, because we're both Type-A workaholics, both of us spent a couple minutes on our phones, setting alarms and scoring one last hit of data. All the usual bullshit.

There it was, an email sent from oopsiedaisy541@juniper-ridge.com. A fake account, but a very real message. I read the words with Vanessa's thigh against mine, her head on my chest.

*Cheating.*

On the CPA exam.

I could have said something then. She was still awake, her breath gently fanning my chest. I wondered if she could hear my heart pounding, sense my visceral reaction to that word.

*Cheating.*

"Wait." Cooper frowns at me. "You don't think she actually did this, right?"

I stare at him. To be honest, I never asked myself this question. That sounds stupid now, but my first thought was about protection. Protecting Vanessa from embarrassment. Protecting our show from scandal. Protecting all of us from the hot, flaming mess that I know these things become.

My thoughts are whirling and none of them are coming out of my mouth, so Cooper tries again. "It says there was an investigation," he says with a lot more gentleness than I probably deserve. "What were the findings?"

"I don't know." I realize I'm grinding my teeth and order myself to stop. "I haven't called the AICPA yet. I wanted to meet with Lana first. See if we need to get lawyers involved before we go that route."

Cooper shakes his head slowly but doesn't say anything.

"What?"

"Let me ask you again," he says slowly. "You think she did this?"

I think about Vanessa. How kind and good and brave she is. How she rescued a scared dog and handled that banker's meltdown with grace and compassion. How she loves her sister and endures her mother and, above all, remains the most caring person I've ever met.

"No," I say slowly. "No. I guess not."

"You *guess* not?" Cooper shakes his head slowly. "There's a fucking vote of confidence."

I throw up my hands. "What do you want me to say? It's irrelevant what I think. The important thing is to protect her from bullshit like this."

"That is *not* the important thing." Cooper sinks into the cushy leather chair in the corner and shakes his head. "Jesus, Dean."

"What?" I know I sound dumb, but I honestly don't get it. "How many times have we seen shit like this pop up? Someone blackmailing you over a DUI or going public with my text breakup or saying they've hacked Lauren's phone for nude photos?"

I'm still furious over that last one. Over all of it, really. Celebrities are prime targets for threats like this, and if there's one thing that makes me rage, it's assholes terrorizing the people I love.

And I do love Vanessa. More than anything, I wish I'd told her that. Maybe it would make a difference.

Or maybe not, based on how Cooper's glaring at me. "Can you take just a second to pull your head out of your ass and think about how this looks from Vanessa's perspective?"

"What do you mean?"

He sighs and tips back in his chair. "You get this anonymous email. This message saying she did some horrible thing that's obviously going to push all your buttons. Cheating, for Christ's sake, right?"

"Right," I say slowly, still not grasping what he's driving at.

Cooper softens his tone. "Anyone who knows you has a damn good idea that cheating is a deal breaker for you. That's the best way to rile you, to leave you questioning the woman you love."

I nod slowly, unsurprised Cooper guessed how I feel before I figured it out myself. "She didn't do it." The fierceness in my words takes me by surprise. "Of course she didn't cheat."

"No shit, Sherlock." He grabs up a Rubik's cube off his shelf, twisting it to mix up the colors. "Did you tell her that? Did you say 'Vanessa, I trust you, I don't believe this bullshit, let's solve this together?'"

"No." Though now that he's saying it, I can see how that might have been a smart approach. "I wanted to shield her from shit like this. I honestly didn't think about the allegation at all. It seemed smarter to gather our resources. Talk to lawyers, get Lana ready to fight this. Nip the whole thing in the bud before it has a chance to hurt her."

Cooper shakes his head a little sadly, twisting the rows of Rubik's cube colors without looking. "You're thinking like a jaded Hollywood asshole." He gives a wry grin. "I know that since I am one. But that's not how Vanessa thinks."

I sink down into his desk chair. It bounces a little beneath me, and the arms are weirdly out of whack with one adjusted higher than the other. Leave it to Cooper to have the world's most uneven desk chair in an office filled with brand new furniture. "So now you're the expert on how Vanessa thinks?"

"No, asshole." He twists the Rubik's cube again, aligning a neat row of blue squares. "But I *am* an expert on being judged without all the facts. On what it feels like to be presumed guilty every fucking time."

I stare at him, letting my brother's words sink in.

*My God.*

Is that what I've done? Is that how I made Vanessa feel? There's a sinking in my gut that tells me I've screwed this up way worse than I realized.

"I just wanted to fix things," I offer feebly.

"Maybe she didn't want you to fix anything," he says. "Ever consider that?"

"Yeah," I mutter. "When she was yelling those exact words at me, it did cross my mind."

He offers a good-natured half-smile. "She wants your respect, Dean. Not your forgiveness. Not your fix-it skills. *Respect*."

The words zap me in the chest like lightning bolts. "I respect the hell out of her," I insist. "She's smart and creative and brilliant with numbers. I have mad respect for all of that."

He cocks an eyebrow, still twisting the cube. He's got all the greens aligned now, and I'm wondering how the fuck he's doing this. "You've got a funny way of showing it."

I sigh, frustrated and stuck and angry all at once. All of that's aimed at me, not my brother. Definitely not Vanessa. "How did I screw this up so badly? I only wanted to help."

Cooper's eyes fill with sympathy as he twists another row of colors. "I love you, man. You know I do."

"But?"

He grins, kindly not making a butt joke. "Want to know what your problem is?"

"I'm supposed to say yes, right? That's what Mari would tell me—I'm supposed to want to learn from my mistakes."

"Mari's not here. Sorry, but you're stuck with the fuckup sibling instead of the shrink."

I start to insist he's not a fuckup, but Cooper waves me aside. "Look, man. You're too damn good at everything. That's your problem."

I frown. "How is that a problem?" It sounds more like he's trying to make me feel better, but that's not Coop's style.

"It's a problem when you get too used to it," he says. "You were the first to ride a bike. The first one to read or drive a car or get laid."

"I'm not sure about that last one," I muse, pretty sure that's not his point.

"My point," Cooper continues, ignoring me, "is that you got used to being the smartest and best and assuming that meant you needed to pave the way for everyone else. Trample the grass, chew down the branches, whatever the fuck lions do in the jungle so the other lions can pass through easier."

"This is the weirdest metaphor ever."

He shrugs and turns the cube to the side, glancing down to check his progress. He's almost got the damn thing solved. "Look, I'm not here to tell you how to run a business. Or your relationship. Those are literally the last two areas where I'm qualified to give advice."

"Isn't it supposed to mean more if I figure it out for myself?"

He cocks his head. "Sure, go for it. What's your best guess on where you went wrong and what you should have done differently?"

I think about that a moment. My instinct is to handle it the same way I always do. Send Vanessa on a spa day and call a lawyer to fix whatever mess she might be in. Hire cops and PIs to nail the son of a bitch who's screwing with our program.

But I'm realizing it's not the right answer.

"Listen," I mutter.

"What?" He looks up from the Rubik's cube. "There's something you want to say?"

"No, I mean *listen.*" It's not a command, it's the answer, though the fact that Coop heard it the other way should tell me something. "That's what I'm supposed to do is shut the fuck up and listen."

Cooper drops the Rubik's cube in his lap and points at me. "Bingo."

"Thanks."

"No, I mean it. You're smart as hell, and everyone knows it. But so are plenty of other people. You've gotta give 'em a chance to do their thing."

I grit my teeth, hating that he's right, but knowing he is. "Which means not rushing in to save the day all the time."

"Sure, let other people wear the cape sometimes." He grins. "They might surprise you and look better in it than you do."

I think about Vanessa in that champagne-colored dress. Or wearing nothing at all, naked and beautiful in her bedroom. It's the last thing I should be thinking about right now. I should be reminding myself she's smart and capable and kind and clever. Obviously, there was some sort of mix-up with the CPA exam, but—

"I need to ask her about it."

Cooper picks up the Rubik's cube again. "You mean Vanessa? The exam thing?"

"Yeah." I rake a hand through my hair. "That was a dick move to just assume." Even if my assumption is that she wouldn't do it, assuming anything at all wasn't the right call.

"If it helps, I can tell you that admitting you're a dick helps cancel out the dick move," he says. "It's in the manual or something."

I laugh for the first time all morning. "Thanks."

"No problem." He watches me stand up. "You gonna go talk to her?"

"If she'll see me." After the way I acted, I wouldn't blame her for not wanting to. "Maybe I'll bring a peace offering. Flowers or something."

He shakes his head sadly. "Flowers won't cut it. Try muffins. Caffeine, maybe."

"Since when are you the expert on women?"

He laughs and plucks the cube from his lap, twisting the last row to line the colors up in perfect formation. "It's possibly my only area of expertise."

"That's not true."

Still grinning, he chucks the cube at me. It bounces off my chest and lands with a clatter on Coop's desk. "Go get your girl, dumbass."

"And now you're the bossy brother. Great."

I turn and stalk out of his office, the echo of Coop's laughter ringing in my ears.

He's got a point, so I make a beeline for the coffee shop. My instincts are screaming at me to go to Amy Lovelin or call the bodyguard or email the AICPA so I can vindicate Vanessa once and for all.

But none of those are the right move.

Nothing matters but telling Vanessa how sorry I am. Not just a generic apology, either. Coop did a fine job pulling my head out of my ass. Now I need to show her, to make it clear I understand where I went wrong.

As I approach the coffee shop, I spot Colleen and Patti through the window. They're hunched over a laptop, pointing at something on the screen. As I push through the door, they both look up.

"Hey, Dean." Colleen frowns. "Everything okay?"

"Yeah." That's a lie. "Actually, no. I was a dumbass with Vanessa. Got anything I can take her as a peace offering?"

Patti perks up. "We've got Nutella banana oat muffins."

"That's a start." That and a side of groveling might get me somewhere, though maybe I've done irreparable damage. I keep picturing that flash of hurt in her eyes when I told her about the email. "Can I have half a dozen? And a vanilla latte for Vanessa."

Colleen picks up a cardboard mug. "We've got this new house made lavender syrup. Made it myself from the lavender patch over on the north edge of the property. She might like that better, since it fits with her goal of breaking out of old ruts."

Old ruts like dating control-freak assholes?

"Make it a huge one," I tell her. "Thanks."

I sink down into the nearest chair, remembering Cooper's words. Have I been so stuck inside my own ruts that I've ignored everyone else's needs? If that's true, odds are good Vanessa isn't the only one I've hurt.

But she's the one who matters most, especially right now. I don't mean our professional relationship, either. It's Vanessa the person I care about, not Vanessa the CFO. Not what she does for my business, but how she makes me feel. Not just me, but everyone she meets. Lana and Lauren, Tia and Mari, they all glow in the light she puts out. I can't believe I didn't consider that I might be snuffing it out.

I'm still digesting that when Patti yelps. "There! I just saw it again."

I look up to see her watching the laptop screen, both her muffin-filled hands frozen over a pink cardboard box. As she gestures at the screen with one of them, Colleen abandons her post at the espresso machine.

"You're sure?" She joins her wife behind the computer. "It's not just a deer or something?"

"You know any deer who wear blue jeans?" Patti sets the muffins in the box and fiddles with the keyboard. "There must be some way to scroll back through the live video feed."

"Want me to try?" Colleen asks.

"Yeah, you've used this system more than I have."

I ease out of my chair, conscious of the nervous energy pulsing off both of them. "Everything okay?"

Patti looks up. "It's one of the wildlife cams. The one on the north edge by Tia Nelson's property."

"One of your foxes?" Not that foxes wear blue jeans, either.

"Definitely not a fox." Colleen taps a few keys on the laptop, and the reflection of the screen flashes in her eyes. "We thought maybe you had maintenance crews out there or something, but Lauren said no. Said there's not supposed to be anyone out there right now."

A ripple of unease moves through me. These two know way more than I do about computers and weird sightings in the area, so I hesitate to ask. "Mind if I look, too?"

"Be my guest." Colleen taps a few more keys. "Hang on, I've almost got it queued up."

All three of us watch as the camera scrolls back, then pauses on a flash of denim. "There." Patti points at the screen. "See? Lower left-hand corner."

Colleen frowns. "It's like they know where the camera is, and they're trying to stay out of the frame."

"Didn't quite make it," Patti murmurs as Colleen hits a key to zoom in on the edge of the image. "Is that a hand?"

I peer closer, barely making out the grainy image. "Looks like a hand. Not a male one, either."

Colleen grunts. "Men can wear pink nail polish, too."

I let that pass, intent on studying the screen. I don't recognize this particular patch of earth, which isn't surprising. The compound is more than 50,000 acres, and I haven't memorized them all. But there's something else niggling at me.

"This borders Tia Nelson's property?" I ask. "How far from there to the residences?"

"A quarter mile, maybe less." Colleen zooms in closer. "It's right up against that gravel road that runs the far edge of her property. It's a real easy spot to slip through if you don't want to be seen."

I lean closer as the hair on my arms starts to prickle. I don't know why, but something's sitting weird with me. Something besides the idea of a stranger sneaking onto our property. Why not use the normal driveway?

"Can you get closer to that hand?" I ask. "Yes, there. Perfect."

I squint at the blurry image and the edge of someone's pant-leg. The heel of a hiking boot that looks new, pink piping around the bottom. And that hand, it's familiar. Not the painted nails, but something else.

"Oh, shit." I blink a few times to make sure I'm not seeing things, but no. That bracelet. I'd recognize it anywhere.

I stand up straight, feeling dizzy.

"Dean?" Patti frowns. "You okay, honey?"

I nod, backing away from the screen. "Call Lieutenant Lovelin," I say then stop myself. "Please."

"On it," Patti says, picking up the phone.

I'm already sprinting toward the door. "I know who's been messing with us."

And I know exactly why she's after Vanessa.

# CHAPTER 18

**CONFESSIONAL 418**

VINCENT, VANESSA: (CFO, JUNIPER RIDGE)

*BIGGEST FEARS, HUH? WE'RE REALLY GONNA GO THERE?* [CHEWS THUMBNAIL] *IT'S NOT THE BALLOONS OR THE SNAKES. NOT EVEN THE SNAKE WITH BALLOONS, THOUGH THAT WAS PRETTY NASTY. YOU REALLY WANT TO HEAR THIS?*

*ALL RIGHT. I GUESS IT'S THE FEAR THAT I REALLY AM AS HELPLESS AS MY MOTHER SAYS. AS HELPLESS AS I THINK SHE'S ALWAYS WANTED ME TO BE. LIKE—SHE'S MY MOM, RIGHT? IF ANYONE KNOWS ENOUGH TO JUDGE IF I'M CAPABLE OF RUNNING MY LIFE, WOULDN'T IT BE HER? SOMETIMES I ALMOST REACH A POINT WHERE I THINK, NO. SHE'S WRONG ABOUT ME. I'M STRONG AND CAPABLE AND I HAVE MY SHIT TOGETHER.*

*THEN SOMETHING WILL HAPPEN THAT MAKES ME SECOND-GUESS EVERYTHING.*

* * *

I'm halfway to my cabin when I hear Lana's voice.

"Vanessa! Hold up; I wanted to talk with you."

Fuck.

I love Lana, don't get me wrong. But the last thing I want right now is a heart-to-heart with one of Dean's sisters. Especially not one he's asked to help shore up my sullied reputation.

But Lana's cheerful smile stops me in my tracks, and I stop walking to wait for her. She's wearing cute pinstriped capris and a white T-shirt knotted at the waist. She's as fresh and bright as a spring flower, and I feel bad for wanting to dodge her.

"Great dress," she says, twisting Roughneck's spare leash around one of her slender wrists.

"Thanks. It's my favorite."

"You have excellent taste." She tucks a lock of honey-colored hair behind her ear. "I was heading over to your place to grab Sir Pups-a-Lot, if that's okay."

I glance at my watch, surprised to see it's almost ten. "Of course. Sorry, I forgot."

"If you're headed that way, I'll walk with you."

"Oh, um, actually..." I fumble for an excuse to be alone. "I was going over there."

I jerk my thumb in some random direction, and her bright gaze follows. She frowns but doesn't ask why I'm visiting the waterpark in a Rebecca Taylor eyelet sheath dress.

"Right, yes, of course." Her eyes fill with sympathy. "Dean filled me in about the situation. I'm so sorry. You'll be in our meeting this afternoon?"

I feel my jaw tighten. "I wasn't invited, actually."

"Hell." Her brow furrows. "I'm sorry. He means well, but sometimes my brother gets a little too focused on running things. He doesn't stop to ask questions." She hesitates, then puts her hand on my arm. "Look, you don't have to answer this if you don't want to, but it would help if I knew the circumstances of the investigation."

It's the kindness in her eyes that undoes me. That, and the way she asks instead of assuming.

"Was that PR-speak for 'did you cheat on the CPA exam, Vanessa?'"

Lana doesn't flinch. "You don't have to tell me anything you don't want to, and there's absolutely no judgement from me if—"

"No." I look down at her hand on my arm as tears spring to my eyes. "No, I didn't. I didn't cheat."

"Hey, Vanessa? Look at me, okay?"

I take a couple deep breaths before lifting my gaze. The fierce friendship I see in her eyes is the closest thing to sisterly affection I've felt since Val left.

"We'll get through this together, okay? We'll take our cues from you, and everything's going to be fine. The important thing is that you feel all right about the process. We'll talk more at the meeting, okay?"

I nod, but I can't say anything. My throat is clogged with tears, while my brain floods with the one thing I'm not saying: I don't plan to be at that meeting. I don't plan to be at Juniper Ridge at all by the end of the day.

I can't stay, not with Dean believing I'm not competent enough to have a say in things. In my career, my security, my safety. My presence here can't be the thing that derails this show before it even gets off the ground. If I leave now, they can find someone new. Someone without all this baggage.

Lana must see in my eyes that I'm not able to answer, because she squeezes my arm once and lets go. "I'll leave you alone. Is it still okay if I take Roughneck for a walk?"

I nod and take a step back. "Of course."

"Take care, Vanessa." Her eyes shimmer with sympathy. "If you need anything at all, call me. Even if you just need someone to punch my big brother in the junk."

I can't help choking out a laugh. "Thank you."

I'm full-on ugly crying by the time I turn away. Crying and fuming and feeling all kinds of emotions I never expected to feel. This is why I was so hell-bent on dodging relationships. Not this precisely, but the sick, awful, balled-up feeling in my gut. The knowledge that a man I care about doesn't trust me one bit. Not with information, not with decisions, and not to do the right thing.

Maybe that means he's a jerk.

Or maybe it means there's something inherently untrustworthy about me.

It's this possibility that sets me crying again, great, heaving sobs that leave me emptied out and aching. I stumble down the cinder path, not daring to stop. It'd be just my luck one of Dean's other brothers or sisters would come along, and then I'd be stuck explaining myself all over again.

Swiping at my tears, I head for the waterpark. I don't know what my plan is, but it involves being alone to think. There's that table where we sat at the base of the big slide. Was that only a month ago? It feels like years. Like a lifetime ago.

As I approach the door, a maintenance guy I don't recognize pushes through. "Ma'am."

The smell of chlorine and nostalgia hits me so hard I stumble. Averting my face, I mumble a greeting and change course to head the other way. The bumper cars are up ahead, so I head for the refuge of the round, rubber-ringed cars.

They're up on a platform that puts them about waist height, so I climb the four short steps and aim for a car near the back. It's quiet here, except for a smattering of birdsong and some distant hammering from the waterpark. There's no one around to remind me I'm not capable of running my own life. That I'm as big a screwup as my mother always said.

Angry as I am at Dean for doubting me, I know some of this is my fault. I should have told him up front about the investigation. I should have come clean about what happened. I should have done a lot of things, starting with never applying for a such a high-profile job.

But what's done is done. Swinging into my chosen bumper

car, I steady myself with a hand on the steering wheel. The seat is polished leather and cushier than I expected, and I feel a sudden rush of sadness that I won't be here to see it up and running.

I can't stay, right? There's no way I can be in charge of finances for a multi-million-dollar community and TV show. Not when the boss doesn't have faith in me. Not when I'm unsure I have faith in myself.

And definitely not when the guy I love doesn't trust me.

*Love.* I never said it to him, but I've known for a while that's what I'm feeling. It's too late now to do anything about it, so I'm grateful I never laid that burden at his feet. Never spoke the words aloud. For now, they'll stay sealed up tight in my silly, battered heart.

Slipping my phone out of my purse, I dial my sister's number. It's close to dinnertime in Paris, so she'll be home. Before it connects, I remember her anniversary plans with Josh. I hang up before it rings and switch to text.

My hands are shaking as I struggle to tap out a message. Between autocorrect and my clumsy thumbs, I find myself on the brink of sending a message that reads, "Can men weaniny get a cheese" instead of "call me when you get a chance," which is not helping.

"Dammit to hell!"

I delete it and hit the voice-to-text key instead.

"Hey, Val. Call me when you're done with dinner. It's not an emergency, so please don't cut the date short. Dean and I are done, and I could use an ear."

I read back through the words, feeling sick inside. What kind of loser can't handle a breakup by herself?

The kind who texts her twin at the first sign of heartache. The kind who hides out in a vacant bumper car arena instead of dealing with the problem.

I delete the words and slip my phone into my handbag. Then I take a few deep breaths. What now?

I'm considering that when I hear footsteps. Turning around, I see a pretty blonde approaching. She's wearing tight designer jeans and a cute pink off-the-shoulder top, her sunny hair ruffling in the breeze.

"Hey there." She waves, but her smile doesn't reach her eyes.

"Hello." I press the heels of my hands to my eyes, hoping she gets the hint. Now's not ideal for making friendly small talk with a stranger.

No dice. "Mind if I join you?"

I drop my hands to my lap and manage a weak smile. "Actually, I kinda want to be alone right now. Nothing personal. It's just…not a good time."

She smiles and eases herself into the car beside mine, turning on the seat so she's facing me. Her glamorously long legs stretch out in hiking boots that look more fashionable than functional. There's something familiar about her, but I can't put my finger on it.

"It's nice to finally meet you, Vanessa."

I blink at her, trying to figure out what's going on. Is she one of the candidates to open an on-site day spa? "Do we know each other?"

She laughs and holds out her hand, which I accept automatically. "I'm Andi. That's a great dress, by the way."

My mind reels as I try to place the name. I definitely recognize her face, though I can't figure out how. Is she a friend of Val's? "I'm sorry, who are you again? We've interviewed so many people that everyone's started blending together."

She laughs like I've said something hilarious. "I'm not a candidate, sweetie. I already have a career. I'm Andi Knight. Andi has more of a casual, Oregon sort of vibe, don't you think?"

I gape at her without forming a response. I honestly have no words. Not until the name clicks in my brain. "Andrea Knight?"

"That's right." She tosses her hair, the blond curtain flowing over her shoulders. "I'm Dean's fiancée."

There's a roaring in my head that I can't quite place. I dig my nails into my palms to clear my head. "Andrea Knight." Holy shit. "Your hair's different."

"You like?" She reaches up and touches her long, golden mane, fingers flowing through it like silk. "I went blond for my last film, and Dean loved it. I figured it's the least I can do now that we're back together."

I stare at her, not sure how to respond. She expects me to be shocked, that's clear. Or jealous. I've got squiggles of both shifting around in my belly, but mostly, I'm suspicious. Alarm bells ring in my brain, drowning out the emotion as reason surges to the top.

"I didn't know you were visiting." My voice comes out surprisingly calm. "Dean's back at the lodge if you're looking for him."

"Oh, we'll catch up." She waves a manicured hand, gold bracelet flashing on her wrist. "I wanted to talk with you, first. Woman to woman. I thought you should hear it from me that Dean and I are working things out. I'm moving here to be with him."

"I see." I clear my throat and hold her gaze. I'm not sure I believe her, but I know better than to respond emotionally. "Well, good luck with that."

This is not the reaction she's expecting. She wants me to break down crying, pleading with her not to steal my man. She expects me to rant and yell and yeah, part of me wants to do that.

But something's definitely off here.

Maybe it's the weird glint in her expression or the fact that she's not quite meeting my eyes. I know I've questioned whether my intuition is busted, but right now, it feels spot-on.

Andrea keeps laying it on thick. "It's been tough on our relationship being apart like this," she continues like this is a friendly girls' chat. "I won't lie; I wasn't a fan of having him move all the way to Oregon to do the show."

I nod slowly, playing it cool. "Long-distance relationships are tough."

She narrows her eyes, studying me like she can't figure out if I'm yanking her chain. I keep my expression bland as I slip my fingers into my handbag and fish around for that mini recorder. I know it's in here somewhere.

"Well, now we won't be long distance." She delivers a cold, calculated smile. "The ranch I'm buying is less than an hour away. Super-cute, with a gym and home theater and everything."

"That's great." Does she think I want to know this? I fumble for the button on the recorder, considering what I'd say if I were really buying her story. "I mean, I'll miss Dean and all, but you two have a history."

She frowns but takes the bait. "Right, well. We had our problems, but I think most of them will resolve themselves once I'm out here."

"Sure, that makes sense."

I can't tell if I've pressed the right button on the recorder, and Andrea will definitely notice if I pull it out to check. I cross my fingers I've got it right as I scan the bumper car arena. We're far from the lodge, far from the cabins, too. My brain flicks to Amy Lovelin and her gun, but she's nowhere around.

I'm on my own.

Andrea keeps talking. "I know you and Dean have had something going on. Look, I don't blame him for wanting to get back at me for...well, you understand, right? But that was a fling. We've planned a future together."

"Absolutely." I start to ease up off the seat. "How about I get out of your hair right now?"

I'm on my feet, but Andrea stands, too. She's much too close, and a good five inches taller. "Where do you think you're going?"

"Um, back to my cabin?" I edge sideways, wondering if I should make a run for it. "I'm sure you and Dean will be really happy together. Good luck with—"

"Don't patronize me." Her green eyes narrow, and she looms over me, her friendly girl-chat demeanor vanishing. "I know you fucked him last night. And I know he's in love with you. He said so in an email to Mari just this morning."

"I—what?" I don't know where to start with that. That he told his sister he loves me? That he didn't mention it to *me*?

Or that Andrea just admitted she's been into the company email.

I seriously doubt she's some hacker mastermind, but money can buy lots of things.

I keep edging away, crossing my fingers she doesn't notice my progress toward the steps. "I don't want any trouble, Andi. How about you go talk with Dean? He's probably in his office. You could surprise him."

"Oh, I will." The smile that spreads over her pretty face is one I've seen in movies. The sexpot assassin preparing to knock off her evil nemesis. Is that how she sees me?

I'm still creeping sideways, aiming for the steps off the back edge of the platform. "It's been great meeting you. Maybe I'll see you ar—"

"Stop right there!"

I freeze, still ten feet from the edge. It's too far to run, but do I really have a choice? "Let's just calm down."

It's the wrong thing to say to an unhinged actress. I see that instantly from the glint in her eyes, the flash of too-white teeth. She slips a hand into her jacket pocket. I jump back, expecting a gun.

Instead, she pulls out—"A needle?"

She smiles and turns it over in her palm. "A syringe, very good."

I frown, trying to make sense of it. "That's actually not one of my phobias."

It dawns on me that Andrea's the one who left the snake on my porch. Andrea, or someone working for her. They spied and sleuthed and dug through private messages to probe for weakness. But what's the syringe for?

"Phobia or not, you should be afraid, sweetie." She flicks the barrel of the syringe with her fingernail, flashing her mean little smile. "Amazing what you can find on the dark web. Did you know it's possible to buy actual rattlesnake venom?"

"What?" I feel the blood drain from my face, but Andrea just laughs.

"A few quick pricks, and it'll look like you tangled with a Diamondback." She laughs again, and it's the nastiest sound I've heard. "Poor Nessie, wandered off the path in her pretty little dress."

Hearing her use my sister's nickname for me makes me want to slap her. She's almost close enough. Would it make things worse or throw off her balance enough for me to get away? I struggle to clear my head, to recall what Val and I learned in our weekend self-defense class. Could I fight if I had to?

Andrea takes a step toward me. "Such a shame."

I brace myself to throw a punch as fear ripples up my spine. "That's not necessary." I edge away, heart drumming in my ears. "Just let me go, and we'll forget this ever happened."

"No dice, sweetie. You think you can fuck my fiancé and not pay for that?" She shakes her head almost sadly. "I need you out of the picture permanently. How could I trust he wouldn't slip up again?"

"Trust seems to be the theme of the day." I grip my handbag, ready to swing at her head if she keeps coming.

She strikes, quick as a snake. One second she's standing there, the next she's got my wrist in a vise grip. She jerks me toward her, catching me off guard. "This will hardly hurt at all."

I kick out at her, but she jumps back and laughs. "I do my own stunts, did you know that?"

"I might have read that somewhere." My two hours of self-defense training is no match for that, but I have to try. I'm drawing my handbag back to swing it, but Andrea grabs it and tosses it on the ground.

"Good idea," she says. "That's where you dropped it when you spotted the snake. Now come on, cooperate. This would look better in your ankle or calf or something."

"Go to hell." I take a wild swing at her, but she ducks back, laughing as she pushes me toward the wall.

The needle flashes in her fist as she draws it back like a knife. "Let's get this over with. If I know Dean, he'll come looking for you soon."

That does sound like Dean, and I hate that she knows him like I do. I hate that I may never get a chance to tell him how I feel.

But mostly, I hate that I'll never know if we might have made it. If I'd told him I love him, if we'd talked it through like adults. If I'd had a chance to fight like hell for the best thing that's ever happened to me.

I'm not done fighting. I kick out again, nailing her in the shin this time. Andrea gives a startled yelp but doesn't let go of my hand. "Goddammit, Vanessa."

She slashes wildly with the syringe, but I bob back and feel the whoosh of air past my face. I'm breathing fast, trying not to panic, as I struggle to break her hold.

"You're insane," I snap, which is overstating the obvious.

"Come on, Vanessa." She's got my back to the wall now, and I wonder if I can use it as leverage to land another kick. "It'll all be over quickly."

Her grip on my wrist loosens, and I seize the chance to swing again. This time, my fist connects with the side of her head.

"Ow!" She shrieks and tries to slap me. I duck, and while I'm down there, head-butt her in the chest.

She goes down hard, pulling me with her. Shit, she's got a grip on my leg.

"Even better," she snarls, fingers tightening around my ankle.

I twist away, throwing another blow that falls short. She's on top of me now, pushing me onto my back. She's got her shin across my windpipe, and I wheeze as stars flicker behind my eyelids.

If I could just shove her off and get to my handbag. There's surely something in there that could work as a weapon. Keys. A candle in a heavy glass jar. A stapler.

I'm kicking and flailing and trying to get her off me. My vision is blurring, and I don't know how long I have before I black out. I drag my brain for the steps to break a chokehold, but all I come up with is my grandma's brownie recipe. I turn my head to the side, fighting for breath, fighting for just enough air to scream.

But Andi laughs and grips my calf, then raises the needle to swing.

# CHAPTER 19

**CONFESSIONAL 422.5**

Judson, Dean: (CEO, Juniper Ridge)

*Did I ever tell you about the first film I was involved with? No, it was in grad school. You were just a kid. Anyway, we couldn't get the actors to sign on, and the director was a hot mess, but I loved that script. Busted ass to find funding, but no one would bite. It was all about redemption and forgiveness and learning to admit when you're wrong. Also, there were zombies. And monster trucks. No, it never got made. The title? Never Too Late to Say Sorry.*

*I still like those zombies.*

* * *

I'm jogging to Vanessa's cabin when I hear it.

Lana's voice chattering away in an odd, growly sort of baby-talk. I round the corner and nearly crash into Roughneck.

"Jesus, Dean." Lana throws an arm out as Roughneck jumps and bounces at the end of his leash. "Why are you running?"

"Gotta find Vanessa." Panting, I brace my hands on my thighs and curse the high desert altitude. I'm still not used to it. "It's an emergency."

Lana's brow furrows. "She's not at her cabin. I was just there grabbing Duke Doggo. I think she was going to the waterpark."

"The waterpark?" I scan the trees on the north edge of the property. We're not that far from the spot I saw in that video, and the thought makes my skin crawl. "Did she say why?"

"No, but she looked upset." She studies my face, a faintly accusing look in her eye. "Please tell me you don't really think she cheated on the CPA exam."

"Lana, I—"

"And please tell me you at least asked her about it before launching into mister fix-it mode."

I sigh. "I screwed up, okay? In at least a dozen ways before breakfast. Happy?"

She smiles. "A little. Want me to help find her?"

Before I can answer, a shrill scream shreds the silence. It bounces off the canyon walls, and I spin around, scrambling to figure out where it's coming from.

Roughneck doesn't need direction. With a fierce yank, he pulls the leash out of Lana's hand and takes off running.

"No!" Lana sprints after him, calling his name.

But that scream ignited his rocket blasters, and the dog zooms off toward the trees. He's growling and flashing his teeth and looking like a damn wild animal, so I take off after him as another shriek pierces the air.

*Vanessa.* I'd know that scream anywhere.

"Oh, God." I sprint past my sister, following the dog toward the waterpark. No, not the waterpark. Roughneck darts left, aiming for the bumper cars. What the hell?

Female voices are shouting up ahead, both familiar, both heated. But only one of them sends my heart throbbing into my throat where it wedges itself tight and painful. I follow Roughneck as he rounds the corner. His stump tail juts like an arrow, ears folded back as his paws whir in a cartoon blur.

I'm ten feet behind him, praying I'm not too late. That Andrea isn't as crazy as I think she is. I'm positive that was her on the video, and I can't believe I didn't figure it out earlier.

I round the corner and skid to a halt at the base of the bumper car platform. "Oh my God."

Vanessa's pinned down with Andrea on top of her, but not for long. She drives a fist into Andrea's stomach, catching her off-guard. Andrea screams as Vanessa rears up like a goddamn superhero and flings Andrea off her. Before I can move, she lands another blow that knocks Andrea flat on her back.

"Fuck you!" Vanessa yells as she presses Andrea into the ground, dress riding up her thighs as she snatches her giant purse. "You picked the wrong goddamn day to try me."

As I stare in disbelief, Vanessa yanks a blunt, wooden object from her bag and raises it over Andrea's skull. Is that a pepper grinder? She's shouting curse words I can barely make out as she wrestles something from Andrea's hand and flings it aside muttering "fucking snakes."

What?

"Get off me," Andrea wheezes.

"You crazy bitch." Vanessa's still gripping the peppermill as her hair falls over her face. "Stop squirming or I'll bash your head in."

The fury in her eyes leaves no doubt she'd do it. Vanessa's not messing around. I've never seen her like this, but one thing's clear: She needs zero help from anyone.

Even if she did, Roughneck's got it handled. He dives into the fray, teeth bared and snapping. He clamps his jaws around Andrea's pantleg with a ferocious snarl. She screams and grabs Vanessa's arm, but Vanessa's not letting up.

"Holy shit." Lana skids to a stop beside me, eyes wide. "Good dog."

But it's Vanessa earning the real ninja points. She's flipping Andrea onto her stomach and binding her wrists with a phone cord pulled from her purse.

"Never come at woman with a handbag the size of Alaska," she barks at Andrea. "Or a woman with zero fucks left to give."

The swearing, the fury, the utter badassery—this shouldn't be turning me on. I've always known Vanessa's competent as hell, but this...this is next level stuff.

Vanessa looks up then, her gaze meeting mine. She doesn't smile, but at least she doesn't glare. Just stares at me for a few long seconds as her dog growls and tugs at Andrea's pantleg.

Then she stands up, grabs her phone, and—cool as a cucumber—places a call. "Hello, police? I'd like to report a crime."

***

THREE HOURS LATER, we're back in my office. Vanessa has changed into jeans and a T-shirt, and she's sipping her second lavender latte as Amy Lovelin stands up and closes her notebook.

"Thank you for giving me so much of your time," Amy says. "I'm sure we'll have more questions, but you're free to go now."

"Thanks." Vanessa stands and shakes her hand, looking a little tired. "You've been great."

"Me?" Amy laughs. "I'm not the one who took down a crazed actress holding a syringe full of snake venom."

"Roughneck gets the credit," she says modestly, even though we all know she had the situation under control before her dog arrived.

"Give him an extra biscuit for me." Amy bends and scratches him behind the ears, earning a groan of happiness from the dog who hasn't left Vanessa's side for hours. When she took a bathroom break, he followed her inside.

"Dean." Amy straightens and shakes my hand. "We'll be in touch."

"Thank you."

And then we're alone. Vanessa stands in the doorway, looking like she's not sure whether to stay or run like hell.

"Vanessa." I hold out my hand, not sure where to start. "I have no right to ask you to stay here and listen to my paltry, inadequate, much-too-late apology, but if you're willing to hear me out—"

"Yes." She drops back into her chair and crosses her legs. "I believe in letting people have their say. In giving people a chance to be heard."

Ouch. "I deserved that."

"Yep."

She's not going to make this easy for me. She shouldn't, I know that. "I'm so sorry," I begin. "I'm sorry for shutting you out. I'm sorry for doing my stupid king-of-the-county routine when it's clear you're the goddamn empress of the universe."

Her mouth twitches just a little, but her expression stays stony. "Thank you. I accept your apology."

It should come as a relief, but it doesn't. Not even a little. She's still hurt, and she has every right to be. I can't expect a few lame words to do anything but patch the roof I've blown off the house we've been carefully building.

I take a deep breath and try again. "For so long, I've thought it was my job to take care of everyone. It's not about being the older sibling. It's feeling like that's the best and only thing I had to offer the people I care about."

"That's not true." Her expression softens just a little. "You have plenty to offer."

I shrug, not willing to accept compliments I don't deserve. "My ability to fix things—I've been known for that since I was a kid. But I realize it's the last thing you needed from me, and I'm sorry. I know it doesn't make it better knowing it came from a place of love, but it did."

"It makes it a little better." She shrugs, glancing away. "Plenty of people do shitty things in the name of protecting the people they care about."

The pain etched on her face is plain as day. "Your mother, you mean."

She turns back to me, expression wary. "What do you mean?"

I take a deep breath. I'm not sure how she's going to take this. "While Amy was questioning you, I made some calls. I should have done that first." Actually, scratch that. "No, what I should have done first was talk with you. That should have been my first move the instant I got that email."

She nods once, still guarded. "It would have been nice."

"For what it's worth, I never doubted you," I tell her. "I never thought you were a cheater. My instinct was to squash the scandal, but it should have been to make sure you understood that I know what kind of person you are. That I trust you completely."

Tears fill her eyes, but she blinks them back hard. I watch her take a few deep breaths, hands clenched in her lap. "Thank you."

I hesitate, choosing my words carefully. I'm not sure how to ask this. "Would you have told me?" I probe gently. "Would you have explained how your mother filed a false report to kill your chance at passing the CPA exam?"

I watch her chest rise and fall as she looks at me, not breaking eye contact. She doesn't answer. Not right away. When she does, her voice is hard as granite. "She wanted me to be a socialite like her. Thought a career in a male-driven field would get in the way of me scoring a husband and settling down like she wanted me to do."

"God. I'm so sorry." I'm not sure if I'm angrier about the 1950s mentality, or that anyone would go so far to control someone they're supposed to love. "I'm sorry I turned out to be every bit as bad. Worse, because you trusted me."

She shrugs and looks down at the knee of her jeans. Amy gave her a chance to change out of her torn dress. It takes my breath away how lovely she is in a T-shirt and faded denim.

A tiny smile flits over her face. "I didn't trust you, so we're even."

I laugh, though it's clear her joke is hiding more hurt. "Hardly. God, Vanessa."

I want to ask about the exam. How she proved herself and passed with flying colors. With a better score than she had the first time.

"I offered to take it again," she says, reading my mind. "Naked. No chance of hiding notes in my bra."

"Seriously?"

She shrugs and looks away. "They didn't take me up on the naked thing, but they did frisk me like crazy."

"I'm so sorry." I sound like a broken record. "I just want to keep apologizing again and again, but I know it won't help."

"It helps a little."

"Not enough. It could never be enough." Neither could the next words I want to say, but I owe it to her to say them out loud. I owe it to myself.

"Vanessa, I love you."

She looks up, startled. I hurry to keep talking so she doesn't feel forced to repeat it. "You don't have to say it back. And I don't mean it as a desperate, last-ditch effort to convince you to give me another chance. I'm telling you because before I met you, I had no idea what it felt like to love someone so completely that it overwhelmed any rational thought."

The edges of her smile tug up just a little. "For an irrational guy, you're surprisingly functional."

"That's just it." I drag my hand through my hair, not sure how much to share.

*All of it. Bare your guts, you idiot.*

"I've been walking around beating my chest and doing what I've always done as the guy in charge. Then you came along, and I realized I wasn't the center of the universe. Not even close. And I realized the most amazing things in my life—loving you, for starters—they're completely out of my control. And that scared the hell out of me, to be honest."

She looks at me for a long, long time. Slowly, she reaches out to lace her fingers through mine. "I shouldn't have walked away."

"You had every right to. You had every right to punch me in the nuts if you wanted to."

She laughs. "Lana did suggest it, but no." She takes a deep breath. "Being brave means sticking around and fighting for what matters. It means having the hard conversations instead of throwing up my hands and saying 'I'm done.'"

"You're the bravest person I know," I say. "Even before I saw you climb a tree topless or beat the crap out of Andrea."

"You're pretty brave yourself." She looks down at our intertwined hands. "Brave is saying 'I love you' when you're not sure the other person's going to say it back."

I suppose that's true, though I hardly deserve credit. "I'm just telling you how I feel. I should have done that a long time ago."

"Maybe." She shrugs. "There's a lot we both could have done differently."

I take another deep breath. I'm still nowhere near making this right. Unlacing my fingers from hers, I reach under my desk and pull out the box. "I can sit here spouting words all day long, but it won't make up for what I did," I tell her. "Words are one thing. Actions are another."

"What do you mean?"

I reach into the box and pull out the first object. "The remote control to my office TV." I place it in her hand as an offering, smiling as she curls her fingers around it. "For the record, I've never let anyone touch it."

She laughs and holds it up to look at it. "I'm honored. Also a little confused." She flicks the power button on and then off again. "How does rendering your television useless solve anything?"

"It doesn't, but I wanted to show I can give up control. It's my lame attempt at symbolism."

"Not that lame." She gives me a small smile and sets the remote aside. "What else?"

Could this really be working? I don't dare hope as I reach into the box again. "My coffee mug." I set it on the desk in front of her. "I've had this for twelve years. It was a present from the first director I ever worked with, and I've always been petrified someone would break it."

She turns it around on the desk, frowning. "You're not giving me this, are you?"

"Yes. I even washed it." That sounded dorky. "Still going for the symbolism, I guess. I trust you with one of my most treasured possessions."

"That's...sweet." She laughs. "A little weird, but sweet."

This next thing stands a good chance of falling flat. I don't know how she'll take it. If I'll be opening up old wounds.

But I have to take a chance. If I've learned nothing else today, that's it. I reach into the box again. My fingers close around bent metal and round, glossy beads. As I pull out the abacus, Vanessa gasps.

"Where did you get that?"

"Is it the same one?" I hoped it might be, but I wasn't sure. "Maybe not identical, but it's like what you had as a kid?"

She nods, tears filling her eyes. She reaches out and strokes a finger over a row of blue wooden beads. "It's just like it."

"I thought so. The way you described it sounded like the one I had growing up. After you told me that, I called my mom and asked her to ship it to me."

Her eyes snap to mine, and her lips part slightly. "This was yours? The one you had as a kid?"

I nod, feeling simultaneously silly and hopeful. "We've got a lot of heirloom jewelry in my family. My mom's always urged me to go through it. That I might want a ring to propose with someday." I never took her up on it with Andrea. It never felt right, handing over a family treasure. "Anyway, I called my mom after you told me your abacus story. I said, 'I'm in love with the most amazing woman I've ever met, and I'll probably want that ring soon. But I need something else.'"

A tear slips down her cheek, and she doesn't bother brushing it away. Instead, she reaches out to touch the abacus. "It's beautiful."

If I didn't already love her, this would be the moment I fell. The instant she looked at my battered childhood toy and found it as precious as any diamond.

Don't worry, I got the ring, too. There's plenty of time for that without scaring the shit out of her. Right now, this means more.

"I love you, Vanessa. I love your brains and your beauty and how the bumps in your road have made you the brave and amazing woman you are. I love that you don't need me, but that you might be willing to make room for me in your life anyway." I pause, grinning. "And I love that you dig numbers as much as I do."

She laughs and wipes a tear off her cheek. "Dammit, I said I wasn't going to cry again today."

"Hey, I'm good with it. No emotion is off-limits as far as I'm concerned."

"Good. Because I love you, too."

"Yeah?" The wave of joy that hits me is so huge, so fierce, that I almost can't find words. But I somehow find a way to get up off my ass and scoop Vanessa into my arms, hugging her so hard she gives a startled squeak.

"I love you so much," I say, breathing the words into her hair.

"I love you, too, you big dummy." She laughs again as I nuzzle her neck. "So much."

"I love you." I seriously can't stop saying it. "I plan to spend every day proving that for as long as you'll let me."

She draws back and smiles up into my eyes. "Sounds like a plan."

# EPILOGUE

## CONFESSIONAL 439

VINCENT, VANESSA: (CFO, JUNIPER RIDGE)

*I NEVER USED TO BELIEVE IN HAPPILY EVER AFTER.*

*ACTUALLY, THAT'S NOT TRUE. I BELIEVE IN IT. I WAS JUST NEVER SURE THAT WAS IN THE CARDS FOR ME. I WATCHED MY SISTER FIND HER PERFECT GUY AND THOUGHT "THAT'S NICE. THAT'S REALLY AMAZING.'"*

*BUT I NEVER EXPECTED TO FIND THAT.*

*SOMETIMES, BEING WRONG IS THE BEST POSSIBLE OUTCOME.*

* * *

"Want some popcorn?"

I plunk the bowl on the armrest between Dean's seat and mine without waiting for an answer, grinning when he shovels it up in one of his massive paws.

We're five months in, and I'm still obsessed with his hands.

"Thanks." He finishes chewing and throws an arm around the back of my seat. "Want another beer before I start the show?"

"I'm good for now." Mine's tucked in the armrest on my other side, hoppy and cool and perfect. "I can't believe we've already got an on-site brewery."

"Cooper knocked it out of the park getting everything set up a month ahead of schedule." The pride in his voice is obvious, and I'm not sure if it's for Cooper or the fact that Dean never flinched handing the whole thing off to his brother. "I can't believe how fast it's coming together."

I nod and help myself to more popcorn. "It's shaping up to be a nice little town."

We're snuggled up in the full-sized theater near the main lodge. Starting next week, it'll be packed with residents turning out to see first-run films and mingle with their new neighbors in the café lobby. For now, we've got the place to ourselves.

Well, us and Roughneck. He's curled on the ground at my feet, and I slip off my sandal to rub toe circles on his belly. He groans in appreciation and rolls over to grant better access.

Dean reaches for more popcorn. "This is good. What did you put on it?"

"A little butter, some salt, and a few big sprinkles of blue cheese powder from Rogue Creamery over in Southern Oregon."

He finishes chewing and gives me an odd look. "They have that in the café?"

"No, it was in my purse." I grin and grab another handful. "I brought it to girls' night at Mari's so I could make dip for the veggies, and I forgot to take it out."

"Of course you did." He kisses the edge of my temple. "Delicious."

"You don't think it's too salty?"

Dean grins. "I wasn't talking about the popcorn."

I laugh and take a sip of my beer. It's been months since the incident with Andrea, but it feels like a lifetime ago. Since then, we've brought on dozens of new community members ranging from doctors and lawyers to florists and hairdressers. There are several couples and quite a few kids, but most are singles looking for a fresh start and maybe a shot at love.

I figure their odds are good. Dean and I weren't looking for it, and see how things turned out?

He kisses me again and snags another bite of popcorn. "I'm pumped for you to see the pilot."

"You already watched it?" I fight to keep the disappointment from my voice. We've planned for weeks to watch together.

"Nope, I waited—I promise." He squeezes my hand. "I've seen a few clips here and there when Gabe and Lauren asked for my opinion, but mostly I've left it up to them."

See? This is what I mean. The Dean I met a few months ago could never have stepped aside and let his siblings run the show. Don't get me wrong, he's still plenty involved with finances and sponsors and real estate decisions. But he's gotten way better at letting go and trusting others to do their jobs.

"I'm sure it's amazing." I lean my head against his shoulder and fish my hand in the popcorn again. "Everyone's been working so hard."

"Nothing's more rewarding than doing the work and watching it pay off."

I laugh and nudge him with my elbow. "Is that a Mari quote?"

"Duh. Remember, she said it in our last couples' workshop? I was taking notes."

He's so damn adorable I can't stand it. "Have I told you lately how hot it is that you're this devoted to mastering communication skills?"

Dean grins and nuzzles my neck. "You're saying it turns you on?"

"I wouldn't go that far," I muse, even though it's totally true. "We're with your sister, after all."

Roughneck looks up and gives a soft "uff," probably because I quit rubbing his belly. Or maybe he's spotted the popcorn, because he looks at the bowl and licks his chops.

"We've been reading Julia Child's 'Mastering the Art of French Cooking,'" I tell Dean as I bend down to feed my dog a small piece. He takes it gently, smacking his lips as he eyes the bowl hopefully. "Val brought it home from Paris."

"For Roughneck, I assume?"

"Of course. He's very into cheese these days."

"Atta boy." Dean fiddles with the remote but doesn't hit play. He's looking at me oddly, like there's something he wants to say.

"You okay?" I ask.

"Yeah, why?"

"You seem nervous. I know the show's been picked up, but a lot hinges on how the pilot does."

He grins and takes a sip of his beer. "Nah, I'm good. Gabe and Lauren seem happy with the footage, and Mari had that awesome idea to sprinkle those one-on-one interviews through each episode."

"I like Cooper's concept, too," I add. "The part about introducing community members with little flashbacks about where they've been and how they ended up here."

Dean's eyes light up. This is his favorite topic of conversation. "Wait 'til you see the promo spots Lana's developing," he says. "We'll have viewers salivating to watch the first season."

"Sounds very unsanitary." I stretch up to kiss him. "Also, I'm proud of you."

"Don't give me credit," he says. "It's been a team effort."

"That's what I mean. You stepped aside and gave them a chance to shine and do all the things they've wanted to do."

He grins. "It helps having a girlfriend who's a good influence."

As opposed to a crazy one who currently resides in the County jail. Andrea's lawyers fought like hell to get her out on bail, but there was too much evidence against her. It's staggering how far she was willing to go to get Dean back. Even without my recording, authorities had plenty of proof to nail her.

I bring none of that up now. I'm too excited about the pilot. "I'm ready anytime you want to hit play."

"Sounds good." He picks up the remote but hesitates. "You good on popcorn?"

I glance down at the bowl. "We've still got plenty." As I fish my hand in for another helping, my fingers touch something plastic. Confused, I pull it out. It's a key. A shiny one that looks brand new, and it's tucked inside a baggie. I hold it up for Dean to see.

"What is this?"

He grins. "A key."

"I see that, Einstein. What's it doing in our popcorn?"

He slips it from my fingers and turns it around so it catches the light. "It's a symbolic key to an imaginary cabin. Well, not imaginary. It's just not chosen yet."

I study his face, not sure I'm understanding. "What do you mean symbolic?"

"Well, I wanted to ask you to move in with me," he says slowly. "But I thought it would be a dick move to just expect you to move into my place. Besides, I figured we'd want something bigger in case we want more dogs or kids or…well, I'm getting ahead of myself."

A hint of color rushes his cheeks, and I realize he's nervous. I lace my fingers through his. "I'm diggin' it," I tell him. "Go on."

He grins as relief floods his features. "You know how we're planning that whole section of cabins meant for couples?"

"Of course."

"I figured we could choose one together. Pick a floor plan we both like, and we both get a say in things like paint colors and furniture."

"I love it." Honestly, I love way more than the idea. I love Dean even more for thinking of it. I throw my arms around his neck, spilling a few pieces of popcorn on the floor. Roughneck hoovers it up it while I plant a big kiss on Dean. "I love everything about it."

He laughs and kisses me, dropping the key into the breast pocket of my shirt. "I'm glad. I'm in this for the long haul, Vanessa. I love you, and I want to build a future together."

"I love you, too." And I love the idea of a future with Dean in it. A future with a house and pets and the whole ball of wax. "Thank you."

He laces his fingers through mine and squeezes. "Here's to fresh starts."

As the house lights dim, the silver screen flickers to life. I snuggle up to Dean, ready for the show to start.

Ready for the rest of my life.

***

Thanks so much for reading this first installment of the Juniper Ridge rom-com series. Want more? Mari's story is next, and it's on sale now in eBook, audio, and paperback. Keep reading for an exclusive sneak peek at *Let it Show*...

Order *Let It Show:*

https://geni.us/myWBcHA

# YOUR EXCLUSIVE SNEAK PEEK AT LET IT SHOW

**CONFESSIONAL 611**

JUDSON, MARILYN, PSYD (PSYCHOLOGIST: JUNIPER RIDGE)

*BECAUSE THIS IS WHAT I'M WEARING. I'M NOT DEBATING YOU ON THIS, LAUREN. THEY'RE NOT SWEATPANTS, THEY'RE CASUAL SEPARATES. LEISURE SLACKS.*

*LOOK, I STOPPED HAVING MY WARDROBE DICTATED TO ME THE MINUTE I LEFT HOLLYWOOD. THEY'RE COMFORTABLE. LIKE A SOOTHING HUG FROM A TRUSTED FRIEND. LIKE A SOFT, HEARTWARMING TOUCH FROM...*

*OH, SHUT UP.*

*FINE, THEY'RE SWEATPANTS. CAN WE START NOW?*

* * *

I shouldn't have stopped for tea.

I was already running late for my coaching appointment with the new brewery manager, and I should have gone straight to the conference room.

But there's this great new Earl Grey in the café, and with seven coaching sessions scheduled back to back, my need for caffeine overrode my good judgment.

The lodge is straight ahead, so I kick up my pace to a run. The pencil anchoring my bun in place flips out and hits the snow on a bounce. I'll grab it later, maybe shovel this path while I'm at it. My low-heeled pump slips on a patch of cinder-studded sidewalk ice, but I stay upright as I whirl through the side door and into the carpeted corridor.

Pressing a hand to the wall, I pause to catch my breath. My fault for abandoning those twice-daily sessions with a personal trainer, though I don't regret it. Not even a little.

I start moving again, reminding myself to slow down and walk like a normal human. No, not *normal*. I know better than to use ableist language, even in my head.

Squaring my shoulders, I bypass my office and aim for the conference room. The hall smells like Lana's cinnamon candles and Dean's burnt coffee, and I gulp back a weird wave of complicated love for my family.

Griffin Walsh is already in the conference room, callused hands folded on the table in front of him. He looks like he hasn't shaved for a week, which is more appealing than it ought to be. His gaze lifts, and the gaslight blue of his eyes makes me trip over my feet.

Catching myself on the table, I offer my most charming Hollywood smile. "Thank you for your patience."

See what I did there? Opening with gratitude instead of apology starts things on a positive note.

Griffin just stares. "Does this mean we can cut it short by five minutes?" He glances at his watch. "I've got a batch of grist that needs to come out of the mash tun."

"Ah." I can't pretend to understand the brewing process, but it's important to show an interest in every community member's role at Juniper Ridge. "Sounds exciting."

"Not really."

I claim the chair across from him, grateful I wore a skirt for a change. Not that I care about conforming to feminine ideals for fashion, but it's important to set a professional tone for these coaching sessions. "You're settling in okay?"

He nods and looks at his watch again, in case an hour has passed since he checked thirty seconds ago. "How is this different from all the other interviews I've been doing this week?" He meets my eyes again. "I mean, I know I agreed to have my life filmed, but I didn't realize it would be so...so..."

He waves a hand, searching for the right word or maybe expecting me to fill it in for him. I fold my hands on the table and wait. In my experience, it's best to let patients take their time forming their thoughts.

I wait a little longer.

And longer still.

After maybe twelve hours, I cave first. "The other interviews are about gathering footage for the actual show," I explain. "Also, for the research aspect of the Juniper Ridge experiment."

I don't bother explaining my plans to publish details of the study in the *Journal of Experimental Psychology*, since I can see Griffin's eyes glazing over. That information was in the paperwork he signed when joining our little self-contained community, and besides—I'm getting a definite "not a fan of shrinks" vibe.

Cementing that theory, Griffin sighs. "So what the hell is this appointment for?"

I've done this long enough to not take his gruff tone personally. "These coaching sessions are about deciding what you want to work on," I explain. "Areas where you'd like to focus your goals for personal growth. It can be something you'd like help with privately or something you're comfortable having as a focal point on the show."

That's key and something I fought for when my siblings and I dreamed up the concept for *Fresh Start at Juniper Ridge*. If a community member wants privacy for his or her growth arc, I'll absolutely respect that.

Griffin gives me a long look. If he's waiting for me to fill the silence again, he's out of luck.

"Beer," he says, leaning back in his chair. "I was hired to be the brewmaster, so that's what I want to focus on."

I stifle the urge to sigh. The bare bones of Griffin Walsh's file are coming back to me, though it's been months since he applied to be part of our thoughtfully planned, self-sustained community. Unlike some, he wasn't drawn by the prospect of fame. It was the fresh start that appealed to him, though the details are fuzzy in my mind.

I've interviewed literally hundreds of applicants and reviewed files for thousands more. Today alone, I've already done five of these coaching sessions and eight yesterday. Nine the day before. It's possible I need a break, but more important to make sure the emotional needs of community members are fully met.

"Beer," I repeat, stalling for time as I slip a hand into my messenger bag to find his file. It would help if I could jog my memory on his backstory. "Do you have a favorite kind?"

He studies me like he's trying to identify a trap. "It changes all the time," he says at last. "I've been playing around with spontaneous fermentation. Fruit lambics, Flanders red ales, even a Belgian gueuze. I've got a cucumber mint sour I'm working on right now."

"I see." I don't, actually. Beer is beer, as far as I'm concerned, which is to say it's not tea.

I'm still fumbling in my bag for his packet, still thumbing through my memories of why we hired Griffin Walsh. What's his story? He's not married, but widowed? No, *divorced*. Or wait. Gay?

Meeting his icy blue eyes again, I shiver. I'm definitely getting a heterosexual vibe. Not that it's possible to tell by looking, but something about him is setting off alarm bells in my ovaries. That's a clinical observation, not an admission of lust. I'm here purely in a professional capacity.

"So, you've come to Juniper Ridge to start over again." I'm deliberately keeping it neutral since I can't seem to find the damn packet by fumbling blindly in my bag. "Why don't we focus there for now?"

He shrugs and spreads his hands on the table. "Not much to focus on. I got the hell out of Sacramento. Had a brewery there that I lost in the divorce, so this is my shot at starting over without going back to square one."

Yes! Divorced.

Not that I'm celebrating his heartache, but I'm pleased I recalled at least some of his backstory. "That must have been difficult." I leave it open-ended for him to choose whether to focus on the loss of the marriage or the loss of his life's work.

"Yep." He nods, dragging a hand through his hair. Hair that definitely needs a trim, though it's not my place to suggest it.

Lauren, she's the one focused on image management. On which community members are framed up as jokesters or heroes or the brooding, serious type. My sister is a master producer, while I'm here to make sure we follow the rules, and no one cracks under pressure.

I study Griffin across the table, seeing no visible cracks. There are webs of fine lines beside each eye, which gives him a rugged look. A guy who's seen too much. Is that why we chose him? I know he brews good beer, but since that's not my thing, I left most of the hiring details to my siblings.

I'm wishing now I'd paid more attention. Wishing I'd taken just five minutes to review his file before walking through the door.

Griffin clears his throat. "There is one thing."

I jump at the roughness in his voice. "Something you'd like to work on?"

He nods, and I pick up my pen. "Wonderful," I say. "Let's hear it."

With a sigh, he scrubs the heel of his hand over his chin. It makes a soft scritch-scritch-scritch sound that gives me the oddest urge to purr.

*Purr*? For heaven's sake.

He's talking again, so I shake myself back into shrink mode. "I guess I'm wondering about..." He rubs his chin again. "About talking to girls."

"Ah." That's right, it's coming back to me now. Gabe and Lauren's hope for a storyline about a divorced man seeking a second chance at love. A rough-around-the-edges beer guy with a heart of gold seeks sweet, sunshiny shop owner or hairdresser or—

"Is it conversation in general you struggle with or just the small talk?" I ask.

He frowns, shaking his head. "No, that's not it. It's just—" The frown deepens, and he drums his long fingers on the table. "I feel like I've lost this ability to communicate, you know?"

"Ah," I say. "So, this is a more recent struggle?"

Brow furrowed, he nods once. "Yeah, I guess. Like she'll act a certain way and sometimes I just want to put her over my knee and paddle her backside until—"

"Oh." I drop my pen, struggling not to show surprise. It's something I've prided myself on as a therapist, my ability to keep a straight face no matter what a patient says.

But Griffin Walsh is throwing me off my game.

"Well, certainly that's understandable." I pick up my pen again, then set it back on the table. The last thing he needs is a fear that I'm writing this down. "We all have things we *want* to do. Basic urges. Needs."

*Kill me now.*

Griffin's staring at me like I just licked the table, so I straighten in my chair. "My point is that there's no shame in having those kinds of thoughts."

He frowns. "I wouldn't really do it. I mean, spanking—that was never my thing. It's a figure of speech."

The room feels blazingly hot, or maybe that's my face. Should I reassure him these desires are totally normal or talk about consent? He's looking at me like I have answers, and I'm not sure I remember my own name.

*Some therapist you are.*

I clear my throat. "Let's start with the basics," I say. "Strategies for initiating more productive conversations."

"How do you mean?"

I tap my pen on the table, then realize I've picked it up again. When did that happen?

"How about dinner?" I say. "Or coffee. Something simple to set the stage and give you both something to talk about. Or beer, how about beer?"

My brain drags one useful bit of trivia from its archives. Besides being a master brewer, Griffin Walsh is a cicerone. I had to google that after reading his application. It's like a wine sommelier, only for beer snobs. Surely that gives him plenty of fodder for conversation.

"Beer," he repeats, frowning. "You mean talking about it or drinking it?"

"Either, really." Anything to get him to open up. "Maybe both."

Griffin shakes his head. "I don't think that's such a good idea."

"Fair enough." Also, interesting. Maybe his love interest is in recovery, or not a beer fan. It isn't my place to judge. "I agree that alcohol consumption comes with its own set of challenges in social settings."

Lord knows I've done my share of dumb things. I start out sipping chardonnay, desperate to have something to do with my hands at girls' nights or family gatherings. But instead of lowering my inhibitions, it just makes me awkward.

More awkward.

It's really hot in here.

"Have you tried asking questions?" I'm still fishing in my bag, and I resist the urge to cheer as my fingers close around the info packet. "Maybe even starting with a list. Easy topics for conversation that you can prepare ahead of time so they're handy when you need them."

There's a flicker of interest in his eyes. He nods slowly, a shock of dark hair falling over his forehead. I set his packet on the table, then sit on my hands to keep from reaching across to brush back his hair.

"Yeah, that's good," he says. "What kinds of questions?"

"Ask about her interests." We're back on safe ground, so I'm warming to the subject. "What sort of things is she into?"

Griffin looks down at the table, chiseled jaw clenching. "Makeup," he mutters. "And hair. She's always messing around with it. Curling it and then flattening it out with this weird clampy thing."

"Careful with the judgment words," I caution, even though I'm with him on that one. What is it with this societal pressure for women to make their hair do the opposite of whatever it's naturally inclined to do?

*Like you didn't glam it up for the cameras.*

I take a deep breath and order myself to focus. "I totally understand that makeup and hair care may not be in your wheelhouse."

"You think?" The faintest hint of a smile tugs those full lips, and my stomach rolls over like a very good dog.

"Right." I clear my throat. "But the point is to ask questions that show you're interested in her, even if the subject itself isn't something that interests you. Something like, 'how do you decide what you want your hair to look like on any given day?' Or maybe you could focus on how she *feels* about her beauty routine."

"How she feels about her beauty routine?" He shakes his head and grimaces down at the table. "Christ, I'm not cut out for this."

His voice is rough, but when he meets my eyes again, his gaze holds an unexpected softness. He's trying, he really is. He wants to get this right, and I want that for him very much.

I flip open the packet, careful to maintain eye contact. We're making progress, and I don't want to derail that.

"You could try taking the pressure off a little," I tell him. "Maybe suggesting a game that lets conversation flow more naturally. Or what about a book of questions that you take turns asking one another?"

He shrugs. "I tried that once. The book thing, I mean. I asked stuff like, 'if you could take a one-month vacation anywhere in the world, where would you go?' or 'tell me what you like best and least about your life.'"

"Those are terrific." I'm seriously impressed he took the initiative. "How did it go?"

Griffin frowns down at the table again. "She rolled her eyes and shut the bedroom door in my face."

*Ouch.*

This is worse than I thought. I'm debating how best to broach the subject of emotionally abusive relationships, but Griffin's on a roll now. He looks up, blue eyes earnest and a little melancholy.

"The thing is, I've tried reaching out. Like, buying her gifts and stuff?"

"Oh?" I swallow back my judgments, knowing he needs to be heard. "How did that go?"

"Not great." He snorts. "Probably my fault. How the fuck was I supposed to know stuffed animals aren't cool?"

"Um, well." Yikes, what do I do with that? "When a gift is given with good intentions and love—"

"And seriously, I've tried talking with her about her period because I know that's a thing, and God knows I don't want her getting bad information from friends, but she shuts me out completely. It's like I'm damned if I do, damned if I don't, you know?"

I stare at him. This is the first time in my psychology career that I've honestly been at a loss for words.

"Griffin." I say his name slowly, stretching it out, stalling for time as a faint buzz begins in the back of my brain. Something's off here.

"Yeah?"

"Are we—" Lord, where do I start? "Um, well. That is, do you think it's possible we're having two different conversations?"

He frowns. "What the hell conversation do you think we're having?"

The buzz in my brain grows louder—hornets, maybe. It's dawning on me that I may have just stepped in the world's largest pile of excrement. "I thought," I begin carefully, "that we were having a conversation about improving your skills talking to women."

Griffin stares at me. "Women? Like—to date?"

My brain rewinds with a squeal as I scramble to figure out where I got off track. I glance down at the first page of his packet, scanning for anything to help me dig out of this hole.

It hits me like a tire iron to the forehead.

"Sophie!" I slap the table so hard he jumps. "Your twelve-year-old daughter, *Sophie*."

He stares at me, unblinking, unflinching. I'm braced for him to stand up and walk out of this room. He has every right to.

Hell, he'd be entitled to his feelings if he threw in the towel right now and quit the show. God knows I've given him zero reason to think his emotional well-being is in good hands.

But instead, a slow, warm smile spreads over his face. Then a sound bubbles up, so deep, so unexpectedly musical, that it takes me a moment to identify it as laughter.

He's laughing. Griffin Walsh is *laughing*.

"Huh," he says, scratching his chin again. He's still smiling, and *ohmylord* the man has dimples. "That's pretty damn funny."

I try to smile back, but I'm mortified. Never, in all my years as a psychologist, has anything like this happened.

"I'm so sorry."

For misinterpreting his question about girls. For making assumptions. For a million other things including the way my heart is flinging itself against my ribcage like a rabid bird.

"Truly, I apologize," I continue. "If you'd like, we could discontinue this session and—"

"Hey, Doc?"

I swallow hard, tasting shame on the back of my tongue. Shame and the unmistakable, irrefutable sprinkle of lust.

Goddamn those dimples.

"Yes?" I manage weakly.

Griffin leans forward, hands stretching across the table. He's close enough to touch me if he wanted, and it's all I can do not to reach for him.

"This was fun." He grins, and my heart flops over and sighs. "Wanna try again?"

***

Want to read more? Grab *Let It Show* here:

https://geni.us/myWBcHA

In the meantime, have you read my Ponderosa Resort Romantic Comedy Series? It's heaped with humor, heart, and hilarious family hijinx. There's even some crossover into the Juniper Ridge world. You can start anywhere, since the books are written as standalones, but here's a glimpse at one of my personal faves, *Hottie Lumberjack*...

# YOUR EXCLUSIVE PEEK AT HOTTIE LUMBERJACK

## CHELSEA

"Here you go, Mrs. Sampson." I slide the pink bakery box across the counter with a smile. "One dozen Guinness chocolate cupcakes with chai spice frosting, and one dozen strawberry with vanilla fondant."

My retired math teacher pulls the box to her chest like she thinks someone will snatch it. "Did you put the penises on top like I asked?"

Her volume is a good indication she forgot her hearing aid, and the chime of my front door is a good indication of how my week's going. I order myself to stay focused on the customer in front of me, but from the corner of my eye I see the new arrival flinch in surprise.

"I'll be with you in just a—*oh*."

Holy shit.

The guy in the doorway of my bakery doesn't look like someone shopping for a dozen vanilla bean cupcakes. He looks like a lumberjack who lost his way to the forest. The scruffy beard, the plaid flannel, and ohmygod is that an *axe*?

I swallow hard and glance at Mrs. Sampson, reminding myself not to alarm her. If we're going to die at the hands of an axe murderer, I'd like her to go out knowing she got what she wanted in that bakery box. "The cupcakes are made to order, just like always," I assure her. "I even slipped in a couple complimentary macarons because I know Mr. Sampson loves them."

She frowns but doesn't turn around to notice the hulking figure behind her. "But the penises," she says. "They're for a bachelorette party for my grand-niece and—"

"You've got your penises." I wince at the sharpness of my words, wishing desperately we could stop saying that word in front of a guy who presumably has one. I'm trying not to look. "And I've got your order for next week's Welfare Society luncheon. Can I get you anything else, Mrs. Sampson?"

"No, dear," she says, finally convinced that I successfully piped one dozen flesh-colored phalluses onto her pastries. "You're a doll, Chelsea. I hope you find a man soon."

As if that weren't embarrassing enough, she reaches across the counter and pats my cheek. Then she turns and brushes past the man who's looking more than a little regretful about walking in here.

I get a better look at him this time, and nope, I didn't imagine the axe. Or the fact that he has to be at least six-five, which means he has to duck to get under the doorframe as he holds it open for Mrs. Sampson.

"Ma'am." His voice is gruff, but his eyes are kind. "You need help getting that into your car?"

"Thank you, Mark," she says. "I've got it. You tell that sister of yours hello."

"Yes, ma'am."

Sister? Mark?

I study the guy more closely but see zero resemblance to five-foot-nothing Bree Bracelyn, the marketing VP for Ponderosa Ranch Luxury Resort. But this has to be the brother she's talked about for months, right?

The door swings shut and Paul Bunyan—er, Mark—turns to

face me. He scrubs a hand over his beard as he ambles toward the counter. "I need cupcakes."

I glance at the axe in his hand and nod. "Uh, you're in the right place for that."

Folding my hands on the counter, I meet his eyes. They're a warm brown like my favorite Guittard chocolate, and I forget for a moment that he could crush my skull with his hands if he wanted to. He doesn't appear to want to, but I don't have a history of being a great judge of men.

I push aside dark thoughts about my daughter's sperm donor and the half-dozen other men in my past who've turned out to be real doozies and focus on the more immediate threat. Or is there a threat? Hottie Lumberjack doesn't look terribly menacing. There's an odd sort of teddy bear quality to the guy, if teddy bears had massive biceps and broad shoulders and sharp pieces of weaponry in their paws.

He catches me staring and sets the axe down beside my display case, leaning it against his thigh. That's huge, too. Everything about this guy is enormous, so why do I feel more turned on than terrified?

The guy clears his throat. "I'm supposed to order two dozen cupcakes for a bunch of tour operators from—"

"I'm sorry, why do you have the axe?"

He cocks his head, genuinely perplexed. "For chopping wood."

For fuck's sake. "I mean why did you bring it into a cupcake shop?"

I'm no longer worried he's here to lop my head off, but still.

He stares at me for a few beats, not answering, not blinking, not even smiling. Not that I could tell, what with the thick beard masking any sort of expression. But I can see his lips, which are full and soft and—

"Sharp."

I blink. "What?"

"The axe," he says. "Had to get it sharpened."

"So you brought it to a cupcake shop?"

The corners of his mouth twitch, but he doesn't smile. "No, I brought it to the shop down the street. Didn't want to leave it in the truck because the doors don't lock. Safety hazard."

"Oh." That actually makes sense.

Sort of. If this is really Bree Bracelyn's brother, he's a freakin' gazillionaire. Not that any of the siblings in that family act like it, but it's common knowledge the Bracelyn kids inherited a lot more than their dad's ranch when he died.

Suffice it to say, Hottie Lumberjack could afford a truck that locks.

"Chelsea Singer," I tell him, wiping a hand on my pink and green striped apron before offering it to him. "I own Dew Drop Cupcakes." As an afterthought, I add, "And I'm not an axe murderer."

His mouth definitely twitches this time. "Mark Bracelyn. Ponderosa Resort. Also not an axe murderer."

"Good. That's good." And interesting. He didn't volunteer his job title, but I know it's something like Vice President of Grounds Management, which Bree told me he *hates*. He might be part-owner of a luxury resort for rich people, but he'd rather be regarded as the handyman. That's what Bree says, anyway.

And don't think I haven't noticed Bree filling my head with Mark-related tidbits.

*Mark built me a new woodshed this weekend.*

*Mark has a major sweet tooth.*

*Mark rescued a family of orphaned bunnies yesterday.*

I'm not sure whether she wants me to date him or just think twice about macing him if we meet in a dark alley, but it's odd this is the first time we're meeting.

"So Mark," I say, leaning against the counter. "What can I get for you?"

"Cupcakes." He frowns. "Two dozen."

"Right, but any particular flavor? Strawberry, peanut butter, kiwi, red velvet, double-fudge—" I stop when I see the dazed look in his eyes and nudge a laminated menu across the counter at him. "We have more than fifty cake flavors and three dozen frosting varieties, plus fondant and icing. There's an infinite variety of combinations."

Those brown eyes take on the ultimate "kid in a candy shop" glow, so I give him a private moment while I turn and wash my hands at the sink. His eyes become saucers as I turn back and reach into the display case to pull out a tray of mini cupcakes. I wouldn't do this for every customer, but Ponderosa Resort is one of my biggest clients.

"This is one of our seasonal favorites right now," I explain as I pluck a soft baby cupcake off the tray. "It's Guinness chocolate, and it's great with the Irish cream frosting. Would you like to try it?"

"Yes." His throat moves as he swallows. "Yes, please."

The gruff eagerness in his voice makes my girl parts clench, which is ridiculous. And a sign of how long it's been since I had sex, which....um, yeah. Let's just say dating's not easy for single moms.

I whip out a pastry bag and do a quick swirl of frosting on top of the cupcake. "Here you go."

Our fingers touch as I hand it across the counter, and I suppress an involuntary shiver. The good kind of shiver, like the one I do every time I bite into a perfect snickerdoodle. Good Lord, this guy has massive hands. He makes my mini cupcake look like a chocolate chip. "See what you think of that."

I have to look away from the expression of rapture on his face. There's something raw and intimate about it, and my belly's doing silly somersaults under my apron. I survey my tray, trying to come up with another good flavor combo.

"Let's see, this is one of Bree's favorites." I steal a look at his face, but if he's surprised I connected the dots to his sister, he doesn't show it. He's too fixated on his cupcake, savoring every little mini-bite like it's an act of worship.

This shouldn't be getting me hot, right?

I clear my throat and swirl some lime zest frosting onto a lemon cupcake. "Bree likes the citrus combo," I tell him. "Is it a family thing?"

Something odd flashes in his eyes, but he takes the mini cupcake and nods. "Thank you."

He eats this one more gingerly, still savoring every crumb. I glance down at the sample tray and try to think of what other flavors to offer. What would a guy like Mark Bracelyn enjoy? I don't make manly-man confections like sawdust cupcakes with drizzles of pine sap or mini-cakes infused with hints of leather and charcoal briquette. But maybe something on the other end of the spectrum.

"These tend to be too sweet for some people, but—"

"Yes." He nods. "Yes, please, I'd like to try it."

I smile and pluck a gooey-looking confection off the edge of the tray. "You're in luck, I had some left over from a kids' birthday party order. This is my coconut caramel chocolate delight cupcake. It's like those Girl Scout cookies—Samoas?—but in cupcake form."

The sheer joy in this man's eyes is enough to make my hand shake as I place it in the center of his massive palm. He lifts it to his mouth, and I swear on my KitchenAid mixer, I have a mini-orgasm. If the way to a man's heart is through his stomach, the way into my pants is through a man's sweet tooth.

What? No, I didn't just think that.

*Holy shit, Chelsea, get it together.*

I smooth out my apron as Mr. Tall, Gruff, and Silent polishes off his cupcake. I consider offering him more—cupcakes, not sexual favors—but what's that expression about free milk and cow buying and—

Great, now I'm thinking about Mark Bracelyn's hands on a pair of udders, which sooooo shouldn't be hot, but it is.

*Stop it.*

I clear my throat. "So what'll it be?" I ask. "You didn't mention when you need the order, but I have several of these in stock. Most will take a couple days, though."

Mark wipes his beard with a sleeve, and I realize I should have offered a napkin. He doesn't seem to need one, though, and his beard is remarkably crumb-free. What's it like to kiss a guy with facial hair? I've only experienced five-o-clock shadow, the sort of sandpaper scruff that leaves your cheeks raw and red. But Mark's beard looks soft, with hints of cinnamon and nutmeg.

*Stop thinking of this man as edible.*

"I'll take four dozen, please," he says.

I bite my lip, not positive I've got that much stock. "I thought Bree only needed two dozen."

"She does," he says. "The extras are for me. A dozen of whatever you've got in stock now, and the rest can wait 'til Friday."

I smile and jot the order on a notepad. "Got it. You want anything specific, or a mixed batch?"

He doesn't smile, but there's a flicker of interest in his eyes. "Surprise me."

*Oh, baby.*

"How about any pupcakes?" I offer.

Mark frowns. "Pupcakes?"

"Cupcakes for dogs," I say. For some reason I just assumed he has a dog. He looks like the sort of guy who'd have a Rottweiler or maybe a blue ox named Babe. "Bree buys them all the time for Virginia Woof."

"I should get a dog." He says this with an earnestness that makes my heart go gooey.

"You totally should." Good Lord, why am I advising this man on his life choices? "The Humane Society has tons of great ones. My daughter and I volunteer there every Saturday."

This is where most guys check out. Or check my ring finger. Or ask some not-so-subtle question about the baby-daddy, even though everyone pretends not to care. Plenty of folks have heard rumors.

But Mark doesn't blink. Just looks me in the eye, calm and steady. "Good idea."

"Which? Volunteering at the Humane Society, or you getting a dog."

"Yes."

I wait for more, but there doesn't seem to be any. His attention shifts to something over my shoulder, and he points one enormous finger. "How long's that been like that?"

I look where he's pointing and see the banged-up handle on the side door leading to the alley. I left it open a few inches to let the spring breeze waft through, and it's obvious even from here that someone messed with the doorknob.

"A couple days." I turn back to face him. "I came in the other morning and found it like that. Probably kids messing around. I haven't had time to call the repair guy."

Mark frowns. "May I?"

I'm not sure what he's asking, but I nod like an idiot. "Sure."

He lumbers around the counter, leaving his axe behind. After a few seconds of fiddling with the lock and muttering, he marches back around the counter. "Wait here."

"I—"

The front door swings shut behind him before I can point out that I've got no place to go, owning the shop and everything. He's not gone more than a minute, and when he strides back through the door, he's carrying a battered red toolbox.

He doesn't ask this time. Just rounds the corner and goes to the door again. There's some hammering and rattling, a few curse words that make me glad it's a slow weekday and there are no other customers around. I busy myself filling a bakery box with cupcakes, slipping in two extras and one of my cupcake-shaped business cards with a few words scrawled on the back.

Then I wander toward the door, watching his shoulders bunch as he works. He's rolled up the sleeves of his flannel shirt, revealing forearms thick and ropey with muscle. The man is huge, even kneeling on my floor.

I don't realize how close I've crept until he turns his head and—

"Um," he says.

He's face-to-boob with me, and we're frozen in the moment. I could step forward and feel the tickle of his beard against my breasts through the front of my T-shirt. He could lean in and whisper warm breath against my nipples, making them pucker through the lace of my bra.

But neither of us does that.

He's first to lift his gaze, meeting my eyes through a haze that looks like the same thing buzzing through my brain. "You're good."

"What?"

"The door." He gestures with a screwdriver but doesn't break eye contact. "That should hold now. No need to call a repairman."

I drag my eyes from his and see he's fixed my damn door. How about that?

"Wow." I step back at last, aware of the dizzy hum pulsing through my core. "That's—wow. What do I owe you?"

Mark stands and hoists his toolbox, wiping a hand on his jeans. "You gave me cupcake samples."

"Maybe a dollar's worth of samples," I point out. "A repairman would charge at least a hundred."

"You can give me a pupcake," he says. "When I get my dog."

He gives me a small smile, but I don't think he's kidding. I do think he's considering kissing me. I want him to, Jesus God, I want him to, and it's the craziest thing ever.

But he turns and lumbers back around the counter. Setting

down the toolbox, he fishes into his pocket and comes up with a battered leather wallet. "For the four-dozen cupcakes," he says, laying four hundred-dollar bills on the counter as my jaw falls open.

How much does this man think I charge for butter and sugar and—

"It was good meeting you." He gathers his axe and toolbox and the pink bakery box, then lumbers toward the door before I can muster any words like "wait" or "your receipt" or "please bend me over the counter."

The door swings shut behind him, and seconds later, a truck engine growls to life. I realize my mouth is still hanging open, so I close it and watch a faded blue and white pickup rumble down the street.

What the hell just happened?

***

# DON'T MISS OUT!

Want access to exclusive excerpts, behind-the-scenes stories about my books, cover reveals, and prize giveaways? You'll get all that by subscribing to my newsletter, plus **FREE** bonus scenes featuring your favorite characters from my rom-coms and erotic romances. Want to see Aidan and Lyla get hitched after *Eye Candy*? Or read a swoony proposal featuring Sean and Amber from *Chef Sugarlips*? It's all right here and free for the taking:

https://tawnafenske.com/bonus-content/

# ACKNOWLEDGMENTS

Thank you to the best street team an author could ask for, Fenske's Frisky Posse. I'm especially grateful to Nicole Westmoreland, Rachel Kennedy, Kim Adams, Jennifer Holter, and Regina Dowling for your help catching typos in the advance reading copies. Big hugs to Adrienne Bird for naming Andrea, and to DeeJay Sakata, DeAnna Caudillo, Dawn Bekenyi, Karen Fernandez Vickers for naming all the Judson siblings.

Much love and gratitude to Susan Bischoff and Lauralynn Elliott of The Forge for being kickass editors (though I should probably consult you on whether "kickass" is one word or two). I'm also super-grateful to Lori Jackson Design for the teaser graphics and banners.

Meah Meow, you're the most badass assistant I could wish for, and I appreciate everything you do to keep me organized and sane. Okay, just organized.

I tip my hat to Pet Evacuation Team (PET) for rescuing the real life Roughneck (now Eli) and to Sharon, Susan, and everyone else involved in rehabbing that sweet boy whose story I got to follow on Facebook.

Thank you to Judah McAuley for the awesome little math sequence in Vanessa's inner monologue in chapter 12. Hopefully my math-challenged author brain didn't warp it too much.

As always, I'm thankful for Michelle Wolfson of Wolfson Literary Agency for talking me off more ledges than I can count.

Huge hugs and smooches to my family, including Aaron "Russ" Fenske, Carlie Fenske, and Mr. Paxton, along with the best parents in the universe, Dixie and David Fenske, and my awesome kiddos, Cedar and Violet.

And to Craig Zagurski for being the best quarantine companion I could have asked for. Let's grow old disgracefully together.

# ABOUT THE AUTHOR

When Tawna Fenske finished her English lit degree at 22, she celebrated by filling a giant trash bag full of romance novels and dragging it everywhere until she'd read them all. Now she's a RITA Award finalist, *USA Today* bestselling author who writes humorous fiction, risqué romance, and heartwarming love stories with a quirky twist. *Publishers Weekly* has praised Tawna's offbeat romances with multiple starred reviews and noted, "There's something wonderfully relaxing about being immersed in a story filled with over-the-top characters in undeniably relatable situations. Heartache and humor go hand in hand."

Tawna lives in Bend, Oregon, with her husband, step-kids, and a menagerie of ill-behaved pets. She loves hiking, snowshoeing, standup paddleboarding, and inventing excuses to sip wine on her back porch. She can peel a banana with her toes and loses an average of twenty pairs of eyeglasses per year. To find out more about Tawna and her books, visit www.tawnafenske.com.

# ALSO BY TAWNA FENSKE

The Cherry Blossom Lake Romantic Comedy Series

Try Me

Charm Me

Hold Me

Ask Me (coming soon!)

The Ponderosa Resort Romantic Comedy Series

Studmuffin Santa

Chef Sugarlips

Sergeant Sexypants

Hottie Lumberjack

Stiff Suit

Mancandy Crush (novella)

Captain Dreamboat

Snowbound Squeeze (novella)

Dr. Hot Stuff

The Juniper Ridge Romantic Comedy Series

Show Time

Let It Show

Show Down

Show of Honor

Just for Show

Show Off

The Assassins in Love Series

Killer Looks (free prequel novella)

Killer Instincts

Killer Moves

Killer Smile

The Sugar & Spice Erotic Romance Series

Eye Candy

Tough Cookie

Honey Do

The Where There's Smoke Series

The Two-Date Rule

Just a Little Bet

The Best Kept Secret

Standalone Romantic Comedies

At the Heart of It

This Time Around

Now That It's You

Let it Breathe

About That Fling

Frisky Business

Believe It or Not

Making Waves

The Front and Center Series

Marine for Hire

Fiancée for Hire

Best Man for Hire

Protector for Hire

The First Impressions Series

The Fix Up

The Hang Up

The Hook Up

The List Series

The List

The Test

The Last

Standalone novellas and other wacky stuff

Going Up (novella)

Eat, Play, Lust (novella)

Made in United States
Troutdale, OR
09/24/2024

23084244R00166